BEING KNOWN

BEING KNOWN

ROBIN JONES GUNN

THORNDIKE PRESS
A part of Gale, a Cengage Company

GALE
A Cengage Company

Thorndike Press, a part of Gale, a Cengage Company

LIBRARY OF CONGRESS CIP DATA ON FILE.
CATALOGUING IN PUBLICATION FOR THIS BOOK
IS AVAILABLE FROM THE LIBRARY OF CONGRESS

ISBN-13: 978-1-4328-8064-4 (hardcover alk. paper)

Published in 2020 by arrangement with Multnomah, an imprint of Random House, a division of Penguin Random House LLC.

Printed in Mexico
Print Number: 01   Print Year: 2020

With much aloha to my closest DOEs, Rachel, Janet, Marlene, Kim, Carolyn, Janna, Manasseh, Jill, Donna, Alyssa, Leslie, and Molly. Thank you for being so generous with your time, words, prayers, and love. It's an honor to be known by you. You are the mothers, sisters, friends, and daughters who have brought the sacred into my ordinary days.
More, please.

CHAPTER 1

Whenever I close my eyes and think of my mother, I see her red toenails. Her perfectly manicured toes flaunting her signature nail-polish color, Oh My, Cherry Pie.

I saw her toes in my mind's eye when I stopped at 19th and Harbor on my way home on an ordinary Thursday. The January sun was hitting the traffic light just right, intensifying the red, scorching my thoughts with visions of cherry red toenails.

In an instant, everything went from feeling normal to a sensation that my heart was being squeezed. *Strangled* might be a better word, as if all the breath, joy, and hope of my life were being choked out by an angry, invisible hand.

I suddenly felt so alone.

The impression surprised me because I was not alone. Rarely am I by myself long enough to even take a decent shower. In the back seat of the car my four-year-old daughter, Eden, was singing one of her sweet and silly songs. In the rearview mirror I could see that her thirteen-month-old brother was enthralled, as always. Alex was rewarding Eden for her performance by kicking his feet and bobbing his head from side to side.

I love my children. I love my husband. I love the house where we live. It's a dream to be so close to the gorgeous Southern California coast. We have wonderful friends and generous in-laws who are both kind and doting. I love our life. Anyone looking in from the outside would say I have it all.

But I don't.

I don't have my mother. And no one can bring her back to me.

The traffic light changed to green, and the great chasm between what was and what is seemed to be closing. I drove into our neighborhood telling myself to breathe and be grateful for all the good things in my life. Choosing gratitude always helped to shrink the raw, gaping ache.

"Mommy?"

"Yes, Eden."

"Are we going to my dance class now?"

"No, honey. We'll go after nap time this afternoon."

"I don't need a nap."

"I know." I pulled into our driveway,

turned off the engine, and looked at her in the mirror. My daughter's dark eyes were so much like mine. "But Alex needs a nap. And so does Mommy."

Eden giggled and put her hand over her mouth. The gesture was new, and I wasn't sure where she picked it up. "That's silly. Mommies don't take naps."

"Don't I know it," I muttered.

That evening as Joel and I were driving to our friends' house for dinner, we stopped at a red light, and I wanted to tell my husband about the way grief had snuck up on me earlier that day. I wanted to hear all the comforting words he had given me over the past six years whenever I talked about how much I missed my mom. I wanted him to know what I was feeling, and most of all, I wanted him to somehow enter the hazy place of loss with me.

But my handsome, always efficient husband was on the speakerphone. He was setting up the training schedule for the new assistant chef who was starting on Saturday. Joel was part owner at the Blue Ginger restaurant in Corona del Mar, and he was also the head chef. The dual roles were ambitious, but then, so was Joel. The only reason he had this rare Thursday night off was because a new stove had been installed that afternoon, followed by a series of spot safety checks.

The light turned green. Joel glanced at me and seemed to notice for the first time that I'd been facing him, waiting for my turn to get his attention. I reached over and smoothed back his dark hair that was growing too long in the front. His clean-shaven face, with his straight nose and intense, amber-flecked eyes, reflected all the best of his Italian heritage. He looked as handsome to me tonight as when I'd first met him nine years ago. I could wait for his attention. Joel was always worth the wait.

Turning away, I looked out the window and quietly watched the familiar sights as we rolled into our old neighborhood. The rows of beach houses lined up like mismatched vintage toys on a shelf.

Coming up on the right was the cottage we rented when we first moved to Newport Beach. Joel and I had packed a lot of good memories into that 950-square-foot, two-bed, one-bath bungalow with the sapphire-blue door. I noticed that the garden boxes Joel had set up still lined the narrow space at the front of the house. They were now filled with what looked like lemongrass.

I smiled, remembering how happy we were when we brought Eden home to her lovingly prepared nursery. I wondered if the hand-painted morning glories still curved up her bedroom wall, or if the new tenant had painted over my handiwork.

Joel had tried out dozens of recipes in that tiny, inefficient kitchen. I sat for hours, watching from the oval table where I painted and practiced calligraphy on dozens — maybe hundreds — of cards and plaques. We hosted many small get-togethers with new friends as well as lively, crowded dinners with Joel's extended family.

Life was simpler then. Joel and I were just becoming "us." We had only been married for a couple of years when we moved to Newport Beach. Our love was new, and we were intent on crafting our careers and starting a family.

I look back now and realize that our happiness and fresh, young love probably had cocooned me from feeling the full impact of the sudden loss of my mom right before we moved. Joel and I had each other, and in that season, I guess I thought that was enough. We were shoulder to shoulder in our quest for courageous endeavors and new beginnings.

Now, in a little more than half a decade, we had accomplished and acquired everything we had only dreamed of back then.

11

Joel owned his restaurant; we had a daughter and a son. We lived in a two-story, newly renovated house with an exceptional kitchen, and I had the space and freedom to pursue my love of watercolor painting and entertaining to my heart's content.

The only problem was, I couldn't think of anything my husband and I were shoulder to shoulder on anymore.

Joel wedged our Lexus into a rare open space by the curb just down the street from our memory-soaked cottage. I got out and softly closed my door. He was still on his call and, from the sound of it, might be for a while longer. Using both hands, I carried the large, heavy wicker basket to Christy and Todd's front door and pressed the doorbell with my elbow.

The door opened, and my lovely friend Christy greeted me with a hug. "Jennalyn, hi! Come in." Christy's blue-green eyes looked down the street. "Is Joel with you?"

"He's finishing a call in the car. He'll be here in a minute."

I made myself at home in the open downstairs of the beach home that had become so familiar over the past few years. Meeting Christy was one of the biggest blessings that came with the early years in our cottage by the sea. While placing the basket on the large kitchen counter, I noticed that Christy had set out only four of her white dinner plates.

"Is it just the four of us?" My hair had been bugging me all day. I stepped into the small bathroom off the kitchen, pulled the long dark strands to the right side, and made a swiftly folded braid. "Is it okay if I use this hair tie on the counter?"

"Yes and yes," Christy called back from the kitchen. "Yes, it's just us for dinner, and what's mine is yours. Or I should say, what's Hana's is yours."

I turned on the faucet and ran my hands under the water, then smoothed back the sides of my thick straight hair. Rolling my shoulders back, I took one last look in the mirror and wished I had put on some jewelry or at least something other than the plain heather-gray V-neck sweater I had worn all day.

Returning to the kitchen, I took note of how fresh Christy looked in her jeans and long-sleeved white top with the sleeves rolled up. She was also wearing one of the darling aprons she sews and sells online and in local shops. This one was made from a mix of pink, green, and blue fabric remnants, with a playful yellow ruffle across the top.

"Sierra and Jordan said they might stop by after eight," Christy said. "I kind of doubt they'll make it, though. Emily called and said she and Trevor are coming down with colds."

"That's too bad. What about Tess?" I reached for the two fresh baguettes in my basket, pulled a long knife from the block by the stove, and began slicing.

"She said she was meeting someone. I asked if it was a client, and she said no, it was a guy."

"A guy?"

Christy nodded and arranged the chunky baguette ovals on a cookie sheet.

"What else did she say?" I asked.

"That was it. She probably didn't want to say much because, you know, she assumed I would tell you guys, and our group is always so . . ."

"Caring?" I piped in.

"I was going to say nosy."

"We're only nosy because we care," I said. "I think we do a pretty good job of looking out for each other."

"Yes, we do," Christy agreed.

A little more than a year ago, five of us friends unexpectedly formed a group and named ourselves "Daughters of Eve" or "DOEs." We liked the connection to the way

Aslan called Susan and Lucy "Daughters of Eve" in the Narnia tales. More than that, the name fit because we could all relate to Eve in some way. My connection was that Eve didn't have a mother to help her figure out how to raise her children.

Recently our group had migrated to another term we liked. It fit all of us, whether single or married. We called ourselves the Haven Makers because we saw ourselves as being a haven for each other.

"I wish all the DOEs could have come tonight. Maybe it wasn't such a good idea to invite our husbands." I glanced around Christy's quiet downstairs. "Speaking of which, where are Todd and your kids?"

"They left almost an hour ago. When Todd heard Emily wasn't coming and no one was bringing dessert, he decided we needed ice cream. Of course, as soon as the kids heard him say ice cream, they ran to the car."

I lifted one of the two large pans of lasagna from the basket and folded back the foil. "Do you think we should put this in the oven?"

"Oh, that smells good." Christy pulled back her long nutmeg-brown hair and leaned in for a sniff. "I feel bad that you and Joel made so much, and now it's only the four of us."

"You won't feel bad and neither will I when we have leftovers for days. This is Gi-Gi's recipe, so we had to make a lot. I don't think any of my mother-in-law's recipes come with ingredient proportions for under twelve people."

Just then the door to the garage opened, and Todd entered with Joel, along with seven-year-old Hana and four-year-old Cole. Cole had telltale signs of chocolate ice cream circling his contented smile.

Hana, their affectionate little blond cutie, dashed over and gave me a big hug. "We got vanilla bean and chocolate chip for you guys."

"And what flavor did you get?" I asked Hana.

"I got a strawberry cone, Cole got chocolate, and Daddy got a mango shake."

"Kids' size all around," Todd said before sliding two containers of ice cream into the freezer.

I watched as he gave Christy a chin-up grin in response to being busted for treating the kids to dessert before dinner. Her response was to lower her chin and offer a close-lipped grin in return. If she was mad at him for his parenting choice, it didn't show. I saw nothing but a field of love between the two of them.

Their exchange intrigued me because if Joel had done that with our kids, I might not have said something, but I probably would have been shooting messages his way with scolding looks. I had to admit, Todd looked pretty happy that he had scored points with his kids. Christy's quiet response seemed to infuse the noisy kitchen with a special sort of peace.

Todd's attention had turned to the pan of lasagna on the counter. "Whoa! Look at this beast!"

Joel laughed. "If we ever add my mom's lasagna to the menu at the restaurant, someone remind me to call it 'The Beast.' "

Christy pulled the warmed baguettes from the oven, and we all joined hands around the counter to pray, as was the Spencer family tradition. It felt so good to be with friends. To be holding hands with Hana and my husband and to feel connected. Included.

I realized it was the first time that day I hadn't felt painfully alone.

CHAPTER 2

The next few hours felt both familiar and odd. Familiar because Joel and I had enjoyed lots of meals with Christy and Todd over the years. Conversation was never a challenge for the four of us. It felt odd, though, because our kids weren't with us and this wasn't the Haven Makers' group dinner party we had planned.

Hana and Cole were too sugared up after their ice cream treat to eat much dinner. As soon as Christy and I finished eating, we slipped into a co-mothering role and got the kids washed and in their jammies. I tagged along as Christy took them upstairs to bed.

The guys ended up out on the deck by the firepit talking about who knows what. They seemed intent and focused, so Christy and I were glad to leave them for what looked like a male version of a heart-to-heart discussion. I hoped Joel was opening up about how difficult things had been at the restaurant over the past six months and how much his work had cut into family time. The one person who might be able to give Joel good counsel was Todd.

Once we put the food away, Christy and I wandered into the living room and sat together on her small but comfy sofa. We were both too full for any ice cream and opted for mugs of steaming mint tea instead.

"I never heard what happened to the idea you had about teaching a watercolor class at the arts center." Christy tucked her long legs under her and adjusted one of the cute throw pillows under her side. Her custom throw pillows and tablecloths along with her popular aprons had provided just enough income over the last few years for her to remain a work-at-home mom while Todd taught at a private high school.

"I'm not ready to teach a class. I thought I was. I went to the arts center a week ago and was going to set up a meeting with the manager. Something didn't feel right about the timing. Maybe I'll consider it once Joel figures out his staff shortage." I took a sip of tea.

"Are you still giving Audra private lessons?" Christy asked. "Emily told me that Audra was loving them."

I smiled thinking of Emily's precocious preteen daughter and her love for arts and crafts. I had been meeting with her every other week starting last summer, nurturing her natural talent.

"We paused the lessons right before Christmas," I told Christy. "She's taking a ceramics class now at the arts center. We might pick up again in the spring."

"I should see if the arts center has any music classes for Hana's age group," Christy said.

"I don't know about music classes, but I signed up Eden for dance lessons. Her first class was this afternoon. Joel had the afternoon off, so he took her, which made her so happy."

"Do you need a leotard?" Christy asked. "I might still have one of Hana's in a box somewhere. I think we already gave away all the toddler-sized tutus my aunt bought her."

"Thanks, but GiGi already has outfitted Eden with everything, including a pink shoulder bag to carry her ballet slippers in."

Christy smiled and closed her eyes. "Where would we be without Aunt Martis and GiGis in our lives?"

"We probably would have a lot less lasagna in our bellies right now," I said with a grin.

Christy patted her stomach and quickly

covered her mouth as a leisurely yawn leaked out. "Sorry!"

"No apology needed. I'm right there with you. Maybe we should make it an early night."

"No, I'm good. Let's talk." She shifted her position and drew in a breath through her nose. "It's been months since you and I have had a chance to do this. Tell me of you."

Christy's effort to play hostess was noble. The wording of her request was sweet, and I repeated it.

"Tell you of me, huh? Well, I don't think there's much to tell."

Christy gave me one of her chin-dipping looks, as if she knew more was going on under the surface. "How are you and Joel doing? Are things still as crazy for him at work as last time we talked?"

"Yes. His hours have been ridiculous. He's never home. It's been a rough six months. Actually, it's more like a year of ongoing transitions at the restaurant."

"Joel has done a lot to turn things around at the Blue Ginger, from what I've heard."

"He has. It's taken longer than he thought it would, and he's still understaffed. He's working on that. I just want him to work on us."

Christy nodded and added in a light-hearted tone, "I feel understaffed around here a lot of the time."

"I know what you mean. When Joel does come home, he's exhausted. We don't have a lot of time to be alone, just the two of us."

I glanced over my shoulder at the guys out on the deck and then turned back to Christy. "How was it for you and Todd? Was it more difficult for you guys to get back in sync with each other after Hana or Cole was born?"

Christy paused and became thoughtful for a moment, and I wondered if what I had asked was too personal. Christy was always respectful and guarded about the intimate details of her marriage. I reached for my cup of tea and felt a familiar, self-inflicted awkwardness that came whenever I was uncertain of where I ranked on her friendship scale. I considered Christy to be my closest friend. I never had told her because the twelve-year-old girl in me didn't want to risk being the one to say, "You're my best friend" and receive no reciprocal declaration.

She didn't appear uncomfortable when she replied, "For me, after Hana was born, intimacy was more difficult because everything was different, you know? My body was more altered than I expected. What I remember most was always being so tired.

"Then when Cole was born, I think Todd and I had figured out how to adjust, so it wasn't as difficult. I know that I didn't feel anxious all the time like I had with Hana. I was calmer around the kids, and I'm sure that helped me relax more with Todd. Having a baby is definitely an adjustment in body and mind."

"Not to mention emotions," I added.

"Yes, emotions! Who was it that called our emotions 'the womanly wild card'? Was that Sierra?"

"Probably. Sounds like Sierra." I realized that maybe it didn't matter where I lined up on Christy's friendship list. Did women in their thirties even think in terms of best friends anymore? Maybe at this age we simply connected at whatever level we could, in whatever way we could, and did our best to let ourselves be known.

"So, I'm guessing it's been more difficult for you since Alex was born," Christy said.

"Yes. My body hasn't adjusted as quickly as it did after Eden. With Joel and me, our timing is off. Sometimes I feel like we're living two different lives." I hoped I wasn't sounding too melancholy. "I just miss us being us, you know?"

"I know exactly what you're saying. I think most couples go through something like that." Christy reached over and squeezed my arm. "You guys can turn things around, Jennalyn. I know it helps if you can be open to all the possibilities of when you can get together. Timing is everything. We sure had to be more creative with our love life and not think of it as an uphill challenge. The good news is that everything is easier for us as the kids get older."

"That's encouraging." I carefully took another long sip of the calming tea. "I don't know why my body hasn't bounced back to normal the way it did after Eden was born."

"I think second babies can do that," Christy said. "I got so big when I was carrying Cole. At least you've lost your baby weight from Alex. I'm still trying to figure that out. Talk about uphill challenges."

"You look really good, Christy. You always do."

"So do you, Jennalyn."

"Let's keep telling each other that." I grinned. "Hopefully we'll convince each other that it's true."

"It is true," Christy said. "We're both healthy, and that's what really matters, right? This might be the new normal for us. The new, thirty-something-mother-of-two normal. I mean, we're not sixteen anymore."

"Sixteen." I laughed. "Do you realize that was half a lifetime ago for us?"

Christy's expression took on a sudden faraway look. "It was, wasn't it?"

"Way back before our bodies ushered two humans into this world and altered us forever."

"Even more reason to give ourselves some grace," Christy lifted her teacup, and I gently tapped it with the rim of mine. We spontaneously repeated in tandem a phrase our DOEs had begun using as our favorite blessing. "Shame off us, grace on us."

We grinned, and I felt a sense of hope rising in me. Sierra had once said that Christy's superpower was compassion. It was true. She had a way of listening, saying just the right little something, and giving a smile or a squeeze. When she did, she transferred just enough courage, hope, peace, or whatever was needed. That's what made her style of compassion so rich.

"What about you?" I was happy to change the subject and decided to add Christy's clever phrase. "Your turn. Tell me of you."

Christy's eyes lit up. "I got my word for the year."

I long had been intrigued with the way Christy asked God for a word at the start of every year. She saw it as a banner to hang over the months ahead. I had done it, too, in a more hesitant way over the past years, but this year I hadn't even thought about it.

"My word for this year is *trust.*" Without further evaluation, she asked, "What about you? Are you going to ask God for a word this year?"

"I should. I'm glad you reminded me." I pulled one of the throw pillows that was behind my back and rested it on my stomach, folding my arms on top of it and feeling vulnerable once again. "My days seem consumed with diapers and naps and trying to figure out how to get Eden to eat something other than cheese."

Christy laughed. "With Hana it was applesauce. Uncle Bob always stocked those lunch-sized containers and kept them on the lower shelf. Every time we went over there, Hana went right to their fridge and helped herself."

"Does she still like applesauce?"

"Not really. Not the way she did when she was three." Christy reached for her phone on the coffee table and read the message that had just come in. "Sierra says they aren't coming by tonight." She looked up. "You know what? We should see if all the DOEs can get together before January is over. We can have a Word for the Year party. What do you think?"

"I'd love it."

Within a few minutes Sierra and Emily had texted back to say that next Thursday worked for them. We decided to meet at my house at seven, and I told Christy that if Tess couldn't come, we would change to a different night.

"Agreed," she said. "Because if Tess is starting to see some guy, she will need helpful input from her self-appointed sisters."

"True. And if any guy wants to pursue our girl, he will have to be DOE-approved!"

Christy laughed. "Aren't you glad we didn't have self-appointed sisters during our dating years?" She paused. "Actually, I guess I kind of did. Katie never held back on her opinions. I appreciate it now, even though at the time I often disagreed with her. She was right about a lot of things."

I adored Christy's redheaded friend, Katie. She lived in Kenya now with her husband and their three sons. Katie was bold and funny, and I knew what Christy meant about how she never hesitated to share what was on her mind. I admired women who could speak up and express themselves well.

"I wish I'd had a friend like Katie during

high school," I said. "I think my life would have turned out differently. At least my dating life probably would have."

Christy looked intrigued. "I don't think we've ever talked about that. Did you date much in high school?"

"Just one guy. For two years."

"Sounds serious."

"I thought it was. He even gave me a ring."

Christy waited for me to continue. I hadn't talked about any of those events in so long.

"It was a small emerald ring. I wore it on a long necklace and kept it hidden under my clothes because I didn't want our parents to know we secretly had promised ourselves to each other. It was very Romeo and Juliet to my artistic way of viewing life. I was so sure we were in love and that it would last for always."

I paused and then decided to conclude my short confession with, "But, hey, what do you know when you're sixteen? Back when we had skinny little bodies brimming with hormones. You're willing to give your inexperienced heart to the first guy who comes along, right?"

Christy's expression made it clear that she felt my pain. "Ouch."

"Yeah. Ouch." I glanced out at the guys

on the deck and saw that the flames in the firepit had died down and they were heading inside.

"I ended up with one of the good ones, though," I said. "So I'm not complaining."

"Yes, you did. You definitely ended up with one of the good ones," Christy repeated.

"We both did," I added. "And that is exactly why we have to make sure we give Tess the wisest advice we can. She'll thank us later."

Christy laughed. "At least we hope she'll thank us."

The sliding door opened, and the guys came inside smelling of woodsmoke. We chatted a few more minutes, and Joel and I collected our basket and part of the leftover lasagna. With the usual round of hugs, the two of us headed out into the chilly January night air.

"Looks like you and Todd were having a good conversation," I said as Joel drove us home.

"Yeah."

"What did you talk about?"

"Work and stuff."

I looked out the window and thought about Christy's comment on timing. Even though Joel hadn't discussed any details about work with me for what seemed like forever, this didn't seem like the right time to try to coax him into repeating everything he apparently had told Todd. It made me miss our early days. We used to stay up until midnight sipping cappuccinos and playing footsie while sitting close on the sofa. We would talk about everything.

Now the few leisurely talks we had were the rare nights when the kids were in bed, and he was in the mood to bake something scrumptious, if we had all the ingredients. Baking relaxed him. Cooking didn't relax him that much anymore since that's what he did every day at work. But getting the crackling-crisp caramelized sugar topping just right on a raspberry crème brûlée brought out his very best smile, and he would talk with me while he was creating his art.

We turned into our neighborhood, and Joel said, "Did I tell you that Eden's dance class will be on Mondays at four from now on? There was a schedule conflict at the arts center."

"Okay, no problem."

"They handed out a flyer. I think I put it on the kitchen counter."

I thought about how cute Eden looked in her pink tutu, and the enthusiastic way she demonstrated her spins for me when Joel had brought her home that afternoon. She also had been very chatty about the new friend she had made.

"What was the name of the little girl in her class?" I asked.

"Violet."

"That's right. Did you meet Violet's mom? Maybe I can set up a playdate."

"Her dad was with her," Joel said. "We talked a little. Nice guy. A playdate sounds like a good idea." He pulled into our driveway, turned off the car, and stared out the windshield. "Our daughter is growing up too fast."

I looked at his profile as he sat in the driver's seat. I wondered if he just now realized how much he had been absent from our lives over the last year or so.

"You know what I'm really looking forward to?" he asked.

"No, what?"

"Little League. That was my favorite when I was a kid. My dad took me to every practice and was at all my games." Joel smiled. "How about if you take it from here with the ballet lessons, and I pick up all the Little League practices?"

I wanted to remind him of what he had just said about Eden growing up too fast and add how much he had missed out on already. Why was he trying to negotiate his way out of ballet lessons? Eden was so adorably happy when he had agreed to take her to that first one. If he saw how serious his parenting responsibility was, why wouldn't he take on all extracurricular activities for both our kids?

Before any regrettable words flew out of my mouth, I thought about how Christy had rolled with Todd letting their kids eat ice cream right before dinner. I remembered how Christy had looked at Todd when he reported on his mango shake.

A simple truth settled on me. Love grows in fields of grace, not in ruts of shame.

If I wanted to see changes in our relationship, some of them could start with me.

CHAPTER 3

The next few days spooled out like so many weeks that had come before. Joel worked ten-hour days. I fell into my usual autopilot mommy mode. The minutes played out at the same pace they had for months. My head had returned to the same fuzzy space I'd been operating in. I didn't make many inroads to improve my communication with Joel, nor did we find a chance to be creative with our time together. But I did try to be less critical of him and of myself.

It lifted my spirits to think that Christy, Sierra, Emily, and Tess would be coming over on Thursday. All five of us hadn't met since before Thanksgiving. I was certain none of them had any idea what a lifeline they had been to me.

My wonderful mother-in-law volunteered to take Eden to ballet on Monday. Eden was excited, and I was grateful for the break. I put Alex down for a late nap and used the free time to take a bath. I will never again underestimate the value of a luxurious twenty-minute soak with lavender bath salts while being enveloped by spa music.

The evening got even better when Joel said he would bring dinner home. Grilled salmon with asparagus and wild rice drizzled with Joel's perfect aioli sauce — my favorite dish on the menu at the Blue Ginger. We put on a movie after the kids were in bed. It had been a long time since we'd had such a leisurely evening.

"Thank you for bringing dinner, Joel. It was perfect."

Joel leaned over and kissed the top of my head. "Thanks for all the encouraging things you've been saying to me the last few days."

I wasn't sure what he was referring to. They only thing I was aware of was that I'd made an effort not to say the words, "you're never here" or "if you were home more." He hated it when I used those phrases, and they had served only as a wedge to separate us over the past few months.

Joel leaned over and kissed my forehead, my eyebrow, my cheek. I cuddled closer. He turned down the volume and encircled me in his arms.

"I love you," he murmured. Joel's kisses

were soothing and persuasive, and I welcomed them. I wanted him to keep kissing me, captivating me.

"I've missed you," he said.

We kissed more intensely, and I started crying the sort of languid tears that come from the deepest wellspring of the heart and are barely noticeable by sight or sound.

Joel drew back, trying to read my expression. "What's wrong?" He looked at me the way he had many times over the last few years. I knew he was trying, really trying, to be patient and to understand my ever-shifting emotions.

"Nothing." I blinked and tried to fix my gaze on his dark eyes that were studying me from beneath his thick eyelashes.

He turned off the TV, slipped his hand in mine, and led me upstairs, pausing halfway to draw our joined hands to his lips. He kissed my wrist, my forearm, and the back of my hand.

"You sure you're okay?" he asked.

I nodded and managed to say, "I've missed you."

He paused before lifting my chin and kissing me tenderly. I responded with a long and lingering kiss. It had been far too long since we had shared a moment like this.

The next morning the welcoming fragrance of rich French roast coffee roused me from my faraway dream and enticed me to return to the real world. My eyelids fluttered open.

"Morning, beautiful." Joel turned on the soft light on the nightstand. He smiled and smoothed back my hair. The mug of steaming coffee waited next to the lamp. I noticed he was already shaven and dressed.

"You're not going to work already, are you?" I propped myself up and squinted to see the clock. "Is it really only 5:30? Are the kids awake?"

"Not yet."

"Joel . . ." I reached for his arm but didn't know what to say. *Stay? I love you? Don't leave me? Can't you call in sick?*

He paused, a half-grin rising on his lips. I knew it amused him that I was not a morning person. I never understood how he could be so coherent and cheerful before the sun was up.

"Joel, I . . ."

He kissed me on the forehead. "I know. Me too. See you this afternoon."

His exit was as quiet as could be, but as soon as the front door closed behind him, I heard Alex call out from his crib. With a sigh, I tossed back the comfy bedding and swung my bare legs over the edge of the bed.

Back to my real life.

Joel didn't come home until after the kids were in bed that night. It was the longest day I could remember him ever working. As soon as I heard the front door open, I left the dishwasher halfway unloaded and went to meet him.

"Hi! What a long day for you!"

"It was rough."

"What happened?" I reached out to take his hand.

He gave my hand a squeeze and let go. "Just a lot going on with the new chef and some other employee issues."

"You want to talk about anything?"

"No."

"Are you hungry?"

"No. I'm going take a shower and go to bed." He paused on the third stair and turned to look at me. "You okay?"

I nodded and forced a close-lipped smile.

He seemed to believe me and continued his climb.

I stood in the entryway for a few minutes, evaluating my options. I tried to see things from Joel's perspective and knew I shouldn't let my feelings be hurt. I'd fallen into that rut too many times.

It didn't take long for me to finish the dishes. I decided this would be a good time to think about a word for the year since the DOEs were coming over in two days. I settled into my favorite corner of the sofa, with my Bible and my barely used journal on my lap. In the past, I'd followed Christy's pattern of asking God for a word and then looking up the verses where that word appeared. It seemed like a good way to pick a word once again.

I felt both expectant and hypocritical, sitting in my quiet house, about to ask God for a word. I wanted God to lead me and reveal Himself to me. Like nearly everything else in my life, though, my relationship with God had been set on cruise control. As much as I wanted to ask Him for a word, I didn't feel right asking for anything right now.

With the dishwasher's faint whirling sound in the background, I closed my eyes and prayed the longest prayer my heart had managed to pour out in months. I felt a sense of calm. The quiet always made me think of God's love, and I suddenly realized why. It was because of my mom's favorite Bible verse, the one my dad had engraved on her headstone. I opened my Bible to Zephaniah 3:17, where I'd underlined it years ago.

The LORD your God in your midst,
The Mighty One, will save;
He will rejoice over you with gladness,
He will quiet you with His love,
He will rejoice over you with singing.

The beefy fist of grief came at me in a rush and sucker punched me in the gut. I should have realized how this passage would affect me. I gave into the pain and folded over, releasing a shoulder-shaking waterfall of tears.

I don't know how long I'd been crying before I looked up and reached for tissues from the box on the coffee table. The purging had waited a long time to be released. I felt spent. Bone weary and solemn. The house was quiet. Joel was undoubtedly asleep by now. I was alone and felt the thickness of the mantle of solitude as it covered me.

Drawing in a breath for courage, I reminded myself how much my mother loved God. She often told others how she surrendered her life to Christ on her fortieth birthday and how she wished she hadn't waited so long. She loved well. I wanted to love others the way she did, with kindness and generosity.

Love.

The word settled on me with a sense of finality.

Is that my word, Lord? Is love *my theme for this year?*

I wrote the word *LOVE* in large swirly letters in my journal and then wrote my mom's verse in block letters, underlining the words *He will quiet you with His love.* I put down my pen and felt exhausted. Poured out.

Putting everything aside, I turned off the lights and stretched out with my favorite cozy throw blanket covering me. I slept all night on the sofa because I didn't want to leave this space. I felt close to my mom there and closer to God than I had felt in a long time.

The next morning I was up before everyone else. The kids woke soon after. I made some coffee and started cooking oatmeal before Joel came down. He greeted me with a warm kiss, but I didn't think he realized I hadn't slept beside him all night or that I was wearing the same clothes I had worn the day before.

"There's something we need to talk about, Jennalyn." He leaned against the kitchen counter and held his coffee mug with both hands.

"Okay." I spooned oatmeal into Alex's

eager mouth. "What is it?"

"Let's talk tonight. After the kids go down." His expression didn't appear as serious as his tone, so I wasn't sure which of the two was the stronger clue about what he wanted to discuss.

All day I wished I hadn't agreed to wait. A slew of possible topics bumped around in my thoughts, and lots of them made me feel anxious.

When our conversation finally started a little after eight o'clock that night, I had narrowed down the possible topics to a short list. Ninety percent of them had a negative vibe. Joel appeared calm. He was stretched out in the recliner with the footrest up. I had made cappuccinos with our fancy machine just in case his mystery topic fell into the ten percent possibility of happy thoughts, the way our cappuccino conversations used to be.

"Everything is going to change, you know," he said.

"What do you mean?"

"Our lives. Vincent is working out great. His training is almost over, and we're ready to bring him on board. This is what we've been waiting for."

"Oh." I leaned back. "That's wonderful. I was afraid you were going to tell me some-

41

thing was falling apart somewhere."

"No. It's all finally coming together, not falling apart." Joel smiled. "So I've been thinking we should take a vacation."

I blinked and let his words sink in. Of all the topics I had sorted through that day, "vacation" wasn't one of them.

"Now that I can finally take some time off, I thought we should get away for a while and recharge. We haven't taken a vacation since . . ."

"Since our honeymoon?"

Joel leaned back. "You're right. That weekend in San Francisco for my cousin's wedding wasn't exactly a vacation."

"No, it wasn't. I don't think going anywhere with a teething baby can be considered a vacation."

"True. So . . ." Joel's eyes locked on mine. "What do you think about going to Hawaii?"

It was as if he had just tossed a handful of confetti into my life. "Hawaii? Really?"

Joel grinned and handed me his phone. "Todd told me about this the other night, and I think we should go."

I swiped through the website's images of pristine blue water, palm trees, and rows of vacant lounge chairs on a white sandy beach. I scrolled back to the top to see the name of the resort and saw the title of the website. All the glittering confetti in my mind vanished.

"The Marriage Rigorous Renewal Conference?"

"It's being held at a four-star resort. They have speakers at night and workshops in the morning. We'll have the afternoons free."

"You think we need to check into some sort of marriage rehab?"

Joel looked hurt. "It's not rehab. It's a retreat. A couples retreat. Did you see the workshop topics? I thought the ones on 'Managing Expectations' and 'Parenting as a Team' would be helpful for us."

I placed his phone on the coffee table and tried to think of the right thing to say.

"What's wrong? Why don't you like the idea?" Joel seemed stunned by my reaction. "I thought you would be all over this."

How could I explain to him that going someplace to work on our marriage was not my idea of a vacation, even if the destination was a tropical island I always had wanted to visit?

Joel added, "Todd said he and Christy are thinking about going to the one over Easter vacation in April. I thought . . ."

"Christy and Todd are going?" I reached for his phone and had another look at the dates and the resort photos.

"Whoa! What was that?"

"What?" I looked up.

"I tell you about the retreat, and you act offended. I tell you Christy and Todd are going, and suddenly you're interested."

"Joel, when you said, 'Let's go to Hawaii,' I thought you meant let's go on a cruise or rent a condo on the beach or something. I didn't expect you to be pitching a marriage conference. Especially one with the word *rigorous* in its name."

"What's wrong with getting some help? Especially with our communication? We obviously need help in that area."

"We do."

"I thought it would be good for us. I honestly thought you would want to go."

"I do! I want to go. I would love to go to Hawaii." My eyes suddenly filled with tears as a herd of rogue hormones broke loose and ran amuck.

"What's wrong?"

"Nothing."

"Why do you always say 'nothing'? It's obviously something."

"I don't know. It's everything lately. It creeps up on me, and I feel overwhelmed."

"By what?"

"Hormones. Exhaustion. Grief." I wiped

44

my eyes and tried to reign in my emotions.

"Grief?" Joel picked out what must have seemed like the least expected word in the lineup.

I nodded and drew in a wobbly breath. "I've been wanting to tell you. I keep thinking about my mom. Little things pop up that remind me of her. I miss her. A lot. Last night I was reading the verse that's on her gravestone, and I couldn't stop crying."

He lowered the footrest and came over to sit beside me, pulling me close so that my head could rest on his shoulder. "Why didn't you tell me?"

"Because . . ." I didn't want to say it was because he was never home.

He stroked my hair and kissed the top of my head.

"I don't know," I said quietly. I reached for another tissue and felt calmed. The tears had come quickly, like a springtime shower, and ceased just as fast. It wasn't like the deluge that had poured out the night before. Still, I felt exhausted. "Grief is a thug," I said as if it were my closing statement.

"Maybe we should get some sleep," Joel suggested. "We can talk about all this later. If you would rather rent a condo somewhere or go on a cruise, we can do that. I just thought it would be good for us to get away.

Just the two of us, without the kids."

"I agree."

Joel stood and stretched out his hand. "Come on."

CHAPTER 4

The next evening Christy was the first to arrive for our Daughters of Eve gathering. I was glad she was early because it gave me a chance to ask if she and Todd were planning to go to the retreat.

"If you asked Todd, he would say yes, we're going. But I don't see how we can. It's so expensive. He's planning to take on side work to earn the extra money." Christy looked embarrassed. "I got mad when he told me because I want him home with us on the weekends, not painting houses or making benches out of surfboards."

"I get that."

"I know you do. The deadline for registration is March 21. Todd thinks we can save up enough before then." Christy sat on a stool at the kitchen counter. "You know what this means?"

"You won't see your husband for the next six weeks?"

"Yes. There is that. It also means that my word for the year is already waving over my life."

I tried to remember what she had told me at her house last week. Lately my memory was so fragmented.

"Trust." Christy graciously filled in my memory gap without missing a beat. "This is my first chance this year to trust God for something that seems impossible. Well, not impossible, but definitely something outside the norm. Something I can't control."

I nodded. "I think I have control issues too. As soon as Joel brought up the idea of a vacation, I wanted to change the plan to something different, like a cruise. Why do I do that? Why couldn't I just let my husband be happy and tell me all about his ideas for our vacation?"

Christy seemed to be contemplating a response while I filled the electric kettle with water. Before she had a reply, a knock sounded at the front door. Christy smiled. "That's definitely an Emily knock. I'll get it."

The two of them returned to the kitchen, and I felt instantly warmed by Emily's trademark gentle smile.

"It's so good to see you," I said as we hugged. "It's been months!"

48

"I know," Emily agreed. "I'm glad you set this up. I've missed being with everyone."

She was standing by the stove, and it struck me that, for the first time in more than a year, Emily and I were together in the same spot where she had held me while Alex made an early entrance into this world. Ours was the most unconventional beginning to a friendship ever. I was home alone when my water broke, and in the quick shuffle, I fell and twisted my ankle. The terror that came from the pain in my foot and my inability to stand up was intensified when I went into labor on the kitchen floor that December morning.

Like an angel, Emily had showed up unexpectedly at just the right moment. She bolstered me up and coached me while the two paramedics handled things efficiently, as if they assisted emergency deliveries every day.

Calm, shy Emily had infused me with her strength in that frightening moment. She convinced me everything was going to be okay, and it was. For such a petite woman, she was an emotional stronghold and added so much to our group.

I heard the front door open with a quick knock added as an afterthought. The atmosphere in my whole house changed when free-spirited Sierra made a grand entrance, having let herself in as usual.

"What smells so good? Did you make your mom's peanut butter cookies, Jennalyn? Wait. I don't see them. Where are they? Are you hiding them?"

As if on cue, the timer on the oven chimed, and I reached for my favorite pie-shaped oven mitts to pull out the two cookie sheets.

"Yum!" Sierra said. "I love coming to your house."

"Me too." Emily moved the spoon rest on the top of the stove so I would have room to put down both cookie sheets.

"I brought tea." Christy pulled several fancy-looking boxes of loose tea from her large bag.

"Oh, I almost forgot!" Sierra headed for the front door and called over her shoulder, "I brought something for everyone. I'll be right back."

Christy lined up the boxes of tea. I pulled the carton of milk from the refrigerator and poured some into my largest glass pitcher. Emily retrieved several glasses from the cupboard. I loved it when my friends made themselves at home in my kitchen. It was the closest I ever felt to my secret dream of having a bunch of sisters.

Sierra returned with a large shopping bag. "I washed them already, but we might want to give them another rinse since they've been in my trunk for a few weeks." She placed the bag on the counter and pulled out five vintage-looking mugs with different initials in a curvy font on each of them.

"I couldn't believe I found one for each of us," Sierra said. "J, C, T, E, and S. They were supposed to be everyone's Christmas presents."

"We'll just pretend you're extremely early this year," Christy said.

"Eleven months early!" Sierra laughed.

"Our initials!" Emily reached for hers. "These are cute. Thank you, Sierra."

"I thought maybe we could keep them here," Sierra said. "If you have room in your cupboard and don't mind, Jennalyn. That way we'll always have our own mugs whenever we come over."

"Of course I don't mind. There's room. I'll keep them on one of the upper shelves."

Emily already was rinsing the mugs under steaming hot water in the sink.

"Oooh! Nice-looking tea boxes," Sierra said. "What's this? Mint? Could be nice. Green tea? Not usually my cuppa tea. Lapsa — can't pronounce ya — so, no. And what's this one? Assam. I've had this one before.

It's good with milk." Sierra looked up at me, her flowing curly blond hair doing a delayed swish. "Please tell me you have milk."

"Right here. And the water's hot. Should we make one pot or several?"

"Let's make them all!" Sierra's typically high-octane energy seemed to be set on full blast tonight.

I pulled down four mismatched teapots and wondered what might pop out of Sierra's mouth next. She had managed to come across as obtrusive to each of us at some point, but we all found it easy to forgive her because she didn't have a drop of malice in her. Her words were like streamers of colorful, flighty ideas, and her opinions fluttered about wildly. They might give you a friendly thwap in the face, but they never were intended to hurt anyone.

Sierra had dared me to try new things and dream about using my love of painting for more than a hobby. I both envied and treasured her enthusiasm for life.

A soft tapping sounded at the front door, and Sierra rushed off to get it. "Tess should know by now she can just come in."

Tall, graceful Tess entered the kitchen with her arm linked through Sierra's. Her toasty brown skin and ocean-colored eyes gave her an exotic appearance that Emily once said made her seem mysterious until she got to know her. Even as a single young professional, Tess was one of us, heart to heart. She never seemed to feel excluded from our mommy conversations. We were the big sisters she never had and always wanted.

Tonight she was wearing a chunky, long fisherman's knit sweater and skinny jeans with a beautiful brightly colored headband scarf to keep her long dark hair back from her face. The ends of the scarf hung down her back, making her lovely looking from all angles. She always was her own best advertisement for her career as a personal stylist.

"Perfect timing, Tess." Christy was drying the mug with the fancy "T" on the front and handed it to her. "Sierra brought one for each of us. And we have some interesting tea from Aunt Marti."

"I love it!" Tess examined her mug. "Where did you find these, Sierra?"

"One of the vintage shops I go to in Orange. Not the one in the circle. It's one that's on the same street as the Victorian house that's being renovated."

"I don't know where that is," Tess said. "You'll have to take me sometime. I have a new client who is crazy about vintage jewelry. I need some new shopping spots to find what she wants. Right now she's into anything that's art deco."

"Can I confess something?" Emily asked.

We all turned to her with matching looks of surprise. I couldn't imagine our sweet Emily having anything in her life that she needed to confess.

"Sometimes I wish you could tell us who your clients are. I know you have to keep your list confidential. It's just that, knowing you have a job dressing people who are wealthy and famous makes me so curious whenever you mention them."

"Me too," Sierra agreed. "I'm always wondering who you're hanging out with."

Tess reached for one of the warm cookies I had transferred to a fancy plate on the counter. "It's not really the way you're imagining it to be. Most of the people I work with aren't well known."

We all seemed to be studying her, deciding if she was trying to underwhelm us as a way of protecting her clients. Christy and I exchanged glances. I was pretty sure Christy was thinking what I was thinking. What we really wanted to hear Tess talk about was not one of her clients. We wanted to hear about the guy she went on a date with.

"What about the nonclients?" Christy asked with a touch of mischief in her tone.

"Is there anyone you would like to tell us about?"

Tess's countenance changed. She gave Christy a "hush" sort of expression and took a dainty nibble of her cookie.

Sierra perked up. "I saw that. What does Christy know that we don't? Tess, have you met someone?"

Tess looked away.

"You have, haven't you? You met someone." Emily leaned in. "Tell us."

Tess lifted her chin. Her gaze swept the circle, as if she was inviting all of us into her secret even though she should be keeping her lips sealed.

"Well . . ." Tess looked at me, and I raised my eyebrows curiously.

"Oh, this is gonna be good," Sierra said. "Quick! Everybody pour your tea, and somebody grab the plate of cookies. We need to be on the couch to hear this."

The five of us clicked into our women-sharing-the-kitchen rumba with ease. In record time our new mugs were filled and we were settled on the two facing sofas, with cookies in hand. All eyes were on Tess, who had been assigned the recliner.

"I don't know if I should say anything." Tess leaned back with her long legs crossed and both her hands bent around her mug of Assam tea.

"How about if we guess, and you can just nod?" Sierra asked.

Christy playfully started with, "Is he tall, dark, and handsome?"

Tess hesitated, staring into her tea before relinquishing a small nod.

"What's his name?" Emily asked.

"I can't say."

"Let's just call him Guy," I suggested.

"Are you going out with Guy?" Sierra asked.

Tess looked up. "No. Absolutely not."

"But I thought you had coffee with him last week," Christy said.

Emily and Sierra looked at Christy as if trying to figure out why she had the inside scoop.

"I thought when you texted that you couldn't come to dinner with everyone, it was because you were meeting a guy." Christy looked around. "Was that not a group text?"

Tess shook her head.

"Sorry!"

"It's fine, Christy." Tess adjusted her headband scarf. "I wasn't sure whether I should say anything tonight."

"Why?" Sierra asked.

"Because it's . . ."

We all waited.

"Okay," she said. "I'll tell you guys, but let me say what I have to say first, before you give me any advice. Promise?"

"Promise," we all echoed.

"I had coffee with Guy last week, but it wasn't like what you're thinking . . ." Tess hesitated. "I met him in October because he was a client assigned to me. The network he was with hired me to style him, but then the production he was in didn't get picked up for the next season."

"Would we know him?" Sierra asked.

Emily nudged Sierra and whispered, "We just promised we wouldn't ask questions."

"No, we didn't," Sierra whispered back. "We promised we wouldn't give advice."

"I don't mind if you ask questions," Tess said. "The answer is, yes. You might know him. He's not currently working on anything, though."

We waited to see if she wanted to give us any more details.

"He's smart and funny and good looking. We go to the same church. And . . ."

"Are you going to see him again?" Sierra asked.

"I don't know."

"You sound interested in him," Sierra said. "If he asked you to coffee, he must be

57

interested in you."

Tess pressed her lips together and looked down. We all waited for her to respond. She lifted her chin and finished her earlier sentence. "And . . . he's married."

CHAPTER 5

Tess held up her palm like a stop sign. "Before any of you say anything, it's not what you think. We're not seeing each other. We're not anything. Just friends. Colleagues. His wife left him last fall and moved across country. He's trying to figure out what to do."

"Do you know why she left?" Sierra asked.

Tess shifted in her seat and paused, staring into her mug of tea while the rest of us shot glances at each other.

"You don't have to say anything if you don't want to," Emily said.

"No, I do. I want to talk about it. I need to. I've been wanting to tell all of you, but I knew this conversation had to be in person. Not as one of our long group texts." Tess sat up a little straighter. "The reason his wife left is because she doesn't agree that he should keep pursuing a career in LA after the show was cancelled. The last few years were overwhelming for both of them. She wants him to go into a different line of work so he can spend more time with her and their daughter."

I glanced over at Christy. She caught my gaze and held it for a moment. The circumstances sounded similar to what I'd told her last week about Joel working long hours for so many months. I couldn't imagine ever leaving Joel or making a demand that he abandon his career. However, I did understand the pain and frustration. I imagined the pressure would be escalated unbearably for someone in the film industry.

"He's good at what he does," Tess said. "I have to say, though, I see his wife's side on this. The show he was on was grueling. I don't know how he kept at it for so long."

My brain spun through all the possible shows where a good-looking actor had done "grueling" work for the past few years. I assumed the other DOEs were doing the same.

Tess took a demure sip of tea and returned the new mug to her lap. "He thinks he should wait it out and see what might open up. I can see why he would want to do that. It seemed like a reasonable next step, but then his wife gave him an ultimatum. She said that if he doesn't leave California to be with her, she's going to file for divorce."

"How long ago did she say that?" Sierra asked.

"Two weeks."

"And he's still here? Without work?"

Emily nudged Sierra.

"What? It's a question." Sierra looked around the circle and turned back to Tess. "Sorry. I'll be quiet. Go ahead. Just say what you want."

"All I know is that at first he was going to leave California and try to reconcile. Then last week he decided to stay. At least for now. The way he sees it, he thinks it might be best to let her take the next step and file because she's been unhappy for a long time."

Tess leaned forward. "Please don't anybody say anything about how unhappiness shouldn't be grounds for divorce. I know that. And before you ask, as far as I know, there was no unfaithfulness or abuse or anything that would be considered an understandable reason for two Christians to end their marriage."

Tess leaned forward even more and said, "And don't quote the verse from the Old Testament about how God hates divorce. He already heard that from his brother, and now he feels like he doesn't have anyone he

61

can talk to. Except me."

The room was quiet.

Tess added firmly, "I'm a friend he can talk to. That's all."

I don't know if it was the mama bear in me or the concerned big sis, but I knew I had to say something and say it as gently as possible. "Tess, please be careful."

"I know. I am. Like I said, we're not seeing each other. I'm just a neutral person he can talk to."

"You might not be as neutral as you think," Christy said.

"Why do you say that?"

"Because you know a lot about his situation."

"I do. But I'm still neutral."

Christy looked skeptical. "I don't know if a woman in your position can ever be neutral when the guy is in the middle of such a big decision."

Tess tilted her head and pressed her lips together. It was her politely frustrated expression. We had all seen it before.

"I'm sorry," Christy said. "I shouldn't have —"

"Will everyone stop apologizing?" Tess spouted. "Just talk to me. I want to hear what you have to say. I do see your point, Christy. Talking with him and meeting for coffee might be taken in the wrong way."

"Do you think he's considering something more for the two of you down the road?" Emily asked.

"I don't know. I don't know what he's thinking."

"But you do know what you're thinking," Christy said. "Or I should say, what you're feeling."

"What are you getting at?" Tess asked.

"I'm saying, based on what you're feeling, how was it last week when you met for coffee?" Christy asked. "Did it feel like a date?"

Tess thought for a moment. Her expression made it clear that the answer was yes. "Listen, I would be dishonest with myself and all of you if I didn't admit that, yes, I am attracted to him. But I never would act on it. And I never would do anything that made him think I was . . ." Tess stopped.

"That you were what?" Sierra asked.

"Available. Interested." Tess looked frustrated. "But then, I guess I already made that clear when I agreed to meet with him."

"I just wonder," Emily said. "Do you think it might be easier for him to walk away from a difficult marriage if it meant he could have a chance to be with you?"

Tess's lips parted, but she didn't say anything.

63

Sierra put her mug on a coaster with a decisive thump. "I have to say something."

I hoped that whatever popped out of Sierra's mouth would be helpful and not one of her well-meaning bursts of passion.

"Okay. Bring it," Tess said with a half-smile, which made me feel like however the rest of this conversation went, it was going to be okay.

"I want to say that I don't think it's fair for him to pursue you while he and his wife are trying to figure out their relationship. It sounds like he's putting you in the middle and looking to you as a future possibility. That could end up shifting his decision-making onto you."

"What do you mean?" Tess asked.

"He could end up saying, 'If I leave her, will you be with me?' That rolls all the weight of his final decision onto you."

Tess shook her head. "No. It's not like that."

"Maybe not," Sierra said. "But I have to say I would feel differently right now if you were sitting here telling us that you met a guy whose marriage fell apart, he's no longer legally married, he's ready to move on, and he would like to get together with you for coffee. That would be different than his using you to help him to process this huge life decision while he's still married."

"He's not using me," Tess said defensively.

"Okay, maybe that isn't the right word. He's stuck, though. He needs to make some enormous decisions about his career and his marriage. I think it's better for you if he makes those choices on his own. Without the possibility of a relationship with you being a factor."

"So, you're saying I shouldn't even talk to him until he figures out what he's going to do."

"That's definitely an option." Sierra's tone softened. "I care too much about you to see you caught up in something that could really be painful."

"I feel the same way," Emily said. "We all want you to be with someone who's worthy of you."

"What does that even mean?" Tess's eyes narrowed, and she put her mug on the coffee table. "Do any of you really think there's some guy out there who is my age or older who hasn't been through a breakup or divorce? Every man I've met in the past ten years has come out of some sort of messed-up previous relationship."

She pushed up the sleeves on her bulky sweater. "I've heard all your love stories. It wasn't complicated for you because you were all young when you met your spouses. None of you can know what this is like for me."

"You're right," Emily said tenderly. "We don't know what it's like."

Tess seemed to be blinking back a few tears that were threatening to come out of hiding. "It just gets really lonely sometimes."

"We love you, Tess," I said. "Just be careful with that beautiful heart of yours."

"I am. I will." Tess leaned back and put up the footrest on the lounger. "Can we talk about something else now?"

"Wait." Emily looked around before asking a final question. "So, what are you going to do?"

"What do you mean?" Tess asked.

"Do you think you'll see him again?"

"Probably. Like I said, we go to the same church. We have a few mutual friends. I don't know. I'm still processing everything." Tess left it there. "Thank you for listening. And telling me what I needed to hear."

"And a few things you didn't want to hear?" I asked.

She nodded, but I thought her expression looked lighter.

At that moment, my hostess instincts kicked in. I eased us on to the next subject, which was an update on the new chef and how it looked like Joel would finally have some time off. Christy brought up the marriage retreat and added how Todd wanted to go and was working side jobs to make it happen.

That rolled into Emily talking about how Trevor, her Realtor husband, had a major real estate deal fall apart right after Christmas. It affected him more than she had expected, and their plan to move out of their apartment into a home of their own was now going to be delayed.

Sierra told us that she and Jordan were talking about moving too. They had been living with his parents in Irvine for several years. Their daughter, Ella Mae, was fifteen months old, and they felt they had overstayed their welcome.

"You know what?" Tess said. "This is great. I like hearing about your problems."

"What could you possibly like about hearing everyone's problems?" I asked with a laugh.

"Sometimes I think my life would be so much easier if I found someone and got married and had a couple of babies," Tess said. "You guys keep it real for me. Married or single, life is just messy, isn't it?"

We all laughed. It felt good to have vented around the circle and now to be reaching for the last of the peanut butter cookies. We talked for another hour, being honest about our messy lives.

Before everyone left, Christy asked if she could pray for us. Her prayer was sweet and comforting. Her sincere words fell on us like a benediction. She asked God to give Tess wisdom. For me, she asked God to restore my soul. Her prayer for Sierra was that God would lead them to a perfect haven, and for Emily she asked God to bless Trevor's work.

"Let's do that every time we meet," Emily suggested. "I love being prayed for."

"Me too." I smiled at Christy. "Thank you. I needed that."

"We all did," Tess said.

Our hugs at the door felt soul deep that night as the DOEs were leaving. Christy pointed out that none of us had shared our word for the year. We agreed on the spot to have another gathering in a few weeks.

My friends had barely made it to their cars before I decided we would make it a Valentine's Day theme. I couldn't wait to hand-make the invitations the way I used to. I envisioned the decorations and refreshments: red hearts strung across the kitchen window and sugar cookies with pink frosting. I decided it would be fun to make valentines for each other. It would be nurturing and affirming. I loved the idea.

The replies to my group text the next morning were unanimous. We set the date for the first Saturday in February. Instead of meeting again at my house, Tess persuaded us to come to her place. We were excited because none of us had been there before. She lived in La Habra Heights, a suburb of Los Angeles. She had told us that her duplex was a hillside haven and that we would feel right at home.

I was still determined to make valentines for all the DOEs; so I made a list of the art supplies I needed to pick up. I hadn't painted anything for a long time and felt eager to create something beautiful. I wondered if my lack of artistic expression for so many months had contributed to the dips in my mood.

My plan was to pick up the supplies before Eden's ballet class. I was glad Joel came home in time to watch Alex; this way I would be able to do the quick shopping trip without lugging Alex along in his heavy carrier.

Right before I left, Joel said, "Hey, let's talk about our vacation plans when you get back."

"Okay." A few days earlier I had told him

I had thought a lot about the cruise or condo possibilities but decided those would be fun to do as a family once the kids were older. We hadn't finalized any plans for the retreat, though.

"Did you and Christy talk about the retreat yet?"

"A little. She said they're going to make their decision by the end of March."

Joel's phone buzzed. He rested his arms on the kitchen counter, stretched them out, and started tapping a reply on his phone.

I leaned across the other side of the counter, wanting him to look me in the eyes. "Joel?"

He looked up at me.

"Even if the Spencers can't make it, I still would like to go. To the retreat. Just the two of us."

"Good." He gave me one of his great smiles. "Because I registered us and booked the flight."

I pulled back, feeling my face warming. "I thought you just said we were going to talk about it. Tonight. I'm sure that you just said, 'Let's talk about it tonight.' "

"I was going to wait till the kids were in bed and tell you I grabbed two spots for us before it was all booked. I wanted to surprise you."

"Joel."

"What? Didn't you just say that you wanted to go?"

"I did. I do. It's just that . . ." I lowered my voice when I realized that Eden had come closer, as if sensing that her mommy and daddy were about to have another one of their "you're not listening to me" arguments.

"We hadn't discussed it yet. That's all." I tried to speak as calmly as I could. "It seems like you made a decision for both of us."

"How is that a problem?" Joel still looked confused. His voice kept elevating. "You said we should do this. Isn't that what you just said?"

"Why don't we talk about it tonight, like you suggested?" I stayed composed and exited the kitchen, heading for the downstairs bathroom.

When I closed the door behind me and looked up, my reflection in the mirror startled me. My hair was a mess. I undid the day-old braid and pulled my hair up into a high ponytail, smoothing the sides as best as I could. I had intended to take a shower, but the afternoon had gotten away from me. If I was going to get to the art supply store, I needed to leave now.

I washed my face for the first time that

71

day and patted it dry with a hand towel that smelled as if little peanut butter–laced fingers had used it last.

When I returned to the kitchen, Joel was holding Alex on his lap at the counter, and Eden was sliding back and forth on the kitchen floor in her ballet slippers, her arms over her head, entertaining the guys.

Joel's gaze followed me as I went to the refrigerator and pulled out a pitcher of water with sliced lemons and cucumbers.

"Would you like some?" I offered, after I had poured myself a glass.

"No, thanks. Isn't it about time for you to go?" he asked.

I glanced at the clock and nodded before taking a long drink. Possibly the first full glass of water I had drunk all day.

"All right then, little ballerina. Time for your lesson." Joel stood and lowered Alex to the floor. "Have fun with your mom."

Alex started to cry. Eden chimed in with, "I want you to take me, Daddy!" She ran to him and clutched his legs.

"I'll be here when you get home." Joel's voice came across stern.

"I want you to take me, Daddy!"

Alex had pulled himself up and was still crying, clinging to Joel's leg.

I secretly felt glad that Joel could see our

72

children in one of their tandem meltdowns. He seldom saw this side of them.

"Come on, Eden." I pulled a baggy sweater from the stack of folded clothes on the couch and pulled it over my head.

"Do you want me to take her?" Joel's forceful voice called out over the squalling, which prompted Alex to wail louder.

I knew if we tried to change plans, the situation would just get more complicated. I didn't try to yell back over the toddler chorus. Instead, I shook my head, put on my "nice mommy" face, and rushed Eden out the door.

She was still wailing as I buckled her into her car seat and started the engine. I put on her favorite sing-along music. Fortunately, it had the desired effect, calming her and stopping the tears before we were even out of our neighborhood.

Why does Joel get so tense about everything? He's like his dad and the rest of the men in his big, hot-blooded family. I wish Joel could relax around the kids.

We were almost to the art supply store when I wondered if Joel's ambitious goals and long work hours would ever really change the way he kept saying they would.

What if the rest of our lives are going to be like this?

Eden seemed to have forgotten all about her tears when we arrived at the store and I told her she could pick one new treat. In her pink tutu, she joyfully bobbed up and down the aisles with me, examining all the options. My basket was soon filled with the items on my list.

To my surprise, she wanted to go back to the aisle with the colorful pom-poms in one of the lower bins. She selected one pink pom-pom the size of a grape. It was sweet the way she took my "only one treat" so seriously.

"I'm glad you found these," I told her. "Because I need twenty pom-poms. And you know what? We can share them."

Her eyes lit up. "And Alex too?"

"As long as he doesn't put them in his mouth, then yes. We'll share them with Alex too."

Life was all pom-poms and tutus for my innocent daughter as she skipped into her dance studio ten minutes later. We were a little early, and I was glad I didn't see anyone I knew. If I ever did apply to teach a watercolor class here one day, I wanted the manager to see me as a professional and not as the harried mom I was this afternoon.

"Where's By-let?" Eden looked around for her new friend.

"Maybe she'll be here in a minute." I pulled Eden's sweater off and pointed to the row of chairs lining the bottom edge of the large window facing the parking area. "Let's sit here. You can watch for her."

Eden climbed onto a chair and turned around, balancing on her knees. She looked out the window and held the back of the chair, watching for Violet. Her waiting lasted only a few minutes before she squealed, "I see her! She's coming."

I turned and watched a darling little ballerina with short blond hair and fancy pink glasses make her way across the parking lot. She was holding the hand of a tall man with strawberry-blond hair.

He looked up, revealing the broad nose and tilted grin on a face I'd once known by memory. My unprepared heart clenched.

Garrett?

CHAPTER 6

It's not possible. That can't be Garrett.

My hand automatically went to my chest as if grasping for the emerald ring that once was hidden there.

Violet and her father entered the studio, and Eden bounded over to greet them. The voice that rumbled from the tall man was unmistakable. I couldn't look away.

He glanced in my direction, and as soon as our eyes met, he froze. My heart gave an uneven thump.

Our daughters took off hand in hand to join the others in the dance floor area. I felt glued to my chair as he slowly made his way in my direction. He stood in front of me, still staring as if he couldn't decide if I were real.

"Jennie?" His voice turned raspy; his eyes narrowed in disbelief.

I nodded, instantly affected by the way he said my name. My mother was the only

76

other person in the world who had ever called me Jennie.

"Eden? She's yours?"

I nodded again.

Other moms and dads had arrived and were settling into the chairs lined along the wall. The class was beginning, and the only place for him to sit was next to me. Garrett remained standing, looking at me as if he expected me to say something or do something that would transport us both out of this wincingly difficult moment.

"Could we . . ." He pointed to the parking lot.

I stayed where I was, looking at him and then turning to focus on the little dancers as they lined up. I didn't know what to do.

Garrett shifted from one foot to the other, his large frame blocking my full view. "I'm going to just . . ." He retraced his steps and went outside.

Drawing in a slow breath, I tried to think. All that came to me was a rush of repressed memories. They were so vivid. Friday night dates to the movies, football games, homecoming dances, late-night talks, shared holidays, birthday parties, the crazy pranks Garrett loved to play. I closed my eyes, and all I could see were summer sunsets. All I could think of were our kisses. Hundreds of shared kisses. Brief, quick, slow, gentle, determined, lingering, convincing, rushed, romantic — we had created a vocabulary of kisses over the two years that we were inseparable.

My hand rose to cover my lips as if I thought that wiping my mouth would make the memories go away.

What is he thinking right now?

One of the moms who had been standing came over and sat in the empty chair next to me. My eyes were fixed on Eden, but my thoughts were focused on Garrett and how he was undoubtedly positioned just on the other side of the large windows behind me, staring inside at the back of my head. He used to love it when I wore my long hair in a ponytail.

I should say something. I can't ignore him. I should go outside.

I reviewed all the options of what I could or should say and decided that I would approach him like any other old friend.

Hello, how are you? How's your family? Your daughter is adorable. Nice to see you. Good-bye.

I ran through the script in my head until I felt confident enough to get up and slide past the other parents. Garrett must have observed my departure because he was standing by the door, holding it open for me.

"Jennie, I can't believe you're here. I didn't know you still lived in this area."

I looked at him and then looked away, forgetting my rehearsed, safe words. His face was too familiar. His voice, his inflections. It felt so strange.

"You look great," he said, nervously filling the void as I tried to find my voice. "I mean, you look the same. I couldn't believe that was you."

I still couldn't speak. Reality had bent like a paper puzzle, and my current life was tucked away in an origami fold for a moment. I was standing in front of him now as an equal in thoughts and emotions to the girl I was back then.

"So, I guess I met your husband here at the first class. Or at least, he said he was Eden's dad. I don't know if he's your . . ."

"He is." My voice cracked as I spoke for the first time. I cleared my throat. "Joel is my husband."

The simple act of saying Joel's name aloud unfolded the emotional paper trick. I was back to the present. I wasn't a teenage girl in jeans standing in front of my high school boyfriend who could talk me into almost anything. I was a wife. A mother. A strong woman who now wore yoga pants and oversized sweaters and went out in public with her messy hair up in a ponytail.

"Joel told me about his restaurant." Garrett seemed determined to start a conversation. "It sounds like a great place. I'm going to try it one of these days."

I nodded. "Good."

"So, how are you?" Garrett looked as if he were in pain.

"I'm good. You?"

"Yeah, good. I'm busy. We live in Irvine. Near the Spectrum. Left Idaho about four months ago. Tiffany started a new business with a friend. She travels a lot. I work at home. Web design. Some photography. And Violet, of course. She keeps me busy."

His rush of details seemed to calm him a bit. He looked around as if to make sure we were the only ones who could hear our conversation. Rubbing the back of his neck, Garrett dipped his chin and in a low voice said, "Jennie, I have to say something to you."

I glanced at the tiny dancers through the big window and then back at Garrett.

"Jennie, I'm sorry."

I never would have expected to hear his sudden statement. His expression was sincere.

"I really messed up. I've wanted to tell you for years. I wanted to apologize and ask you to forgive me for treating you the way I did. I'm sorry. I don't know if you can forgive me, but I hope you will. I was wrong."

This show of humility was something new in this man-version of Garrett. I didn't know what to make of his honesty and vulnerability.

"You don't have to say anything," he quickly added. "I just need you to know that I'm really sorry, and I apologize." Garrett placed his large hand over his heart and gazed at me.

We stood in silence, both of us blinking, looking at each other. I nodded. That's all I was able to manage in that unexpected moment. I nodded again.

"Okay." He turned to look into the studio. I did the same. We remained standing three feet apart in front of the window as if we were complete strangers and it was only natural to ignore each other's presence.

All I could think of right then was the way his car smelled that night when we had sat in the parking lot behind the two-story office building. A sickening sweetness came from a pineapple-shaped piña colada air freshener he had hung from his rearview mirror. When I had teased him about the unusual addition, he said "someone" had given it to him.

I was so naive.

Blinking, I focused on the sight of my daughter and his daughter, our daughters, twirling in their pink tutus. My thoughts cleared.

"Garrett?"

He turned to look at me. His eyes were misty.

"Garrett, I forgive you. I did a long time ago." I felt my throat tightening. "Thank you for saying what you did just now."

He nodded and attempted a conciliatory expression. "I'm sorry I didn't reach out to you when your mom passed away. I wanted to. I wish I had."

"Thank you."

"My mom said she saw you there, at the memorial service. I wish I had gone. Your mother was a very special person. She was always so nice to me."

I managed to nod. I was going to echo that indeed she was a very special person and she had been very nice to him, but the words stuck in my throat.

"Well, I guess . . ." He looked lost.

A bit of my mother's kindness and hospitable spirit seemed to override my emotional reaction to the last ten minutes. "We should probably go back inside."

"I'm going to stay here," he said.

"Okay." I didn't look back as I opened the door and slid into the back corner of the studio. I stood for the remainder of the class and opened my arms wide when Eden dashed to hug me and receive her accolades.

Violet was right behind her, looking around for her father. I was grateful that Garrett appeared instantly, scooped up Violet, and exited before Eden realized her friend was gone. I kept the praises going and pressed to hurry home so she could tell her daddy all about her lesson.

"And show him," Eden said once I had her strapped in her car seat, pink tulle sticking out in every direction. "I want to show him my dance."

"He will love it," I promised.

"And the pom-poms. I want to show Alex the pom-poms. But he can't eat them."

"That's right. Alex may not eat the pom-poms."

Joel met us at the door and smiled at Eden, asking her about class. As she jabbered, he shot me a repentant glance. I knew it was his way of apologizing for the tension right before I left.

I gave him a close-lipped smile. It was the

best I could muster and seemed to be enough to settle our earlier tussle and get us moving on with dinner, baths, and bedtime. I somehow had managed to stuff down all the emotions that had raced through me during the Garrett encounter. I knew I would tell Joel about it eventually. But not tonight.

Tonight would be all about settling the plans for our Hawaii trip. At least that's what I thought. Joel didn't bring it up. Instead, we talked about which car had the most gas so he would know which one to take to work in the morning. Then he asked if I could get him some toothpaste for sensitive teeth because he didn't like the kind we had. He said that once he finished training Vincent, he was going to make an appointment to see the dentist. And get a haircut.

We went to bed with our backs turned to each other, and as usual, Joel had no trouble falling asleep.

Sleep seemed to be standing over me but refusing to cover me. I curled inward, pulling the comforter up to my chin. It felt as if my whole being had crawled into a memory-padded cave where it was dark and lonely. So lonely.

I reviewed the events of that evening and lingered in the cave as I thought about how

Garrett had apologized with such sincerity. That would have made my mother happy. She would have told Garrett that she was proud of him. I could see her smiling at him.

Oh, Garrett. What might have happened if you had found your humility all those years ago? Would you and I have gotten back together?

I brushed the thought aside. Everyone knows the futility of pondering too many what-ifs. I thought of how Christy had referred to them one time as "the Land of If Only." Perhaps my melancholy cave was a hidden entrance to the Land of If Only.

What felt confusing, as I stayed in a tucked position under the covers, was that I knew my real life was outside, waiting in suspension while I tried to feel my way through the cave. I could leave. I could walk out into the light at any time and go back to being me. Jennalyn. Wife, mother, friend. Artist.

But I didn't want to leave this strange place that had opened to me. I wanted to stay in the deep quietness, staring into the darkness, because for the first time in many years, I could see shimmering memories of my mom floating around me. She was there. Garrett was there. His voice, so familiar and echoing afresh in my ears, bounced off the walls.

The odd thing was that his voice, the reality of his presence in my current life, brought a dimension of vividness to all the images of my mother. I felt closer to her than I had in years. And it seemed to be because of Garrett and the way time had folded inward when I saw him.

Over the next few days, I moved around in my real life with a placid rhythm that must have masqueraded as contentment because Joel gave no indication that he saw any changes in me.

At night, however, I returned to the cave. Each time I did, the dark space became more familiar. The memories etched on the walls like petroglyphs linked to more memories until both my mother and Garrett were there, together, in my thoughts and in my dreams. And it brought me comfort.

Joel's long hours, our choppy communication, and his seeming disengagement with anything connected to my feelings made it easy for me to stay sequestered in my melancholy cave where I found it easy to hide. The week slid by without my telling him about seeing Garrett. We didn't talk about Hawaii either. His goal was to get his new chef ready to run the Blue Ginger, and

I told myself I was supporting him and helping him reach his goal by not bringing up anything that might sidetrack that objective.

On Friday morning before Joel left for the restaurant, he said, "Today's the last day of training with Vincent. I plan to be home all weekend. Why don't we do something?"

"Like what?"

Joel shrugged. "I don't know. Something fun. A family outing. You pick. We can do whatever you want."

He closed the front door behind him, and I stood with my feet planted in the entryway, swaying Alex on my hip. Our chunky thirteen-month-old son was teething, and I was pretty sure it was his first molar, based on the amount of gnawing, drooling, and fussing. A runny nose had been added to Alex's symptoms that morning, and all he wanted was to be held. The shoulder of my shirt was soggy, and my lower back ached.

"Whatever I want." I repeated Joel's line and looked at Alex. "Your daddy drives me crazy sometimes. Did you know that?"

"Why?" Eden asked. I didn't realize she had padded down the stairs.

I quickly changed the subject. "Let's get you dressed. What do you want to wear today, Eden?"

"I wanna wear my rain boots."

"It's not raining."

She thought a moment, looking adorable in the princess-style nightgown GiGi had given her for Christmas. "I'll wear my bathing suit."

"It's not summer yet, sweetheart. How about a pair of pants and a long-sleeve T-shirt?"

"My kangaroo shirt?"

"Kangaroo shirt? Eden, you don't have a kangaroo shirt."

The news seemed to shock her, but her four-year-old logic took over. "I need one." She burst into tears. "Please, Mommy. I need one."

Alex joined in the outburst. I herded Eden upstairs, still jostling Alex on my hip. I knew what kind of day this was going to be. I wondered how Joel would respond if I told him my idea of picking "whatever I want" for the weekend was to close my bedroom door and sleep for two days without a single interruption. He could be the one who tried to make a kangaroo shirt hop into Eden's closet, appearing out of thin air.

The morning was as bumpy as I anticipated. But that afternoon, to my surprise, both kids ended up napping at the same time. I had a feeling they were both coming down with colds, which explained their willingness to go to bed. If they were getting sick, it would certainly alter any possible "fun" plans for the weekend.

Once the house was quiet, I seized the opportunity to do something that had been on my mind since Monday. I pulled a large plastic bin out of the garage and hauled it next to the sofa in the family room.

Inside was a collection of memorabilia I had placed there a lifetime ago. I found a photo of my mother I had forgotten about. She was standing next to my camera-shy dad, and she was leaning close to sniff a fully opened rose. The rose was deep red, like her favorite Oh My, Cherry Pie nail polish. Her eyes were closed as she drank in the fragrance.

She loved life. She appreciated everything. Oh, Mom, you were a lovely, lovely woman.

I studied her profile for a long time and then tried to read the expression on my dad's face as he watched her. I think my mom was always a mystery to him. A puzzle he didn't try to solve too quickly but rather left all the pieces where they had landed and studied them individually before trying to connect any of them with a matching piece.

His way with people was very much like his pastime of sitting for hours at our old folding card table, contentedly working on a thousand-piece jigsaw puzzle. He always chose puzzles of landscapes and idyllic scenery. Never anything with people, buildings, or animals. He would sit for a long time without moving any pieces, as if he merely wanted to take in the vista and gaze at the horizon.

It wasn't that much of a surprise after my mom's death when he chose to move from crowded Orange County, California, to Whitefish, Montana. He had lived within the same two-mile radius his entire life. The lure of having his own attached cottage at my brother's home in Big Sky Country seemed to soften the great loss of the love of his life. He handled everything quietly and efficiently, which was always his way. Never in a rush.

The night before he left, he came over for dinner, and Joel made all his favorites. My dad gave Eden a stuffed puppy with floppy ears. When he kissed us all, he handed me an envelope. It was a check for more than half the profit he received when he sold his house with the rare quarter-acre backyard. His only wish, his handwritten note said, was that we would consider using the money to purchase our own family homestead.

We followed his example and took our time until we found this house. We paid cash and had enough left over to make a small investment. The investment doubled in the first year, and that became the money we used to buy the Lexus. I knew he was pleased with our decision.

I put aside the photo of my parents and continued to sift through the bin. I found a half-dozen of my old artist sketch pads, a shoebox full of my early attempts at hand-made watercolor birthday cards, and a ribbon I was awarded for winning an art contest in eighth grade.

I dug deeper through old souvenirs, more photos, and our wedding guest book. I hoped that what I was looking for was in this bin and not any of the containers that had been wedged onto the garage storage shelf that required a ladder to reach.

When I came to the bottom of the bin, I was disappointed to see that my yearbook wasn't there. Just then my phone chimed, and I saw that I had a call coming in from Christy.

"Hi. Did I catch you in the middle of something?" she asked.

"Not really. I was just . . . looking for something." I wasn't ready to admit to anyone that I was on a hunt for my high school yearbook since it contained the only pictures I had of Garrett. Everything else associated with him had been destroyed in a memorable ceremony with my mother.

I flashed back to the day when my mom and I watched the movie *Emma.* A few months had passed since Garrett exited my life. When Jane Austen's character, Harriet, finally destroyed all her mementos of Mr. Elton, my mother looked at me with an impish grin. Our little firepit ceremony at the beach that night was one of my favorite moments with her and made us closer than ever.

That was the night my mother taught me the valuable lesson of forgiveness and how to be free. I released everything to the Lord that night, and I know that's why my heart was open and ready to fall in love with Joel when he came along.

"Jennalyn?" Christy's voice brought me back to the present.

"Yes, sorry. What's up?"

"I just said I'm taking my kids to the park. Do you want to meet us there?"

"They're both sleeping. I have a feeling they're coming down with colds."

"We're recovering from colds around here. That's why we need to get out of the house. I hope yours don't develop a cough. Todd is finally just past the coughing stage. He sounded like a barking seal for almost a week."

"That's awful. I didn't know you guys had been sick."

"The kids had runny noses and were sneezing for about three days. It wasn't bad. If that's what your kids have, hopefully it won't last long. I somehow managed to dodge the germs."

I glanced at the monitor and saw that Alex was standing up in his crib. The sound was off, but I could hear him crying upstairs.

"Alex is up. I should go."

"Okay. Let's talk soon. I want to hear what's been happening with you. I hope the kids aren't sick, but if they are, please let me know if you need anything. I've had a lot of practice making chicken soup this week."

"Thanks, Christy."

"Love you, Jennalyn."

"Love you, too, Christy." My throat tightened as I hung up.

I had a friend who cared about me — loved me — reached out to me. That realization settled on me as both comforting and disturbing. I had begun to retreat to my cave whenever I could because I believed I was all alone. The two familiar specters that haunted me in the secrecy of that cave somehow felt like enough companionship for now.

I realized that if I let Christy or Joel or anyone else into my hidden world, I was afraid the closeness of my mother's memory would vanish, and I would never be able to summon her back. For now, I wanted the cave with its unlikely residents to remain just as it was, with no intruders into my private world.

I don't think what I'm feeling is normal.

My phone buzzed again. Someone had left a message. I thought I'd turned off my notifications since I was so rarely on my social media pages anymore. I tapped the screen as I headed upstairs to Alex. The message was from GAREBEAR.

I stopped midway up the stairs.

The stupid nickname I gave him at Lake Tahoe. He remembered it.

I swiped his name without reading the message and was about to tap delete. A what-if thought made me pause.

What if he knows something about the girls' dance class that I don't know? What if this is the only way he could alert me?

Alex's cries prompted me to keep walking toward his room. I paused at the nursery door, phone in hand.

If I accept his message, I don't have to read it. He won't know if I opened it or not. It will just be sitting there in case I ever want to see what it says. Then I can delete it.

Pressing my lips together, I placed my finger over the screen and drew in a deep breath.

Chapter 7

A week later, at about the same time on Friday afternoon, Christy called again and asked how everyone was feeling. She and I had exchanged a few texts during the week while our home was on lockdown, with the cold and flu bug tormenting everyone but me.

I had stepped out on the back deck to talk to her because the late afternoon felt surprisingly warm for the first week of February. Joel was watching TV with Eden, and Alex was still napping. I brushed the leaves off one of the loungers and stretched out on the padded chaise. The fresh air and change of position felt good.

"I'm glad you didn't get sick," Christy said. "How did you and I both manage to avoid the bug when everyone else in our families got it?"

"I have no idea, but I'm so grateful. It hit Joel hard. He missed four days of work and pretty much slept through two of them. His new chef, Vincent, saved the day. It's a good thing he was trained and ready to take over."

"Do you guys feel ready to make a final decision about the marriage conference?" Christy asked.

"I didn't tell you. Joel registered us and booked our flights."

"So you're going!"

"I guess so." I leaned my head back and took in the view of the pale blue sky. A sheer layer of vaporous clouds stretched across the sky like a veil.

"You don't sound very excited," Christy said.

Even though the sliding door was closed, I glanced over my shoulder to make sure that Joel couldn't hear me from inside. "It's just that we didn't really talk about it. He moved ahead and decided for both of us. I guess that proves how much we need this conference. Our communication has been awful. Now that he's feeling better, I hope we'll have a chance to talk about it and both get on the same page."

"I think we're the opposite of you guys," Christy said. "All we've done is talk about it. We've over-communicated. For us, that can be as frustrating as what you and Joel are going through."

Christy added, "Todd is planning to take students on another outreach trip to Nairobi in June, so that means more time that he won't be home with the kids. Plus, those trips always turn out to be expensive."

The sliding door opened, and Joel appeared, holding Alex, who looked sleepy but was already wiggling to get out of Joel's arms.

"You want him out here with you?" Joel asked.

"Sure," I told Joel. To Christy, I said, "Hey, I need to go. I'll see you tomorrow."

"I almost forgot to tell you. I can drive all of us to Tess's, if you want. I thought it would be fun to take Gussie."

"Yes! I love it. Pick me up at seven."

I hung up and looked at Joel, grinning. "Christy's driving us to Tess's. In Gussie."

I wasn't sure he would put together all the pieces of what I had just said or if he knew I had always wanted to go somewhere in Todd and Christy's VW van. It didn't matter. He eagerly deposited our squirming baby tank on my lap and said, "I'm going to call China Palace for dinner. What would you like?"

"My usual."

He stood by the door with a blank look on his unshaven face.

98

"Lemon chicken and brown rice." I didn't mind refreshing his memory; the poor guy still looked wiped out.

"Okay. I'm going to call it in now so we can eat early tonight."

After Joel went inside and Alex was squirming to get off my lap, it did strike me as odd that Joel didn't remember my usual. Every time we had ordered from China Palace for the last half-decade, I'd always gotten the same thing.

How did he not know that about me?

Alex kept reaching for the chaise lounge chair next to mine. I picked him up and stretched awkwardly to plop him on the cushion. He put his little hands on the armrests and stretched out his legs like a child prince, ready to rule from his cushy throne.

With my young rajah content to sit by himself and kick his heels on the cushion, I reached for my phone and debated whether I should open the word-game app I had loaded earlier that week. I glanced over my shoulder to make sure Joel was inside and then stopped myself and put my phone down.

Drawing in a deep breath, I tried to understand the round of conflicting emotions sparring inside. The boxing match began last Friday when I chose to "accept" GAREBEAR's message.

It had been such a simple tap of the finger and yet what a rush of unexpected memories and rogue emotions had run through me as a result of that one decision.

Even though I accepted Garrett's invitation to connect, I didn't look at his note right away. I thought all that afternoon and evening about what I should do. It wasn't until late that night when everyone was asleep that curiosity got the best of me.

His message was, If having me there is uncomfortable for you, I can enroll Violet in a different class.

I didn't reply. I kept thinking about the conversation we'd had at the last DOE gathering and how Tess was trying to figure out what to do about "Guy." Her situation was different. Very different.

However, to be on the safe side, I maintained the boundary of not responding to Garrett. My thinking was that he didn't know I had seen his note, and since he would probably be at the class on Monday, I could make it clear that his presence didn't affect me one way or the other. He didn't need to take any heroic actions to ensure my comfort.

That was the end of it. Or so I thought.

When Monday came, Eden stayed home from ballet class because she was still sneezing and coughing. I noticed that night that Garrett had messaged me again right after class. Apparently, he could tell that I had accepted his invitation and that I had read his first message. He wrote that he was concerned because we weren't there and wondered if I had gone ahead and enrolled Eden in a different class. He said he was willing to pull Violet out and put her in another class, but now he wanted to make sure he didn't put her in the same one I might have moved Eden to.

Oh, brother.

That's all I could think about for the next four or five hours. Right before I went to bed, I was tired of thinking about his message, so I finally typed back, No need to change classes. My kids were sick this week.

I was surprised at how normal it felt to reply. Why had I made such a big deal of this? It was like sending a text to my brother or giving one of Joel's sisters a quick update.

Garrett came back right away with a message that said, Kids??? More than one?

I typed back that we also had a son who was almost fourteen months old. I added a line that I often included when I told anyone about Alex and said that he had

101

been an "unexpected home birth baby."

Garrett replied with three question marks.

I immediately wished I hadn't added that last part. I closed the app and decided I didn't need to answer his question marks. If he was at the next class and if it felt natural and not weird, I could explain then how Alex was born.

Better yet, if his wife was there and if the topic came up, she and I could swap birthing stories. It would all be as normal as with any old family friend I happened to connect with after a long absence.

That plan made sense for a while. But the more I thought about it, the more it seemed that the most natural way to ensure that things didn't feel weird the next time I saw him was to answer the question marks and not ghost him. It's what I would have done if any other high school pal reached out to me and we were catching up on our lives.

So late Wednesday night, while my ailing family was sleeping, I pulled out my phone and typed, I slipped in the kitchen and sprained my ankle. Paramedics delivered our son.

I was alone downstairs on the couch. I had set it up as my bed for the second night in a row. Joel preferred it that way when he was sick. By his own admission he was a terrible patient. He was rarely sick, but when he was, he wanted everyone to go away so he could hibernate.

I felt resolved after sending the message to Garrett and was about to put away my phone and turn out the light. I noticed, though, that Garrett had quickly replied, which surprised me.

Why does that remind me of the time you took a digger on the dock at Lake Tahoe? No paramedics involved but plenty of drama.

His words lit off a string of firecracker memories of the shared family vacation that had ignited our teenage attraction to each other when I was fifteen. I vividly remembered how Garrett had grabbed me by the shoulders and was teasing that he was going to push me into the lake. I pulled away, lost my footing, and tumbled into an awkward heap on the splintered wooden dock.

He helped me up and kept his arm around my waist all the way back to the condo, where our parents combined their first aid skills and made sure I was comfortable on the couch.

That was the first time Garrett kissed me. When no one else was in the room, he bent his tall frame over me and brushed his lips across my forehead as a sort of apology for being the initiator of my pain. Then he found Scrabble, the only board game in the vacation rental, and challenged me to a game. We played for hours.

I realized I was smiling when I typed back, How could I forget? Scrabble saved that vacation.

He responded with one word: Rematch.

His next message was a link to the Word Wiz app. I downloaded it, and lying on the couch in the stillness of the night, I played an innocent first round and won. He initiated another rematch, and we started a second game. A green dot appeared by my name. When I clicked on it, I saw that he had messaged me through the comment feature on the game.

I let you win that first round.

Oh really? My quick reply felt quite natural.

Between Tuesday and Friday I had won four games. I also had typed out several long replies to questions he asked in the comment section, where only the two of us could see. I told him how I had met Joel at a church event and how my husband had worked hard to get to where he was in his career.

Garrett told me about the three miscarriages Tiffany had experienced and how Violet had been premature and had to stay in the hospital for the first two weeks. He told me that he and Tiffany had decided to move to Irvine so that she could pursue the career she had put on hold when they married.

I knew how much Garrett always wanted a large family. "At least four boys," he had said more than once when our conversations in high school had cautiously approached the edge of dreaming together about our future. I could almost hear the sadness when he typed out the words, Violet will be our one and only.

Yesterday, through the private messaging feature, Garrett asked me about my love of painting. He said he hoped I hadn't put it aside because I had too much talent not to keep it up. I told him art was only a hobby for me. He suggested it should become more than a hobby.

I wondered if he had told his wife the same thing and that was why they had moved, for her to pursue her dream.

Then he wrote a line that tore at my heart. Your mom would have wanted you to develop your gift to the fullest. I hope you think about doing more.

I responded with a thumbs-up emoji and put away my phone. My family was starting to feel better, so I knew this silent escape from my real life needed to come to a close. It was time to step away from the conversation. That's when the sparring of my emotions began.

Did I give Garrett too much information? Too much access to my life? What would Joel say if I showed him the messages and told him Garrett and I were playing an ongoing word game?

After so many days of being the nurse, cleaning woman, cook, and comforter to Joel and the kids, I told myself that the communication and the game had been little more than two old friends catching up on each other's lives. I was sure this was as far as our touching base would go. It had been a boon, really, because now when we saw each other again at Eden's ballet class, all the uneasiness would be gone. We could simply be two parents saying hello without any uncomfortable conversations.

I held to those conclusions and hadn't checked the game app since last night.

But now that I was here on the deck, relaxed and watching my son on the lounge chair next to me, I felt the emotional sparring come back. I liked playing the word game. I liked feeling that I was winning at something. I wanted to keep the Word Wiz game going. It didn't matter if it was with

Garrett or someone else. It would feel relaxing to play it right now, on this lovely evening, as I stretched out on the chaise lounge on our deck.

Maybe later.

I put my phone away and turned all my focus to my son, who had grown tired of being an infant Grand Pooh-Bah on his throne. He was on his belly, wiggling his way off the lounge chair with his chubby legs dangling over the side.

"You can do it," I told him. "Come on, clever boy. You're almost there."

Alex finally committed to the descent, landed both feet on the deck, and turned to me with a victorious grin. He patted my leg, drooling and stealing my heart the way he was so good at doing.

"Come here." I scooped up my darling boy and covered him with kisses. Kisses on his cheeks, his ears, his tummy, the top of his dimpled hands. My efforts were rewarded with the world's best belly laugh. My son could laugh himself to tears in seconds. It was the most delightful sound in the universe.

The sliding door opened again, and Eden hopped over to us, adding her sweet little tickles to keep her brother giggling.

I love my children so much. I love our

little family and felt full of gratitude for all the ways that God had blessed us.

I don't need to develop my art to the fullest right now. Garrett was wrong. My mom would have wanted me to have this — to focus on my little ones while they're young. I'm not missing out on anything.

I glanced through the sliding door and could see that Joel was nearby. I tried to get his attention because I wanted him to come outside and join us. I wanted us to feel like a complete family. We had been living such separate lives for the past year. Something needed to change.

He saw me. I motioned for him to come be with us. He shook his head. I told myself there could be a dozen reasons he wanted to stay inside. It didn't matter. I wasn't going to let it stop me from enjoying the adorableness of our two happy and now healthy children.

Even though I tried not to fall into a funk because Joel wasn't part of this moment, my joy felt cut in half. I rationalized that if he could choose to stay inside, I could choose to mentally return to my cave at night. I could keep sleeping on the couch and play word games all night if I wanted.

When our Chinese food arrived, Joel readied the plates and put Alex in his high chair. I pulled all the boxes of delicious smelling food from the two bags and opened them on the counter.

"Joel, I don't see any lemon chicken."

"Lemon? No. I ordered orange chicken for you. Isn't that what you asked for?"

"I asked for lemon."

"Sorry."

I let it go. It didn't matter. Not really. But as I ate, I realized how often I brushed aside little things for the sake of peace in our home. There was nothing wrong with the orange chicken. Everything I had ever tried from China Palace was good.

What kept rolling through my thoughts that night when I was giving Alex his bath was that Joel wasn't listening to me. Our communication wasn't great. We knew that. But did he realize how often my words, my requests, were running past him like white noise?

Would Joel ever tell me that he believes I have a gift with the art I create? Would he want me to develop it to the fullest?

It was a painful question to ask, so I put it out of my thoughts and drew inward, as was becoming my habit.

Joel went to bed early. I decided to go downstairs and start a playlist that I usually didn't listen to. It included all the top hits from my high school years.

I easily moved around in my beautiful kitchen since I didn't have two little ones or their toys underfoot. I hummed along to the music and mixed the ingredients for sugar cookies that I planned to take to Tess's. When the double batch of dough was ready, I rolled it into several small lumps and covered them with parchment paper the way my mom used to do before putting them in the refrigerator. The dough could chill through the night and would be ready in the morning for Eden to help me turn into oodles of heart-shaped cookies.

I knew the DOEs would be talking about our words for the year since we didn't get to them at our January gathering. I thought about how, if my word was *love,* was my verse the one from Zephaniah? I felt a little unsettled about having the verse from my mother's gravestone as my word for the year. I reached for my Bible and journal. With a couple of taps, I changed the high school nostalgia music to some relaxing classical guitar music.

After opening my journal, I wrote 1 Corinthians 13 across from where I had written the Zephaniah verse. Some of the verses from 1 Corinthians 13 had been read at our wedding. I looked them up in my Bible and wrote them down.

Love is patient and kind. Love is not jealous . . .

The familiar sound of Alex crying came through the baby monitor. I checked and saw that he was thrashing around in his crib, so I hurried upstairs. When I opened the door, I could smell the reason for his trauma.

"It's okay, sweet baby boy. It's okay." I took care of the especially awful diaper and realized I had been pumping the poor little guy with extra juice for a week to help battle the cold. Now that he was better, I needed to cut back on the fruit.

Once Alex was settled, I closed his bedroom door softly and stood in the dark hallway. I felt a familiar tug to go back downstairs and check my phone to see if Garrett had made another move on the word game. It struck me in an eerie way that this was where I had been standing a week ago when I tapped to accept his invitation.

What if I hadn't?

I decided that all the communication with Garrett had been innocent. It was no big deal. But it was over. I needed to reenter my normal life now.

Instead of sleeping on the couch and

111

checking the word game, I returned to my bed and slipped in next to my peacefully sleeping husband.

I knew that Joel planned to make an early exit in the morning to get to the restaurant and oversee the prep for the weekend. But I longed to curl up next to him and pull his arms around me. I wanted to be warmed by his bare chest and feel his even breath against my neck. I wanted to kiss him. It felt like it had been so long since he had kissed me. Now that his cold had rescinded, I wished we could be the way we were when we were first married and fell asleep tangled in each other's arms.

Once I was under the covers, though, I knew that if I made any movements toward him, he would wake. Joel needed to sleep. I told myself I could wait to feel fully known and loved once again by this man I had married.

After all, love is patient.

CHAPTER 8

The next morning I got up at the same time Joel did. He was running late and gave me a rushed kiss.

"I'll have time off soon," he said. "I promise."

"I know. I'm patient," I said.

He glanced at me for a moment and grinned. "Yes, you are."

It wasn't exactly a declaration of his love, but I accepted his affirmation like a tasty bread crumb. He noticed. At least, when I reminded him, he saw me and realized that I was really trying my best.

It was a good day. The kids were back to their energetic selves, and that made our morning cookie-making session a bigger mess than usual. Eden especially loved squeezing the frosting tubes and decorating her own special heart cookies. She decorated one for me, for her daddy, for her brother, and then moved on to one for GiGi and one for Poppy. When those were done, she reached for one more.

"I think that's all, Eden," I said.

"No! I have to make one for By-let."

I felt a pinch in my gut. How could I tell her it would be best if she didn't get too close to her new friend?

She reached for a second and a third cookie and added, "And for Hana and Cole."

I was glad her list of friends wasn't limited to only Violet. I smoothed back her dark hair and leaned over to kiss the top of her head. "You're a good friend, Eden. It's sweet of you to think of your friends and decorate cookies for them."

She turned her face to me and beamed. "I love my friends."

"I know you do, honey. I love my friends too."

I selected the best of the best sugar cookies that remained and smothered them with pink icing. When Eden was done, I used what was left of the accent frosting and added white dots and squiggles. In keeping with Sierra's contribution of the initial mugs, I made sure there was at least one cookie with the first initial of all the DOEs.

The finished cookies looked so cute on my floral-rimmed serving plate, a jolly little tea party waiting to happen at Tess's nest that evening. I covered the plate with clear plastic wrap and had them ready to go when Christy arrived to pick me up. She texted that she was in our driveway with Gussie's engine running. Sierra and Emily already were in the van. Joel was at work, and his parents had come over to watch the kids.

As much as Eden and Alex loved GiGi and Poppy, tonight they weren't having any of it. They wanted to come with me. They begged for me to ask Daddy to come home so he could read them a bedtime story.

Even though I felt like the worst mother in the world, GiGi pushed me toward the door. I made my exit and winced when I could still hear Alex crying. The side door of Gussie slid open, and Emily welcomed me onto the back seat with her.

"Sorry! Meltdown at the last moment." I clicked my seatbelt in place and was grateful for the affirming comments from the other moms in the van. They understood. They knew the routine.

"What's on your lap?" Sierra asked from the front passenger's seat.

"I made some cookies."

"Yum! What kind did you make?" Emily asked.

"Sugar cookies with almond extract. And

with lots of gooey pink frosting."

"No wonder your kids didn't want you to leave the house," Sierra laughed. "They saw you taking the treasure with you."

For the first time since I had gotten in the van, I took in the customized interior. Behind our bench seat was an open space with built-in cupboards. The windows had curtains, and the biggest surprise was that the floor was carpeted. It was too dark to tell, but it looked like a vintage shag in avocado green.

"Gussie is adorable," I said. "It's really comfy back here. Did Todd make all these customized changes?"

"Most of them," Christy said. "We have a platform that fits in the back and a mattress."

"The carpet is an unexpected touch," I said.

"Todd loves it. I'm not so crazy about it. I think he planned for it to be a soft place to load up his surfboards. He ends up strapping them to the roof, though, because he usually takes a bunch of guys with him when he goes surfing, so he needs to keep the bench seats in."

"Have you guys ever gone camping?" Emily asked.

Christy merged onto the freeway, and I

noticed the way Gussie chugged. As updated as she was, she still sounded like an old Volkswagen when she sped up.

"We haven't gone camping since before the kids were born. Our big trip was up the California coast to Oregon to see my brother. He was working at a conference center near Glenbrook. That's where he met his wife."

"You stayed with us on that trip," Sierra added. "Remember? When we were in Santa Barbara."

"Yes, we did. That was so fun," Christy said. "You guys were renting a sweet cottage."

"I know. We didn't know how good we had it! I loved the big patio area." She turned to Emily and me. "Our bungalow was on the grounds of a gorgeous estate in the Santa Barbara hills. It was a groundskeeper cottage near a big swimming pool. Jordan lived there before we met. When we were married, he did the landscaping for the family in exchange for rent. It was a tiny cottage but such a great place for us."

"You had it fixed up so cute," Christy said. "It was tiny but adorable."

Sierra turned to Christy with an exaggerated pout. "I know. I can't wait until we get to move out of my in-laws' house someday.

I look forward to fixing up a place like that again and making it feel like home for us."

"Any leads on a place to live?" Christy asked.

"No. We looked at three places last week, but we were so discouraged over the prices of everything. Oh, I didn't tell you guys yet. In an effort to contribute to our housing fund, I found a part-time job yesterday."

"You did?" Christy asked. "Where?"

"I get to work at home. I'll teach English to students in Brazil.

"How do you do that?" Emily asked.

"Through video calls. The organization provides the curriculum with homework and tests. All I have to do is go through the lessons with each student and answer questions the best I can. I think I'm really going to like it."

"That sounds like a great job for you," Christy said.

"It doesn't pay much, but I needed something where I could work from home. You know I was selling stuff, but that hasn't really brought in much moola. I can see why Tess does well with her side hustle of selling the oils. She has a built-in customer base. After I saturated Jordan's family and mine, I ran out of customers." Sierra turned toward Emily and me. "Have you guys ever been to Tess's place?"

None of us had.

"I have a feeling it's going to be really impressive," Sierra said.

"I picture it being boho chic," Emily said. "With lots of colors and sheer curtains fluttering in the breeze."

"That's interesting because I always pictured her going with midcentury modern," I said.

"Really? Not me," Christy said.

She and Sierra both thought Tess's place would be traditional.

"I know that she has a leather couch," Christy said. "So I bet it's either traditional with lots of accent pieces to make it look super classy, or it's clean traditional with a white leather sofa and a thick rug."

"We'll find out soon enough," Emily said.

"Not at this speed," Sierra said as the freeway traffic slowed to only thirty miles per hour.

"Do you think there's been an accident?" Emily asked.

"No, I think it's always like this on the 55 freeway," Christy said. "I probably should have taken the 405."

"You should be fine once you hit the 22," I said. "Or were you going to take the 5?"

Christy glanced in the rearview mirror.

"The 5. What do you think, Jennalyn?"

"You could take the 5 but then jump off on the 57 instead of taking Beach Boulevard."

Emily laughed at us. "You do realize, don't you, that you guys sound like a comedy sketch with all the freeway numbers. Obviously, you've both lived here a long time. In the year and a half we've been here, all I know is the name of the street I live on and how to get myself to work and home."

"That's why I rely on my secret weapon!" Sierra pulled out her phone. "I am dependent on my apps. Here. It's set with Tess's address. Do you want me to start it?"

"Sure." Christy merged into the carpool lane.

I looked out the window at the familiar buildings and billboards visible from the illumination of all the car headlights. "My dad grew up not far from here. His dad was born back when the city of Orange still had lots of orange groves. My grandparents both came from families that were ranchers."

"I didn't know that," Christy said. "You're a third-generation Orange County girl."

"Fourth, actually. My great-grandparents owned part of the orange grove that was sold to build the Angels' baseball stadium."

"That's amazing," Sierra said. "You always

astonish me, Jennalyn. You are a woman of many hidden surprises."

I laughed self-consciously. "I don't know about that. You were the one who surprised me when we first met. I didn't believe it at first when you said you had lived in Brazil for five years."

"Believe it. Those were some refining years, for sure."

The traffic jam had let up, and we had clear sailing in the carpool lane most of the way on the 5 freeway. Sierra told us some interesting stories about her time in Brazil. My friends all commented at the looming arena when we sped past Angel Stadium.

"Can you imagine this whole area being orange groves and dirt roads?" Christy asked. "I've seen pictures of what Disneyland looked like before they started building it. All of Orange County is a concrete jungle now."

We talked about life and changes and wondered what this world would be like when our kids grew up. Christy got off the freeway, and Sierra's phone kept interrupting us, giving advice on where to turn so we would miss the congestion. We found our way up into the hills, winding through a beautiful area with tall trees and gated driveways.

"You know what I appreciate?" Christy asked. "I appreciate that Tess is willing to always be the one who drives to see us. She's a lot farther away than I realized."

I glanced at my phone. It was 7:45 and we had told her we would be there at 7:30. I sent Tess a text and told her the street name of the intersection where we were waiting for the light to turn green. I noticed I had two texts from GiGi. She had snapped a picture of my little ones, content on Poppy's lap as he read a story to them. Her message said, All is calm here. Have fun.

I turned the phone screen to show Emily. She smiled.

"That's honey to a mama's heart, isn't it?" she asked.

I nodded and glanced at my phone again. Tess had replied with a smiley face. I also noticed that I had two messages waiting for me on my Word Wiz app. I slid my phone back into my purse and felt an odd tightening in my gut. Knowing that Garrett was trying to contact me now felt different from the late-night back-and-forth messages when I was home in flu-bug mode. He didn't belong here in Christy and Todd's Gussie. He didn't belong in my circle of haven maker friends.

"Looks like it's up here on the right,"

Christy said.

The gray, one-story duplex with its flat roof was unimpressive at first glance and not at all what I had expected.

"Tess warned me about her driveway," Christy said. "She wasn't kidding about its being steep." Christy inched her way into the sliver of a parking space next to Tess's white SUV.

"Well done," Sierra commented.

"Only one slight problem," Christy said. "I can't get out my door. I'm too close to this retaining wall. I'll have to go out your door, Sierra."

Sierra had opened the passenger's door a half a foot but couldn't open it any further without hitting Tess's car. "Guess again." She closed the door. The interior of the car went dark. "Looks like we all go out through the sliding back door."

Christy got out of her seat, lowered her head, and bent over as she tried to squeeze through the opening between the driver's and passenger's seats. She reached for her shoulder bag on the floor to loop it over her arm as she came toward where Emily and I were sitting. However, she somehow had put her foot through the long strap so, when she pulled it up, the strap snapped up between her legs.

"Ouch!"

"Christy, you're giving yourself a wedgie!" Sierra laughed. "Here, hand me your purse. Now lift your right leg. Sorry. No, I meant your left leg. Bend your knee. Not that much. Wait."

"Don't make me laugh." Christy repressed her chuckles. "I mean it. Don't make me laugh. I've had two babies."

She really did look funny hunched over and trying to stay in place on one foot. Sierra's unhelpful directions made it even more comical. Emily and I glanced at each other, and we couldn't help it. We burst out laughing.

"You look like an arthritic flamingo!" Sierra spouted, which was no help at all.

"Don't make me laugh!" Christy yelled. "I'm not kidding! Not on my husband's precious vintage shag carpet!"

"Here," Emily said. "Take our hands."

The moment Christy leaned forward to take hold of my hand and Emily's, Sierra pulled on the purse. It was like watching a slow-motion mousetrap game. The strap tugged at Christy's raised leg. The tilt of the van added to Christy's imbalance. With an unladylike squawk, she came toward me headfirst, her chest landing on the plate of cookies in my lap.

"Got your purse!" Sierra held it up triumphantly.

We all laughed so hard we could barely breathe.

Christy had sunk to the floor at my feet, laughing and wiping her tears with the back of her hand. She smoothed her hand over the front of her top. "Did I ruin the cookies?"

"Forget the cookies," I said. "Did you break any bones?"

"No, I'm fine."

Emily let out a startled shriek and then started laughing again.

We all turned to see Tess standing by the window of the sliding door, peering inside, trying to see what in the world was going on. I reached over and pulled the handle, sliding the door open.

"What are you guys doing?" Tess asked.

"We were trying to get out," Christy explained, "but then Sierra —"

"Hey, don't blame me!" Sierra protested. "I was helping."

"Helping?" Emily started laughing again. "That was the funniest way of helping I've ever seen."

I handed Tess the plate of cookies through the opened side door. With my brightest smile, I said, "I brought crumbs."

She looked confused. "Pink crumbs?"

"They used to be hearts." Inspired by a sudden pun, Sierra said, "Oh, Christy, you're such a heartbreaker!"

"I'd rather be that than a . . . What did you call me?"

"An arthritic flamingo."

We burst into another round of laughter, much to poor Tess's confusion.

"You guys better come in," she said. "My neighbors are going to think I'm throwing a wild party and call the police."

It took the four of us in a team effort of uncoordinated moves and assistance from one another to get out of the van and make our way to the front door. The laughter had calmed down but not the jovial teasing.

"I think we should try synchronized swimming next," Sierra said.

"Absolutely not!" Christy, Emily, and I answered as a chorus.

"Hey, that was pitch perfect," Sierra said as we approached Tess's front door. "Maybe we should start a girl band. We could introduce the world to a new dance move."

Sierra imitated Christy's bent-over, balanced-on-one-leg position and cracked herself up with laughter.

Tess stared in disbelief.

Just then the neighbor's porch light turned

on, and Tess put a finger to her lips to hush us. She opened the door and pushed us inside. "I'm serious," she whispered. "They'll call the police!"

Chapter 9

I was the last to step inside Tess's home because I wanted to take a moment to admire the entryway. The front door was painted black, and she had two potted plants on either side that were trimmed the way a champion poodle might be for a competition — precisely and artfully, in the shape of a teardrop. The ornate vintage black iron lantern hanging over the entry, along with the door and plants, gave the feel that we were about to step into a Parisian shop.

I entered an open area that immediately felt luxurious and simple at the same time. My earlier guess of Tess's style being mid-century modern was close. True to everything else about Tess, her home wasn't just one style, nor was it predictable. Inside we were met with a surprising mix of styles that all worked together in beautiful and inviting ways.

On the left was a small, and I do mean small, galley-style kitchen. A narrow floating island with a white marble top separated the kitchen space from the living room. A stunning blue leather couch dominated the space along the edge of an oversized ivory rug.

I especially loved the lighting. I wanted to ask her what watt bulbs she had in the various lamps positioned around the room. They seemed to have the same strategic balance of proportion and shape as the many lush green houseplants. The glow of the soft lights bounced off the gold accents in the picture frames, the hammered brass bowl on the end table, and the curios that dotted her built-in bookshelves. Tucked up against the wall under one bookshelf was a table for two, with narrow high back chairs upholstered in a rich blue and gold tapestry that seemed like maids-in-waiting for the queenly sofa.

"I don't know what you guys were drinking before you got here," Tess said, as she pulled a glass pitcher of water from her narrow fridge. I noticed the cucumber slices bobbing in the water, which was something I loved to do with my water too.

"It might be hard to believe, but we didn't have anything to drink," Sierra said. "Hey, are those Fenton or hobnail?" She took one of the filled glasses from Tess and examined the light blue goblets that had rows of raised polka dots on them.

"I have no idea. They came with the house. I love them." Tess's voice was especially low, as if she were setting an example of the level at which we needed to communicate in her duplex.

"These are collectibles." Sierra took the cue and lowered her voice. "Just so you know. They are true vintage pieces. I don't think I've ever seen them in blue."

"Your home is beautiful," Emily said. "If Trevor and I are ever able to buy a home, could I pay you to come over and make decorating suggestions for me?"

"Of course. But you can't pay me," Tess said with a look of mock offense. "Don't even say things like that. I'd be happy to give you some ideas. We're haven makers, remember? We agreed long ago that this is what we love to do and love to do together."

Christy lifted her goblet. "To us haven makers."

We all raised our glasses, echoed her sentiment, and sipped in unison.

"Besides," Tess said, "I've been to your haven, Emily, and it's so cozy. Whenever I'm there, I feel loved. I really do. It's the same for your homes, Jennalyn and Christy."

"We feel it here too," Emily said.

Tess grinned as if that's what she was hoping to hear. "I haven't been to your place, Sierra, but I'm sure it would feel the same."

"It might. It's different, though, since it's not our home."

Christy quoted a saying as if we all had heard it before. " 'A house is made of brick and stone, but a home is made of love alone.' "

"Did you just make that up?" Sierra asked.

"No. My grandma did a cross-stitch of that saying when she was a young girl. It's on a piece of linen with a border of little houses. Really sweet. When she passed away, it was sent to me. She knew I always loved it. I need to reframe it and find a good place to hang it."

"Sounds like another vintage treasure." Sierra held up her goblet again. "This water is so refreshing. What did you add besides cucumber?"

Tess showed us one of her bottles of essential oils and explained how she prepared a large container of infused water every morning and kept it in her refrigerator. She said she always took a water bottle with her whenever she left the house and that way made sure she drank enough throughout the day.

"I'm going to start adding oils to my water," Sierra said. "I love this."

"Make sure you check first," Tess said. "Not all of them should be ingested. My go-to edible oils are peppermint, lemon, and grapefruit. There are others you can add, but those are my favorites."

I slowly peeled back the clear wrapping from my plate of cookies Tess had placed on the counter. The others watched as if I were demonstrating a delicate surgical procedure. "What do you think? Are they still edible?"

"Of course." Tess opened one of her cupboards, revealing tidy stacks of plates, mugs, and bowls. She put five small plates on the counter.

"We can use spoons if we need to," Emily suggested. "They'll still taste the same."

"I put together a charcuterie board for us." Tess took two steps toward the narrow refrigerator.

"A what?" Sierra asked.

Tess pulled out a round tray on which cured meats and scrumptious-looking appetizers had been artistically arranged.

"That's beautiful," Christy said. "Tess, you design everything."

Tess smiled. "I love doing things like this."

"Joel would be impressed," I said. "What am I saying? I'm impressed. What a feast." I began assessing the items, trying to memorize the way she'd placed them to create such a gorgeous mix of colors, shapes, and patterns. I probably should have taken out my phone and shamelessly snapped a photo.

Tess had anchored the design with a circle of plump green olives in the center. A line of square crackers plus dark orange cheese cut into small rectangular slices was fanned out next to a clump of glistening cherry tomatoes. Extra color came from yellow and green peppers, sliced horizontally to keep their natural flower shape, positioned next to a cluster of baby carrots. Rounds of salami formed rosettes, and sticks of jicama and plump red grapes dotted across the entire arrangement.

"I almost don't want to take something because it will mess up the mosaic," Emily said.

"No, please. Enjoy it. Does anyone want something hot to drink?"

Even though we were in a new place, Tess's haven soon felt like home to all of us, and we were nibbling and chatting the way we love to. We stood encircling the counter as we snacked. But once the tea was ready, we headed for the sofa. Tess pulled the two chairs over and the space was just right for the five of us.

Before I sat down, I went over to the sliding glass door that dominated the back side of her duplex. All was dark, but I could see that she had a narrow deck. "Do you sit outside much?"

"Not often. My neighbor and his wife do. They have bird feeders and sit out there with their binoculars. Beyond the deck is a bank of trees full of special birds. I know nothing about birds, but my neighbors update me on their latest sightings."

"That's sweet," Emily said.

"It is." Tess tilted her head. I recognized her body language and knew she was frustrated.

"Not an ideal situation?" I asked.

"Let's just say that sometimes I feel like I'm living in a retirement home. I've thought of moving, but my rent is lower than anything else I could find that's this nice and this close to both LA and Orange County. For now, I'm okay."

I took the open seat next to Emily on the sofa and leaned back. The couch seemed to fit the way a favorite pair of slippers would. I leaned my head on Emily's shoulder and sighed contentedly. Emily chuckled and leaned her head on mine. Peace reigned around our sweet circle.

Tess started the conversation by saying, "I have a small confession to make."

Emily and I straightened up, and we all tuned in. I'm sure I wasn't the only one wondering if her confession had anything to do with Guy.

"I confess that I don't have a word for the year. I know the plan for tonight was to share our words, but I don't have one. So, who wants to go first?"

I leaned over and gently removed a bit of pink icing from Tess's hair. The rest of us were drinking tea and hot cocoa. Tess had filled one of her coffee cups with the broken heart crumbs and was eating them with a spoon.

She grinned at me, and I grinned back. I don't think any of the others knew that when we were together like this, each of them was filling up the place inside me that had gone dry when my mother left this earth. She had been so in tune with my heart and so in touch with my daily life. It now took four exceptional women to fill the missing space. I wanted to tell them, but as was often the case, my feelings came at me in a big gush in moments like this. I kept quiet, not knowing how to put the enormous emotions into tiny words.

Sierra spoke up, and I was glad of it. "I'll go first. My word is *wait,* and I'm mad."

"You're mad about your word for the year?" Christy frowned.

"Not really mad. It's more like I'm bummed because who wants to wait for anything? Not me."

"I think *wait* is a great word," Emily said. "It means something is coming. You're just supposed to patiently expect that at the right time it will come. You wait for God to work it out."

"Well, all I know is that I'm waiting for our own place to live. I want to feel settled."

"I know that feeling," Emily said. "A big house isn't everything, though. We had that in North Carolina before we moved here. I like what you said, Christy, about a home being made of love alone."

I almost spoke up, taking my cue from Emily's last sentence to share that my word was *love.* But Christy shared next.

"Sierra, I get what you're saying about being bummed about your word. My word is *trust.* I've already had to trust God in deeper ways in some areas, and it makes me nervous."

"Nervous? Christy, I can't believe you're saying that your word makes you nervous."

Sierra went into the kitchen and filled her empty mug with cookie crumbs, as Tess had.

"Well, it does." Christy grinned. "It's like I'm waiting for something difficult to happen. I didn't feel that way in January when it settled on me. I think I'm looking for problems."

"But you're the initiator of all this," Sierra said. "I never would expect you to feel that way."

Christy shrugged. "We all have our moments."

"You guys," I leaned in. "I don't think these words for the year are like fortune cookie messages or prophecies that we're supposed to somehow go out and self-fulfill."

"You're right," Christy said.

All eyes were on me, and I realized I sounded more assertive than usual. I softened my tone. "Don't you think we should see our word for the year as sort of a whisper from God? Christy, you told me one time how your word for the year was like a love note from the Lord. I always loved the poetic imagery of that."

"That's because you love to bring the sacred into everyday moments," Tess said.

I wasn't sure what she meant.

"It's your superpower," Sierra said.

I must have still looked confused because Tess explained, "You like things that are set apart and celebrated. That's why you started inviting us to gather. You showed us how to go deeper and create community that has substance to it."

"It's true," Emily said. "We've all felt it, Jennalyn. You bring beauty and a sense of reverence to our gatherings, and we all started copying you in one way or another."

I felt my face warming at the compliments.

"Now I'm curious to hear your word," Tess said.

I cleared my throat. "My word is *love.*"

I got a couple of "oohs and aahs," as if I had picked the cutest puppy in the litter.

"Since you guys made those generous comments about sacredness and doing things on purpose, I have to say in full disclosure that it's not as if I spent a lot of time thinking about my word. I also realize I may have been influenced by all the valentines and pink hearts in my world lately."

"Don't diminish it," Emily said. "You asked Him for a word, didn't you?"

"Yes."

"Then it's yours," Emily said. "After all the ways you DOEs have influenced me, I now happen to believe that God can use anything or anyone to impress specific thoughts on us. Even heart-shaped cookies."

"Or crumbs," Sierra said before spooning the last of hers into her mouth.

"You're right, Emily," Christy said. "And Jennalyn, what you said about the love notes — that was a good reminder. I shouldn't be nervous. I'm glad you said that."

Christy turned to Emily with an open palm gesture as if handing off an invisible baton. "What's your word?"

"I like my word, *peace*," Emily grinned. "I found it when I was reading Proverbs. The chapter talks about seeking wisdom, and the verse says, 'Her ways are ways of pleasantness, and all her paths are peace.' I love that verse. It's so poetic."

"Say it again," Christy said.

Emily repeated, " 'Her ways are ways of pleasantness, and all her paths are peace.' "

"That sounds like the essence of you, Emily," Christy said.

"What verse is that? Proverbs what?" Sierra pulled out her phone and had the answer before Emily could reply. "Oh, I see it. Proverbs 3:17. It might be talking about wisdom, but it really does sound like you, Em. Your ways are ways of pleasantness, that's for sure."

"I liked the part about 'all her paths are peace.' " Emily grinned. "I've walked down plenty of paths that have not been peaceful at all."

"Right there with ya, sister," Sierra said.

I noticed, as I had more than once, that Emily had a subtle beauty to her. More of a loveliness than a beauty. It was her countenance. She was quiet and petite, unobtrusive and kind. Her hair was short and thin, with a tendency to spiral in ways that made her appear as if she had been out in the rain. I liked the winsomeness of her demeanor and the way she had become such a pillar of strength in our group by simply always being there for each of us.

Artistic possibilities spun through my mind of how I might paint a small gift for each of my friends that would include their banner word.

"I may not have a word," Tess said. "But I do have a thought. May I share something, and you tell me what you think?"

"Of course," I answered for all of us.

"I read this the other day, and I keep thinking about it. Let's say you're seeking God about something, and you sit by a window and open your Bible. A breeze turns the pages to exactly the verse you needed.

Would you think that was a coincidence?"

None of us answered at first.

"What if, from the beginning of time when God put every weather pattern into motion, He already knew you would sit exactly where you did, when you did, with the questions you had on your heart? What if He knew precisely when the breeze would come to turn the page and that your eye would fall on that verse?"

"Then it wouldn't be a coincidence," Christy said.

"That's what I'm thinking," Tess said. "God already knows. He's already there before things happen."

"That's intense," Sierra said.

"I know," Tess agreed. "What you guys were saying about how you got your words for the year made me think it's not capricious, is it? I mean, you're asking; so when a word is impressed on you in whatever way, for whatever reason, God's fingerprints are on it."

"Like a love note," Emily said.

Tess stood and sauntered into the kitchen where she poured another glass of cucumber water. "God knows us by heart, doesn't He?"

Again, none of us answered with words.

Our response was a mutual nodding of heads.

Tess returned. "Here's my next question: Do you think it's not a coincidence then, that I met Guy? I mean, met him when I did? When his marriage was coming apart?"

"I don't think it's a coincidence," Christy said. "But I think we always have the ability to choose what we do in a situation. How we respond. Do we honor God and follow His Word? Or not. That's always the tension."

"Do you guys agree? Does it come down to our free will?" Tess asked.

"I think so," Emily said.

The room felt hushed as both Sierra and I nodded our agreement to what Christy and Emily had said.

"Interesting." Tess didn't say any more. I wanted her to open up. Instead, she changed the subject. I think we all were feeling unsure about whether we should ask more in-depth questions about Guy or wait and let her tell us what she wanted, when she wanted.

"I haven't shown you the rest of the place. Do you want a tour? It won't take long. Two bedrooms and one bathroom." She stood and motioned for us to join her.

She showed us her bedroom first. The first

thing we noticed was the dramatic head-board.

"It came from Spain," Tess explained. "At least that's what the guy at the Pasadena Swap Meet told me. It's the door of an old hacienda."

I wasn't as crazy about the carved wood headboard as I was about the poufy and inviting ivory comforter. "Eden would want to jump on your bed."

Tess laughed. "Christy made the pillows for me for Christmas. I love them. I kept dropping hints to her that I needed something fresh and white with texture."

"They're made from old linen tablecloths that I bleached and then added the extra details from scraps I had."

"Gorgeous," I said. "Now I know to drop hints to you for my next birthday."

We took turns peeking into the bathroom. It was small and badly needed a renovation. The original salmon-colored tile ran across the small counter and up the wall. Tess had hung a huge, framed mirror so that it covered a lot of the tile wall, but not enough.

"And here's my office." Tess opened the door to the second bedroom, which was larger than hers. Three standing racks were packed with outfits that were neatly hung and labeled. One wall had floor-to-ceiling shelves with labeled bins.

Under the small window was a file cabinet with a basket on top filled with loose papers. Above the window was a shelf lined with matching white binders. The built-in closet doors were full-length mirrors. The reflection made it seem as if the racks of clothes continued into another matching space.

"This is amazing!" Sierra took it all in as if she were at one of her favorite shops.

"I'm trying to get organized enough to have clients come here sometimes so I can style them on the spot rather than always hauling outfits everywhere." Tess straightened the sleeve of a white blouse on its hanger and adjusted the collar.

"I'd love to come here and be styled," Sierra said. "How much do you charge?"

"For you," Tess tapped her finger at the side of her mouth and looked up as if she was trying to calculate the price. "How about a personal tour of all your favorite vintage shops in Orange?"

"I'm serious," Sierra said.

"So am I," Tess replied. "Here. Let's start on you now." She pulled an expensive-looking leather jacket from one of racks. "I think this is your size. Try it on."

"Are you sure?"

Tess looked like she was in her happy

place, and Sierra was about to become her newest runway model. I secretly hoped Sierra wouldn't be the only one who would be blessed tonight with a Tess styling consultation. If she was, I told myself to be happy for Sierra.

A thought from the 1 Corinthians chapter on love came to mind. *Love is not jealous.*

I watched Sierra pull her mane of free-flowing blond curls out from the back of the jacket and catch a glimpse of her classed-up image in the mirror. She looked stunning.

I'll admit, I was a teeny bit jealous.

CHAPTER 10

Sierra turned to the right and left, admiring her reflection in the fitted cocoa brown–colored jacket. "I look rich."

We all laughed and then hushed ourselves, remembering the neighbors.

"I always wear flowy, earth-child outfits," Sierra said.

"I know." Tess grinned. "And I love you in them. Just realize that you are a woman with options. One day you might need something different to wear, and when you do, think classic."

"Classic," Sierra repeated.

"You have a perfectly proportioned figure. That's why you can wear clothing that's more fitted, with classic lines. If you ever do want to look a little more LA than Laguna Beach, I would put you in this jacket, a pair of dark-wash skinny jeans, a nice quality white tee, and a single long chain necklace. Preferably gold. Like this one."

Tess put a necklace over Sierra's head and pulled her bulky shirt back so that the jacket became the featured item and not her many-layered cotton top.

"Wow," Emily said. "You're so slim!"

"Not really," Sierra said.

"You do look classy," Christy said.

"I feel classy in this jacket." Sierra lifted the price tag. "Whoa! I've never spent that much on clothing, ever. Why would you tempt a thrift-store girl with something like this?"

"Here's the thing," Tess said in her professional-sounding voice. "If you invest in a few classic pieces that don't go out of style, they will last for a decade or more. You'll find you're actually saving money by not having to replace lesser-quality items that fall apart quickly."

"Makes sense." Sierra took off the jacket carefully and handed it to Tess. "It's a beautiful jacket."

"It's a great color on you too." Tess looked at me. "Jennalyn, do you want to go next?"

I felt a little shiver of happiness and immediately repented of my jealousy. "You were reading my mind."

Tess held up a black boatneck top in a stretchy fabric. "This could be a classic go-to with your hair. It will show your collar bones, which are actually a very attractive feature on a woman, if the top fits snuggly and doesn't gap or show any cleavage. Again, quality, well-fitting jeans always work best. Try boot-cut, Jennalyn. They'll keep the proportions working well for you. Especially if you wear boots with heels. And then earrings. Are your ears pierced?"

"Yes. They may have closed up. I don't know. I stopped wearing anything dangling when Eden was born."

"Well, I suggest that on your next date night with Joel, you wear a top like this and dangling earrings — not too long — and if they have a little shimmer, so much the better." Tess turned to the others. "Go for accessories that shimmer, not sparkle. There is a difference."

Sierra picked up the fun of being tutored by Tess and turned to Emily. "Did you hear that? No more borrowing Audra's bedazzled necklaces to wear when hostessing at the pie shop."

"Got it," Emily said with a grin.

"Here's an idea for you, Emily." Tess reached for a short white jean jacket. "Always a winner year-round in California. You can do all kinds of tops underneath. I think you should avoid yellows and tiny printed fabrics that are in billowy tops. Nothing gathered at the neckline. No ruffles. Lean toward straight lines that fall to your hips, and try darker shades like navy blue, emerald green, or the right kind of true red. Like . . ."

Tess seemed to be searching for the best descriptor for true red, so I offered, "Cherry-pie red?"

"Yes, perfect! Cherry-pie red."

"What made you think of that?" Christy asked. "Peggy's Pies, where Emily works?"

"No, my mom," I said in a low voice. "Her favorite nail polish was called Oh My, Cherry Pie. It was the perfect red for toenails."

Christy didn't reply because Tess was holding up a V-neck sweater in front of her that was a color I wasn't sure I could describe.

"It's kind of bright, don't you think?" Christy asked.

"A little. But I want you to see that you can wear this shade of persimmon. With your hair and skin tone, you can pull off all the oranges, reds, and blues that I can only dream of wearing. Pair it with black or white. Avoid most beiges and tans. They'll wash you out. And try this." Tess had Christy slip into a white jacket that zipped up the front and had a stand-up collar.

"Cute," Sierra said. "Very Newport Beach, 'let's go out on my yacht' looking."

Christy tucked her hands in the pockets. "This is really nice cotton. It's so thick."

"It will last at least five years, even with constant wear. I put a lot of my clients in that brand when they're going on vacation."

For the next half hour we asked questions and held up colors and styles that we wouldn't normally pull off the rack when shopping. I learned so much. Tess amazed me. I never had been around someone who knew so much about fabrics and styles, body shapes and clothing brands.

She convinced us that we were "women of options" and should be thoughtful about how we dress and present ourselves.

"It sort of goes back to our free will," Tess said. "You can wear anything. Why not focus on quality and be true to what best fits you rather than what everyone else says is fashionable?"

She shared about what it was like to always be the tallest girl in the room and how her cocoa skin tone had prompted racial comments when she was younger. When she made peace with who she was — her height, shape, skin, and hair — she started figuring out how to best adorn what God had given her.

"When I first realized I was a woman of options," Tess said, "clothes and accessories became the door to walk out of feeling inferior and self-conscious. Now the clothes are just the fun bonus. The truth is that I'm comfortable with who I am on the inside. That, of course, is because of what God has done in me. I always liked that verse about how you'll know the truth, and the truth will set you free."

"This is so good," Christy said. "All of it. I wish the girls at the school where Todd teaches could hear you say all that."

"Do you speak at schools and events?" I asked.

Tess shook her head. "I've never been asked. I think it would be fun. I always wanted to pull a rack of clothes on stage and pick random girls from the audience and style them. I saw that on a TV show once, and I loved the spontaneous way the teens responded."

"Would that be your dream job?" Emily asked. "You said one time that you loved styling actors. I guess that's why we always picture you driving off to a film studio in your SUV loaded with clothes."

"Not every day. Rarely actually. I do love working on projects like that. At this point, though, I'm open to anything. Business has been slow the last few months, and I need more clients."

"Well, get ready for your phone to ring," Christy said. "If you're serious about speaking, I'm sure that between Todd and Aunt Marti, they'll have lots of gigs lined up for you in no time."

"I'd love it." Tess glowed like a woman who was about to have more options open up to her.

It was nearly midnight when we all hugged Tess at her "Parisian" front door and whispered our goodbyes. We tried to be as quiet as possible entering Gussie through the side door. As soon as we had our seat belts on, Christy started the engine, and the rumble seemed amplified in the confined space. Gussie chugged loudly as Christy slowly and carefully backed up. She had almost made it to the top of the steep driveway when the neighbor's front light turned on again.

"I have a feeling Tess is going to hear from her bird-watching neighbors in the morning," I said.

My prediction came true. Tess texted the group Sunday afternoon to let us know that her neighbor had reported the disturbance to their landlord. I might be house hunting soon.

Being the Haven Makers that we are, we all jumped on the group text with suggestions for Tess. By Monday afternoon Emily's husband, Trevor, had two housing options for her in nearby Santa Ana. I was watching for Tess's reply when a text came in from Eden's dance teacher. The flu bug had caught up with her, and she had to cancel class.

For the first time in a couple of days, I thought about Garrett. I felt relieved that I wouldn't see him. Fortunately, Eden wasn't in her tutu yet, so she didn't realize it was ballet-lesson day.

I started Eden on an art project, making paper valentines for GiGi and Poppy. She loved sitting at the counter and working on crafts of any sort. I leaned against the kitchen sink while Alex was in his high chair, contentedly eating his new favorite organic baby crackers.

Tess finally replied with appreciation for Trevor's house hunting efforts but assured us that her landlord would never kick her out. She said she was only kidding when she said she might be house hunting.

I typed, Any updates on Guy? Then I deleted it.

Tess's next text read, We didn't make plans for our next gathering. How about a picnic?

A long string of messages followed, as we chimed in with all our ideas. Sierra described her vision of the five of us lounging on colorful blankets and pillows in a field of wildflowers under a billowing canopy that she was sure Tess could design.

Where do we find the wildflowers? Emily wanted to know.

I can bring lots of pillows, Christy offered.

Sierra said she could hunt up some vintage-style picnic hampers, if the rest of us agreed to fill them with all kinds of delicacies.

What kind of delicacies did you have in mind? I asked. Keeping up with the slightly unrealistic Downton Abbey–type theme that was emerging, I jokingly added something I had seen on a cooking show Joel had tuned into a while ago. Quail eggs and figs with cream?

How about pie? Emily asked and then volunteered to bring an assortment from Peggy's Pies.

Tess pitched for us to have a picnic on the beach. She insisted that the photos would be "scrumptious" if we caught the "golden hour" of light.

Sounds like we're setting up a photo shoot for a magazine, Sierra replied.

Tess's response was immediate. We could.

I know people. What do you think? Should I make a few calls?

I felt like it was time that someone intervened with a voice of reason, so I reminded everyone how we had gathered at my house last year under the big tree in the backyard. I had hauled a long table out on the grass and set it with my white dinnerware. The table was encircled by mismatched chairs with pillows on the seats. It was very simple. The only decorations I had managed to put up were a half-dozen Mason jars with battery-operated votive candles. I hung them on wires from the tree limbs, and when the sky darkened, the candles were like fireflies flitting over us. Somehow, being outside together had an enchanting effect on us, which was probably why the instinct was embedded in all of us to do something special outside for our Spring Fling get-together.

Gazing out the kitchen window, I waited for the others to reply to my suggestion to set up something simple at my house. I knew it would still take extra effort on my part since nothing from last year's event remained. The table had been removed when the deck was built last summer. The Mason jars had all come down when the unstable limbs had been cut back significantly by an expensive tree specialist.

I heard Eden giggling and looked up.

"Eden, no!"

She had taken a red marker to her baby brother's face and drawn an uneven heart on his cheek, which she was now coloring in. Alex posed for her, contentedly eating his crackers.

Eden looked surprised at my strong reaction as I reached for the pen and took it away from her. "You may not draw on your brother."

"But he's my Bal-intime."

Alex was grinning so happily and Eden seemed so proud of her artwork that I had a difficult time staying in a disciplinary frame of mind. Even though I had read all the mommy blogs and I knew I would probably regret it, I held up my phone and snapped a couple of pictures before returning to my stern mama voice.

Eden asked me to take more pictures. She posed next to her brother. She held up her valentines. She said "cheese" six times before I finally said in the sternest voice I could muster that I was not taking any more pictures.

My words had little effect. She seemed determined to capture my attention with her cuteness.

The streak continued over the next few days. She kept doing things she knew she wasn't supposed to do. As soon as she completed her shenanigans, she would call for me to come and take her picture.

On Tuesday morning she used an entire roll of toilet paper to wrap, or as she called it, "make a present" of, all the books she could find. Then she hid them throughout the house and told her brother to find them. All he found was the first one she pointed out to him, and when I came into her room, Alex had a fistful of toilet paper in his mouth.

On Wednesday she got into a box of Alex's diapers. After peeling back the tabs on every single one, she stuck them all along the upstairs hallway. I snapped a picture when I thought she wasn't looking and sent it to Joel at work. In a way, it was the best inroad I had to connect with him throughout his long days. He had replied to the pictures I sent with an emoji of a laughing face or a single word, such as "Nice."

The moment of reckoning came on Wednesday afternoon when Eden dumped a container of almond flour onto the pantry floor. When I found her, she had gone from finger painting in it to urging Alex to follow her and walk barefoot through it so they could make footprints throughout the house.

I came down hard on her, and she burst into tears. I felt like a terrible, mean mother. Remaining firm, I made her help clean up the mess, all the while talking to her calmly and trying to explain why everything in our house is not a toy. She told me she was "souwee," and we hugged. I thought her reign of terror had ended.

That evening, though, I discovered she had "made a picture" with toothpaste on the closed toilet seat in the master bathroom. Before I was aware she had done it, though, Joel came home. She called to her daddy, and he came upstairs to find us. I picked up Alex and discovered his diaper was so wet he squished when I rested him on my hip.

Joel joined us in the master bathroom and looked around. "What's everyone doing in here?"

"I made a flower," Eden said proudly, holding out her open hands toward the toilet seat as if she were a hostess on a game show.

Joel laughed and tickled Eden, calling her his "clever little artist."

She was ridiculously cute; I had to admit it. But I was so irritated by his response. I wanted him to join me in my firm-parent crusade and help me crush the rebellion of toddler antics.

As soon as the kids were in bed that night, I followed Joel into the bathroom, where he began brushing his teeth with the tiny bit of toothpaste that was left. The bathroom still smelled minty fresh.

"I don't know what to do," I told him. "She didn't have much of a terrible twos phase. It's as if she saved it all for her fours, but I can't keep up with her. And Alex is so mobile I can barely keep up with him."

"Mobile, huh?" Joel garbled.

"Yes! He's fast, Joel. You've seen how he charges across a room. I can't put him down at the grocery store like we used to do when Eden was his age. Remember how she used to like to push the kiddie shopping baskets, and she would stay right beside me? Not Alex. He bolts. Every time I put him down, he takes off. When he starts running, I'm in trouble."

Joel rinsed out his mouth and turned to me with a grin. "You have to admit, our kids are cute."

"Cute has nothing to do with them turning into wild little hooligans."

"They're just kids."

"But they need to behave. Eden doesn't

159

get it. She's determined to make huge messes every day."

"It can't be that bad. Are you sure you're not exaggerating?"

"Joel, you don't know what it's like here with them every day." It frustrated me that he wasn't sympathizing with me.

"Yes, I do. I understand."

"No, you don't. How could you? You're never here. You said things were going to change, but they haven't."

His countenance changed instantly. He stared at me, his eyes narrowing. He turned off the bathroom light, said nothing, and went to bed.

I turned the light back on and finished getting ready for bed. A few minutes later, once I had calmed down, I got into bed and placed my hand on Joel's chest. "I didn't mean to sound like I was attacking you for not being here. I just feel like I'm all by myself sometimes. I'm trying hard, but it's never enough."

"Trying hard?" His voice came out in a low growl. It wasn't a tone I had heard from him very often. "Try working ten- and twelve-hour days for months so you can provide for your family. That's trying hard. But that's not enough for you, is it?"

"Joel, I didn't mean . . . I just . . ."

160

"Look around, Jennalyn. You have a nice place to live, all the food and clothes, and anything you and our two healthy children could ask for. I can't feel sorry for you that they're so normal and do childish things and make your life so miserable."

"Joel!"

"I'm not going to talk about this now." He pulled away and turned his back to me, my hand slipping off his chest. "Leave it alone."

Even though he was indicating that I should leave the topic alone, in my frustration I heard that he wanted me to leave him alone. I grabbed my pillow and slammed the bedroom door shut as I marched to the stairs. My heart was pounding.

Why did he think I was trying to attack him? What's his problem? How did we get this messed up?

Stomping down the stairs, all I could think was that if I had woken the kids by slamming our bedroom door or from my thumping footsteps, it would be up to me to go to them and comfort them.

Everything falls on me.

I knew that statement wasn't fair. Joel was the one who worked such long hours. When he was home, he did a lot with the kids. But that was when he was home, and my comment was accurate about him rarely being home.

He keeps saying things are going to change at work, but it won't happen this weekend. Not when Valentine's is one of their busiest times of the year.

I pulled a blanket from the basket by the sofa and threw my pillow next to it on the couch. I didn't know what to do. Should I go upstairs and apologize? Should I try to make things right?

Why couldn't he just sympathize with me about the kids? That's all I wanted. A simple hug would have been enough to make me feel like he at least heard me. Understood my feelings. Cared about me.

Settling in under the blanket, I felt so alone. So confused. *Why is everything coming in as a ten on my stress meter? I need to talk to someone.*

Something deep inside me whispered that if I needed to, if it was really important, I could reach out to Christy, Sierra, Emily, or Tess. Any of them would take my call, even though it was after ten o'clock. They would understand the churned-up emotions. They would have comforting things to say, the way my mom used to say just the right thing when my mood went low.

I thought about going back upstairs. If Joel

was awake, I would apologize and try to smooth things over. If he was asleep, I would curl up quietly on my side of the bed and try to sleep. There was wisdom in not tumbling back into the cave where, a few weeks ago, the melancholy I had felt over the loss of my mother had threatened to grow around my heart like moss.

In the darkened room, I saw a glow coming from the kitchen counter and then go out. It was my phone. I always plugged it in downstairs so that I wouldn't scroll through it in the dark when I was in bed. My phone lit up a second time, indicating a text had come in.

It might be important.

I got up, went over to the counter, and reached for my phone.

Who would be texting me at this time of night?

CHAPTER 11

The text was from a local business letting me know that I had three days before my BOGO coupon for frozen yogurt expired. I deleted it.

I was about to turn off my phone when another text came through. This one was from Tess. She hadn't sent it to the group. Only to me.

You still up?

I typed yes and waited. After thirty seconds, I typed, You okay?

Tess replied with an emoji of a girl shrugging.

Anything I can do?

Are you able to talk right now? Or tomorrow?

I pressed the call button and returned to the sofa, pulling the blanket over my legs and leaning against my pillow.

"Hi," Tess said. "I hope it isn't too late. I know you guys usually go to bed early."

"I'm still up. What's going on?"

"I have a new client. It's actually a production company that wants to hire me to style one of the TV personalities on a talk show."

"Tess, that's amazing. Isn't that something you've wanted to do for a long time?"

"Yes, it is." Her tone was still somber.

"So, why don't you sound excited?"

"Because Guy got me the job."

"Is he the client you're styling?"

"No, it's not anything he's involved with. He just recommended me for the position. I had the interview today, and they offered me the job on the spot."

"Why does it feel unsettling to you? I think I'm missing something."

"It's because he's part of it. I feel like he's finding ways for us to stay connected. A couple of weeks ago I told him that he should try to figure out his life without the two of us meeting or talking on the phone." Tess paused.

I quickly said, "I've been wanting to ask how everything turned out with him."

"I know I should have said something when you were at my place. I didn't want to dominate the conversation."

"We wouldn't have minded," I said. "I'm sure I'm not the only one who has been wondering. I mean, it's a big deal, Tess. Or

165

it could be a big deal. It's a lot for you to sort out by yourself."

"There wasn't that much for me to sort out," Tess said. "At least, until I was offered this new job."

"Do you feel like he's using the job to sort of corner you into talking to him more?" I wasn't sure what to say.

"I didn't tell you guys, but he and I had spent a lot of time talking. On the phone. For a while there around Christmas and most of January, we talked almost every night."

Her comment caught me off guard. In her earlier sharing, her connection with Guy had seemed much less involved. "That explains why you felt so connected to him emotionally. It was a lot more than just a single coffee date."

"It was. I tried to be neutral, but it's like Christy said, I was too involved in his whole situation. You guys were right. I needed to pull way back so I wouldn't be an influence."

"I think the others would like to know this, if you want to tell them."

"I will. It's just that I feel like I'm back in the middle of it now with this job offer. He called an hour ago. It was the first time he's called in about three weeks. I didn't pick up. He left a message saying he wanted to know how the interview went. I feel like if I tell him that they offered it to me, I'll owe him for the referral."

"You don't owe him anything, Tess."

Tess was silent.

"Listen, it was his choice to refer you, right? You didn't ask him to do that."

"No, I didn't. I didn't even know he was putting my name out there."

"Okay, so, you got the job on your own merit, not his. You are a woman of options, right?"

"That's right, I am."

"You have the option of taking the job or turning it down. He's not part of any of that. You don't owe him, Tess."

"You're right. Yes. I needed to hear that. I'm going to turn it down."

"You are?" I hadn't expected that to be her conclusion.

"Don't you think I should? That way I won't be connected to him at all."

"True. But it's business, isn't it? It's a job you really want. And need."

"I know. But I'm thinking that since I managed to land this offer based on my work, then I can put myself out there on my own and find a similar position."

Once again, I wasn't sure what to say. Guy

and his industry connections were still a bit of a mystery to me.

"The way I see it," Tess said, "I never tried to apply for a position like this before. I didn't know how to break in. As a result of the interview process, I found out the name of the agency that sent the other applicants. What if I went back to that agency, let them know I was offered the position but turned it down, and then see if maybe they would represent me. The agency would be the one sending me out for interviews."

"That makes sense. It sounds wise."

"It puts me back in the position of being a woman of options," Tess said.

"Exactly."

"Thanks, Jennalyn. I'm so glad you were able to talk right now. I feel a hundred pounds lighter."

"Good. You're quite amazing, you know. Amazing and courageous." As I said the affirming words to Tess, I remembered when I was in ninth grade and had submitted a painting for my very first art contest. My mother had said the exact same words to me.

"Thank you, Jennalyn. I love you."

"Love you too. Sleep well."

"I will."

I hung up and leaned back against my pillow. It felt richly satisfying to be there for Tess at just the right time and to give her words that my mother had given me years ago. At the same time, I felt unsettled. I wished I'd been equally transparent with Tess and told her what I was struggling with. She might not understand the tension between Joel and me, but she would definitely understand if I told her about Garrett.

Why wasn't I courageous enough to open up to Tess the way she opened up to me?

For a long time I sat alone in the dark room, thinking. I remembered when Tess had talked at her place about how God orchestrates everything so there are never any coincidences. Had that been the case when I came downstairs? Was it just a fluke that I saw my phone flash when I did and was able to call Tess when she needed to talk?

I never had pondered God's timing and His omniscience much before. Surely He didn't set things up so that Joel and I would have a fight and I would end up downstairs. I wondered if He merely knew what was going to happen and when it would happen. That made sense to me.

So, how much does God really leave up to us and our free will? When and how does He step in and intervene? And how does prayer factor into all of it?

The questions were enormous, and my brain as well as my emotional capacity were operating on reserve mode. Sleep was what I needed. Lots and lots of sleep. It struck me that maybe a big part of the angst I had struggled with lately was related to the ongoing sleep deprivation. I was a night person by nature, so before Eden was born, I stayed up late and worked into the wee hours of the morning on the things I really wanted to do.

That pace made sense when I was younger and could sleep in a little. Since I had become a mother, I rarely managed to stay in bed much past six thirty. I counted it as a victory if both kids actually slept or at least stayed in their beds until seven.

Determined to make sleep a bigger priority in my life, I decided to start here on the couch tonight. I would sleep better here than next to Joel since being with him would make me all the more aware of his frustration with me.

I reached for my phone, intending to make sure it was turned off. My thumb accidently tapped the game app and opened it. I saw that I had seventeen messages. I stared at the screen, telling myself that most of the messages would probably be like the BOGO ad for frozen yogurt. I convinced myself that I could scroll through all seventeen messages, unaffected.

Then I would delete the app.

Sixteen of the seventeen messages were from Garrett. Only one was a video ad trying to convince me I needed new car insurance. That one I deleted. Then I leaned back and read the rest. Garrett's first few messages were, Hey, your turn. And Ready to admit defeat so soon?

Since I hadn't replied to those friendly chides over the week or more since I had started playing the game, he added more wordy messages about how he and Violet were holding down the fort for the next week while Tiffany was in San Francisco for a trade show.

On Monday he wrote, No class, I guess. I'm taking Violet to the park. She really misses Eden. You're welcome to join us.

Early that evening he had added a long message. He said he hoped he hadn't said anything to upset me or offend me. He was concerned that maybe something was wrong, and he asked me to reply so he could quit worrying. He promised that after that he would stay out of my life, if that's what I wanted.

Without thinking, I typed, I'm fine. Just busy.

I sent it, and his reply was almost immediate. He said he was relieved. Then he sent another, longer note about how he had found some photos and wondered if it would be okay to mail them to me. Or, if it would be easier, he could just drop them off at Joel's restaurant this weekend.

I quickly typed back, You can mail them. The last thing I wanted was for him to show up at the Blue Ginger and deliver a package to Joel with my name on it.

My thoughts clustered as I typed: What pictures? If he had kept any photos from our years together, I didn't want copies of them. What purpose would they serve? I had gotten rid of all of mine.

They are of your mom and a few of the two of you together. I thought you might want them, in case you don't already have copies.

I stared at my phone screen, trying to figure out why in the world Garrett would have pictures of my mother. Even though I felt like a gullible fish going for the bait, I typed back, Where did you get them?

I came across them when I was going through my mom's things.

His answer sounded strange. What was he doing going through his mother's stuff? Had he gone hunting for pictures of me after we saw each other at the dance studio?

Then I remembered how I had searched for my yearbook.

As if he could sense my uncertainty, Garrett messaged back, I found them when I settled my mom's estate.

My throat tightened. That could mean only one thing.

Garrett, I didn't know. When did you lose your mom?

Last summer. July 5.

I am so, so sorry. I didn't know.

Thanks, Jennie. I know you understand what it's like.

For the next hour we messaged back and forth. I opened up to Garrett at the same speed that he was typing, as we shared about the pain of losing our moms and the huge void their absence from this planet had left in our souls.

I cried as I typed. For him and for me. I told him things about my mom that I had never told Joel. After 1:00 a.m., I finally said I had to go due to sheer exhaustion.

The last words he typed were, Thanks for spending tonight with me, Jennie. Love you.

I closed the app, turned off my phone, and sat alone in the dark. I realized I had never turned on a light and had been tapping my now-sore thumbs all that time without moving from the same hunched-over position on the couch.

I put down my phone, stretched out on my back, and stared at the ceiling.

I thought about how he had signed off with "Love you." Of course he meant it in a brotherly way, after all that we had shared in our messaging conversation. And because of all the ways our families had overlapped years ago.

It was only his way of saying that we're friends. That's all. Tess and I expressed our love for each other on the phone. This was the same thing.

Exhaustion on every level overtook me, and I fell into a deep sleep.

When the early morning light broke through the sliding glass door and flooded the great room, I tried to turn away. It was no use. As soon as I turned, I felt a sharp pain in my neck. The exhausting feelings that had gone to bed with me last night now felt oppressively close, confusing, and sticky. An uneasiness clung to me, reminding me of the falling-out with Joel and the heart-to-heart, intense conversation with Garrett.

I didn't know where to fit the conversation with Tess into the rest of it. All I knew was that I needed a hot shower to ease my tense muscles. It was going to be difficult to face Joel and then take on a normal day with my two busy babes.

What happened with my resolution last night to get more sleep?

My head pounded as I folded the blanket and returned it to the basket. Taking the stairs as light as a fairy, I made it past the closed doors of the kids' rooms without hearing any peeps from them. I opened our bedroom door as quietly as possible and was relieved to see that Joel's back was to the door and that he appeared to still be sleeping too.

I knew the sound of the shower running might wake him, but I had to get the hot water on my neck. I stepped into the steaming flow from the shower head and let it minister to my throbbing, tight muscles. I wished it would wash away the emotional pain from the night before. With my eyes closed, I turned my face to the stream of water and cried the last of the tears that had risen in me last night but had not leaked out.

I heard the bathroom door open. I didn't move.

A moment later the door to the shower opened and Joel entered, wrapping his arms around me, holding me, kissing my tensed shoulders.

"I'm sorry," he murmured in my ear.

I melted into his familiar embrace. "I'm sorry too."

The warm water fell on our faces as we kissed.

CHAPTER 12

The week that followed was filled with starts and stops. Joel worked long hours through Valentine's Day and was elated to tell me that it was the best holiday revenue the Blue Ginger had ever brought in. Most of his innovative new items on the menu had been a big hit.

The kids and I had Valentine's Day spaghetti dinner at GiGi and Poppy's. Eden loved giving them the cards she had made, and my in-laws had cute stuffed animals for both the kids. As much as I wished I could have spent the official "love" day of the year with my sweetheart, I knew that in his line of work that might never happen again.

Joel made me feel loved, though, by having a dozen red roses delivered to the house. The message on the card read "For my one and only."

I had made a valentine for him and left it on the bathroom counter with a ribbon-wrapped box of his favorite aftershave. That way I knew he would see it when he went into the bathroom to shave and shower. He kissed me warmly before he left and thanked me for loving him.

As much as I told myself that I understood this was the season of life we were in right now, I still felt waves of loneliness and abandonment. I knew those feelings could be linked to the same emotions that kept triggering me when I thought about the loss of my mom.

The day after Valentine's, while Joel was home trying to catch up on some sleep, I reached out to Christy and asked if she was available to meet at the park with the kids. She couldn't get away, so I tried Sierra. She was locked in with her English lesson video calls.

I buckled my noisy kids into their car seats and headed to a mall. I had been thinking about Tess's recommendation of boot-cut jeans and wanted to try some on. We ended up at the Irvine Spectrum, a large upscale area with outdoor shops. I hadn't been there in a long time and wasn't sure why that had been my mall of choice, since I had several options within a ten-mile radius of where we lived.

As I was unfolding the double stroller, I

realized Garrett had mentioned the Spectrum last month. He said he lived nearby. I felt a little shiver as I wondered what it might be like to run into him here instead of at dance class.

I knew the odds were slim to none that I would see him. Instead, I focused on all the bodybuilding moves required to move two toddlers out of their seats and into the stroller. We were barely out of the parking lot before Eden asked for snacks.

"Not yet, Eden."

"When?"

"Soon."

"I'm hungry."

"Later, Eden. Please don't fuss." My routine had always been to bring snacks whenever Eden went shopping with me to help keep her occupied. I was pretty sure that my coping mechanism would come up later in her life if she ever needed to go to counseling for the inability to disassociate food with shopping.

For now, I wouldn't worry about the many ways I was imprinting my children for life. I needed to let their daddy sleep for at least two more hours.

As we made our way through the Spectrum to one of the department stores, I noticed that people were smiling at my children and leaning in and waving at them. I pulled back the cover so I could see what they were doing. Eden was waving like a princess in a carriage and was flapping her brother's arm so that he was getting in on the grand procession.

"Are you having fun, Eden?" I asked.

"Wave, Mommy. We're in a parade!"

I spotted a bouquet of colorful balloons on a kiosk selling mobile phone covers, and I wanted to see if they would part with one of their balloons. The kiosk attendant was insulted that I asked and said I had to buy a phone cover. I didn't need a phone cover.

"Pleeeeease?" Eden begged.

He was unaffected by her charms, and I moved on, wishing I hadn't initiated the possibility of a balloon. Now I had two wailing children, and no one was slowing down to smile or wave at them. Instead, people were glaring at me.

As soon as we entered the women's clothing section of the department store, I caved and broke out the snacks. I handed the bag to Eden. "Share with your brother, please. And if you have to go to counseling one day, I'll pay for it."

She stopped fussing and turned into the cute big sister who was showing anyone who glanced at them that she was helping her brother.

We arrived home two hours later with several shopping bags and crumbs everywhere. Neither of the kids was interested in lunch. They just wanted to wiggle and move and get out all the energy they had stockpiled on our outing. Fortunately, Joel was up, and he was happy to get on the floor and wrestle with them.

We slid through the weekend with more normal days like that. Joel was home all day Monday. Our plan was to take the kids to a park, but it turned out to be a cooler than usual, with clouds that threatened rain but never delivered. We stayed home, Joel napped, I caught up on laundry.

Around three thirty Joel was up. He had the cooking channel on and was folding bath towels on the sofa. "What time is Eden's class?" Joel asked.

"Four."

"If you take her, I can finish the laundry and make dinner."

"It's a deal."

Eden had no preference about who should take her, unlike her strong opinion on the matter several weeks ago. I was glad because getting out the door was drama-free. I was also happy that Joel hadn't suggested he take her. I'm not sure how it would have been if Garrett was there and struck up a conversation with Joel since I still hadn't told Joel about him.

As I pulled into the parking lot, I realized that Tiffany might be there with Violet this time. If she was, would she know who I was? What if both Tiffany and Garrett were there with their daughter? Would it be awkward to carry on a conversation with both of them? Or would seeing them together normalize everything? Maybe if I thought of them as a couple, the way Garrett probably thought of Joel and me, it would change the imbalance that might come from seeing Garrett alone again.

Tiffany wasn't there. Garrett came alone with Violet, and she and Eden were elated to see each other. The vision of their tutus being squished into a halo of fluffy pinkness as they threw their arms around each other was adorable.

Garrett greeted me with a shy grin. "Playin' hard to get, are ya?"

"Excuse me?"

"I messaged you a couple of times. You didn't reply."

"Oh. I, uh . . ."

"I just needed your address," he said. "To send you the pictures of your mom."

I had completely forgotten about the

182

photos. "Why don't you just bring the pictures next week?"

"Okay." He followed me over to the folding chairs lined up under the window. "Mind if I sit here?"

"No, of course not."

Garrett's large frame didn't exactly fit on the chair. I crossed my legs so that we wouldn't be touching. He leaned closer and in a low voice said, "I hope I didn't make you uncomfortable by talking about our moms."

"No. It was good, actually. I appreciated the chance to talk about my mom."

"It's painful to lose someone you love," he said.

I glanced at him and looked back at the tiny dancers. I nodded but didn't say anything.

Garrett shifted uncomfortably and in almost a whisper he said, "Did you feel like that, in a way, when we broke up?"

A burst of adrenaline shot through me, and I stood up. I didn't mean to, but it was as if he had struck a nerve. "I think I left my phone in the car," I mumbled, and hurried out to the parking lot.

I wasn't going to share with Garrett how I felt when he broke my heart. Not now, not ever. He didn't need to know. I didn't need to revisit that time in my life. I refused to describe to him or to anyone else the humiliation and deep gut-wrenching pain that his choices had caused me.

I unlocked the car, slid into the driver's seat, and locked the door. Leaning my head back on the headrest, I tried to slow my breathing. I didn't want to think about the past. I didn't want to go back into the studio. I didn't want to talk to Garrett. I didn't want to be near him.

This is too difficult. I should have told Joel about Garrett weeks ago. I wish I hadn't shared all those deep feelings about my mother with Garrett. He's acting as if he now has access to all my feelings.

I hated that I was back into an unstable place with my contrary emotions. The last few days with Joel had been so good. I wanted to move ahead, not fall back.

A tap on the car window made me jump. I turned to see not Garrett, thankfully, but Emily. I couldn't roll down the window without putting the keys in the ignition, so I awkwardly opened the door an inch.

"Hi," Emily said.

"Hi."

She seemed to be trying to figure out what I was doing, sitting alone in my car.

I pointed to the empty passenger's seat

184

and unlocked the door. She went around the car, slipped into the seat, and said hi again.

"Hi."

We both smiled.

"Eden is in dance class."

"Oh." Emily pointed at the chain clothing store that anchored the small shopping center. "I was going to see if I could find a jean jacket like the one at Tess's."

"That's funny because I just bought a pair of boot-cut jeans a few days ago as a result of Tess's advice."

"She had quite an effect on all of us. Christy told me at church yesterday that she cleaned out her closet and tossed all her blah beige tops."

I realized that Emily's presence brought an immediate calm to me, the same way she had when Alex was born. I wondered if she knew that was her superpower, as Sierra would call it.

"Do you want to shop with me?" Emily asked.

"I probably should go back inside so that Eden doesn't notice I'm gone."

"Are you okay?" Emily asked.

"Yeah. Just . . . you know, tired, I guess. I probably shouldn't sit here in the warm car, or I'll fall asleep and not wake up until

Wednesday." I forced a laugh out of my tightened throat and fiddled in my purse on my lap.

"I won't keep you." Emily looked at me closely.

Of all the women in the DOEs, Emily had seen me at my most frantic moment. When a woman has participated in the delivery of your baby, it's difficult to simply slap on a smile and expect her to believe everything is as it should be.

I realized that Emily knew me. She knew something was wrong.

She was timid, though. Reserved and thoughtful. True to her nature, Emily gave my arm a squeeze and said, "Call me if you want to talk or anything."

"Thanks, Em."

She started to get out of the car but leaned in and said, "Did you see the text Sierra sent about us going to the movies next Wednesday night?"

"No, I didn't."

"It's a movie that will supposedly inspire us for our spring picnic because of the elaborate setting and cinematography." Emily smiled.

"Oh, okay. I'll check her text." I glanced out the windshield toward the studio. "I feel like a horrible mother for leaving Eden in there. I should go."

Getting out, I locked the car doors, and Emily and I walked through the parking lot together. I slipped back into the dance studio and stayed by the door, keeping my gaze on Eden. I was aware that Garrett was still in his chair next to the one I had vacated. I was also aware that he looked over at me a number of times.

I was resolved to move on. No more personal conversations of any sort. This would be Eden's last class. She wouldn't come again. I would delete the game app. Garrett could keep the pictures. Or throw them away. I had loads of photos of my mom. I didn't need to rely on him for anything, including a few fragments of my mom captured in a picture.

With my shoulders back, I kept looking straight ahead, fixed on my graceful little ballerina.

When class was over, our girls clasped hands and scooted over to where I was standing. Garrett came and stood beside me, but not too close. Our daughters were beaming. We both gave them lots of praise and ended up walking out the door at the same time. I held Eden's hand, Garrett held Violet's, and then the two girls linked hands. We walked across the parking lot as if the four of us were connected. Like best friends. Or a family.

We reached my car first. Garrett and Violet lingered as I settled Eden into her car seat. The two girls were jabbering with each other. I pulled back, ready to close the door as the girls merrily waved their good-byes.

"I'll bring the pictures next week," Garrett said. "And sorry about the, you know, the comment. I just want to make sure we're all good."

I looked at him for only a second, trying my best to appear calm. "Yeah, we're good. Nothing to pick apart or review from the past. I'm all about the future."

I sensed his surprise. My tone was brusque compared to what I had written during our long messaging session. But that's the way I wanted it to be now.

"Right. The future," he repeated with an odd grin.

I walked over to my door and was about to get inside when Garrett called over the top of the car, "To infinity and beyond!"

I clenched my teeth and refused to look at him. That had been my line. Our line. Our way of secretly messaging that our relation-ship would go on and on — to infinity and beyond. That one day we would marry and be together for always.

Why did he toss that line at me? What is he thinking? This has gotten too personal.

I felt the tears brimming as I realized that Garrett knew me. He knew intimate details about my thoughts and my feelings from the past, and because I had opened up to him so easily through our messaging, he knew more about what I was going through than Joel did.

The understanding of what I had done by letting Garrett into my heart then and now unnerved me. I drove home angry at myself and determined that I would tell Joel everything tonight.

Joel had dinner on the table when Eden and I arrived back home. I had managed to develop a pounding headache. After the meal, in a gesture of prioritizing my self-care, I asked Joel if he would mind putting the kids to bed. I retreated upstairs, where I took a hot bath with bath salts and went to bed.

I could hear Joel coaxing Eden to get in bed and promising one more story if she didn't stall. I heard Alex cry at some point for only a few minutes. My eyes were closed. My heart was aching, and my body was limp. I slept for nine hours without waking even once. I was pretty sure it was a new record for my mommy years.

The world was a different place when I got up on Tuesday morning. I made buckwheat pancakes with blueberries for breakfast and covered the top of my short stack with apricot preserves. Scrumptious.

Joel made me laugh as he interacted with the kids as they ate. He was full of funny voices and big grins. He reminded me of his dad.

Joel had the day off again. It was so rare. The promise of more time together seemed to be coming true. We ventured out, all four of us, to the beach around eleven o'clock. The weather was clear, warm, and as perfect as a summer day in a movie. It had been months since the four of us had done anything like this, especially something spontaneous. The beach in Newport was practically empty. A random Tuesday at the end of February was not a day that anyone planned to go.

We parked near our old rental house out of habit. Since the house was so close to Christy's, it took great restraint for me to not persuade Joel that I should knock on the door and invite her to join us.

This day was for us. Just us. I brought a blanket and a diaper bag with an assortment of helpful items for the kids. Joel spread out the blanket near the lifeguard tower, and Eden squealed with joy when she found a plastic bucket partially buried in the sand. The kids played together with the bucket, Eden did twirls, and Alex settled into a pocket of warm sand where he wiggled his toes. He seemed fascinated with the seagulls as they soared over the water and picked their way across the firm wet sand on toothpick-thin legs.

"Come here." Joel was stretched out on the blanket with his elbows bent and his fingers folded behind his head.

I scooted closer, casting a quick glance at Alex, who was only a few feet away. I wanted to make sure he had caught on that the sand was not for eating.

Joel reached over and ran his hand down my back, gently twisting my long hair around his fingers. "Remember when we moved here, and we would come to the beach every chance we got?"

"Um-hmm." I tilted my face up to the pale February sky. The sun felt just right. Not too hot. The breeze was gentle. Not too cool, not too windy. It was a perfect Southern California beach day.

"How many sunsets do you think we watched, sitting right about here?"

"A hundred," I said.

"No, four hundred," Joel countered. "At least. Every one of them was different."

I opened my eyes, checking on Eden, who was bending over, drawing in the damp sand with her finger. Alex was putting a handful of sand in the bucket and then dumping it out.

"We had so many dreams back then," Joel said.

"And here we are," I added. "Watching two of those dreams that came true. Three," I added, "if you want to include the dream of your being a full-time chef and part owner in a successful restaurant."

"What about you?" Joel slid his hand under the back of my shirt, resting it on the curve of my lower back. That spot was one of the few places that hadn't retained stretch marks or extra ripples or cellulite. I was well aware of all the changes to the landscape of my body whenever Joel touched them. Where his hand now rested somehow made me feel feminine. Alluring and desirable. An easy smile found its way to my lips.

"You make me feel lovely," I said softly.

Joel rolled on his side and propped himself up on his elbow, keeping his hand on my undimpled skin. "You are more than lovely," he said. "You are the most beautiful woman I know."

I let his words, his gaze, his touch fill up all the places in my soul where so much emotional shrapnel had left gouges. I felt the same way I did when I first fell in love with him. My heart had been skeptical. What if he left me, the way Garrett had? What if I was only fooling myself that this handsome, talented, loving man cared for me?

Joel had been so patient. I had revealed very little to him of my past heartbreak. All Joel knew was that I asked for time to let our relationship grow slowly. He gave me months before he even kissed me. A full year and a half before he proposed and a ten-month engagement. It was perfect. All of it. Just enough time. Just enough confidence. Just enough mystery.

The day we walked down the aisle and looked each other in the eye and said, "Yes," we were both overwhelmed by love. We were in love with each other. In love with love. In love with us.

I longed to feel that way again.

But something seemed to still keep us at a distance. I didn't want to believe that the space between us was filled with the secret of my communication with Garrett, crowding out the flow of my love for Joel. Instead, I wanted to attribute our communication issues to Joel's career and his rarely being around this last year.

The reality was that he wasn't working right now. He was here. Very present. Very attentive. Very kind.

I looked out at the expansive blue of the ocean, lost in a sea of unexpected sadness.

CHAPTER 13

"What are you thinking right now?" Joel asked me.

"I'm thinking . . ." I hesitated. This did not seem like the ideal moment to open my heart to him. But then, when was the ideal moment to tell your husband that you realized you had been unintentionally attaching yourself to another man?

"Joel, there's something I've been wanting to tell you."

His amber eyes peered at me above his lowered sunglasses. "Is it by any chance how much you love me? How patient you've been all these months, and how I should smother you with kisses to show my appreciation?"

"Well . . ." It always amazed me how my husband could go from zero to physically affectionate in two seconds.

Joel's hand moved to my side and he tickled me. I leaned into him, laughing and

195

protesting, but only a little.

Eden took our mirth as an invitation to a family free-for-all and dove onto the blanket with sprinkles of sand flying everywhere. Poor Alex didn't know what to think of the mayhem and burst into tears.

I untangled myself from our giddy little octopus girl and turned to gather up Alex.

"It's okay, sweetheart. We're just playing. Do you want to play with us?"

Alex kept wailing over Eden's shrieks of delight and Joel's deep laugh. I lifted Alex and made a surprised face, then pulled him close and kissed his check. His sandy fingers went into his mouth, and a smile emerged. Soon he was laughing with the rest of us.

The burst of joy prompted Joel to rise to his feet and lift Eden. I turned away and used my hand to shield Alex as another flurry of sand blew our way.

"Let's have a race." Joel put her down where the gently foaming waves had made the sand moist and firm. "Ready? Set?"

Eden shouted, "Go!" She took off with her arms bent and her face forward as if she were a trained athlete, determined to come in first.

I held Alex close, brushing the sand from his face and hands and watching my charmer of a husband and daddy pretend to be puffing along, trying to keep up with Eden's pace.

She stopped suddenly and turned around, running back toward me with the wind pulling her dark hair behind her like many tails to a soaring kite. I wanted to take a picture so I could capture her face. Her gleeful expression was priceless.

Rummaging in my purse with one hand while I still held Alex with the other, I pulled out my phone and clicked haphazardly, trying to seize the moment as best as I could. I tried to coax Alex into a selfie, but he was only interested in pulling off my sunglasses, so none of the shots were successful.

A text message came in just then. The sun had slid out from behind the blessed veil of clouds that had been over us since we got there. I squinted to read the text in the brightness.

Checking in on movie for next Wednesday. I think we're all in but Jennalyn. You in, Jennalyn? Hey, that rhymes!

Sierra followed up her text with a string of emojis including a big chunk of broccoli.

Broccoli? I replied.

Oops, texted Sierra.

I smiled and replied, Yes, I'm planning to come. Remind me of the time.

Sierra responded with: We can go at 3:20 or 7:10. What works best for everyone?

The usual stream of pings and buzzes followed as the others discussed what would work best for each of them. I put my phone back in my purse because I knew Joel had mentioned earlier that he planned to take two days off again next week. I left it to the others to decide on the time for the movie.

Joel lowered himself to the blanket and lay back. Wind-tossed Eden fell on his chest, dramatizing along with her daddy how worn out they were after their race. Thirty seconds later, though, Eden had popped up and reached for my hand.

"Come on, Mommy. Your turn. Let's race."

"I need to hold your brother," I said.

Eden made her most dramatic, chin-lowered, "my world just caved in" pout. Joel burst out laughing.

"That's a new look," he said.

It was, in fact, an old look and one that had lost its charm on me months ago. Apparently, she hadn't pulled it out of her bag of tricks when Joel was around.

"Pleeeeease, Mommy? Just one little eenie meenie teenie tiny race?"

Joel sat up and took Alex from my lap. "Let's all race!"

I reluctantly rose and brushed the sand from the backside of my new boot-cut jeans. I rolled up the cuffs so they wouldn't get soaked if a wave curled up over my feet. We all took our marks, with Alex perched on Joel's shoulders while he clutched Alex's chubby, bare legs.

"Ready? Set?" Joel gave me a nod, letting me know that it was going to be only Eden and me racing.

"Go!" Eden took her racing seriously and shot ahead of me. Instead of turning around as she had with Joel, she kept running, and I kept chasing her.

I glanced over my shoulder and saw that Joel was standing beside our blanket with Alex balanced still on his shoulders. He was grinning like the happiest man who had seen all his dreams come true.

We continued the frolicking for another half hour before folding up the blanket, collecting all our shoes and the diaper bag. Joel carried Alex and the other items while Eden led the way to the outdoor shower and begged me to help her turn on the water so she could wash her feet. I obliged, and Joel put Alex down. I gave both of them all the usual mommy instructions, which were nearly worthless. My children were elated to splash around, and in all the fun they did manage to wash off most of the sand.

They were soon a sparkling, soggy mess. I caught Joel's expression. He was smiling, and that made me happy. It had been so, so long since we had had a spontaneous day like this. I couldn't remember ever doing anything with both kids. On the rare occasion when Joel was home, our plans usually were complicated by Alex's nursing schedule or a diaper blowout or Eden scraping a knee and being inconsolable.

I think it was the first time I felt that we were a functioning family of four and everyone was content. I wondered if Joel was thinking the same thing.

He had reached for my shoulder bag that I had placed on the small bench next to the showers. Strapping it over his shoulder he asked, "What do you carry in this thing? It's heavy."

"Just the basics."

Joel seemed to evaluate the "basics" I carried around. "With your purse, the diaper bag, and our son . . . how do you do it?"

With a bit of a smirk and a wink, I told Joel, "Us mommy magicians never reveal our secrets."

He grinned broadly and leaned in to kiss me. In that tiny moment, I felt as if Joel saw me. He had a bit of understanding of what my daily life looked like. I enjoyed that he was thinking of me. I liked it a lot.

As we made our way back to the car, I thought about how I used to take Eden for stroller rides on the sidewalk along all the beachfront homes. I loved to study the various patios, noting the widely varied decorating touches.

As we passed one of the familiar houses, I noticed that the flower boxes along the edge of the second-story balcony were highlighted with bright red and orange bougainvillea. It always amazed me how the soft petals were able to keep clinging to such a thin, gnarly, thorny vine. They were as colorful as they were hearty.

I knew growing plants and vegetables in the coastal climate was difficult. Joel and I had spent plenty of money on a variety of plants in our raised box garden. I tried to remember which herbs we ended up having some success with. I recalled that our zucchini proved to be hearty enough to survive the climate.

We should start a garden in our backyard. Eden would love it.

On the drive home, I thought through the steps needed to prepare a corner of our backyard for a garden. Alex had been too young for me to think about doing anything like that last spring. Joel's big project last year was setting up his fancy new barbecue once the deck had been completed.

I think one of the reasons I liked the idea of our planting a garden was that, if we could work shoulder to shoulder on it during Joel's days off, it would be a way for us to plant new seeds of togetherness in our marriage. Our time at the beach had been so fun. Working as a family on a garden would be ideal.

I knew that if I mentioned the garden now, Joel would want to work on it right away. The kids needed naps, and I needed to finish the small art project I had started several weeks ago. I had bought nice cardstock and planned to calligraphy everyone's word for the year on a card. The project had stalled when I remembered that Tess didn't have a word.

Maybe she has one now. I'll call her to find out. It would be fun to surprise everyone with the cards on our movie night.

Once our house was quiet that afternoon, I texted Tess. And she said she didn't have a word. She also told me that she had applied at the agency, told the truth about how she had turned down the earlier opportunity, and hoped they would have another job referral for her. They didn't. She said she may have made a big mistake.

My reply to Tess was Wait, trust, be at peace. I realized after I sent it that I had just given her Sierra's, Christy's, and Emily's words for the year.

The coincidence wasn't lost on Tess. She texted back that she recognized those words, and maybe instead of one word for the year she needed to borrow all of ours and try to make a banner sentence out of them.

I smiled and replied, Then don't forget love.

Tess texted back with a question mark and then typed, I thought the point of all this is that you DOEs are helping me not to fall in love with Guy so I won't do something stupid.

Love is my word for the year, I replied.

Oh, that's right. I forgot. Wait, trust, be at peace, and love. It's sort of like the "keep calm and . . ." saying.

I replied with a smiley face and said a little prayer for Tess. She was figuring things out, and so was I.

By that weekend I knew I couldn't wait any longer to talk to Joel about Garrett. I started the conversation when we were in bed Saturday night. It was late. He had worked a full day plus taken the dinner shift, and we were sitting up in bed talking about what we would plant in our garden on his next day off. Ever since I had tossed the garden idea at him, he had been excited to start the project.

"Carrots would be good," he said. "And maybe lettuce. I want to plant things that Eden will eat."

"Then we'll have to plant some cheese."

He gave me an odd look.

"Haven't you noticed that our daughter still has a fixation on cheese? I coaxed her into apple slices the other day. That was a major breakthrough."

Joel still looked mystified.

"About Eden," I took the plunge with a now-or-never determination. "I've been wanting to tell you that at her ballet class —"

"I can't take her on Monday. I'm working."

"I know. I was just going to say that at her class, one of the other students, Violet —"

"I met Violet. Have you set up a playdate for them yet?"

"No. Joel, please."

"What?"

"You're interrupting me."

Again, he looked mystified. "Okay, sorry. Go ahead. But wait. I forgot to tell you. My mom wants to have my dad's birthday lunch at the restaurant. They want to use the back room and have the whole family there. It'll be on a Sunday."

"Tomorrow?"

"No. In two weeks, I think. I'll write it on the calendar in the kitchen." He slunk down and pulled the covers up. "Keep talking. I need to stretch out."

My mind had already moved on to trying to figure out which Sunday, what to wear, if the time they decided on would interrupt Alex's usual naptime, and whether anyone at the party would notice that our daughter only ate cheese.

"Joel?"

"I'm listening. What were you going to say?"

I drew in a deep breath. "When I took Eden to her ballet class, I met Violet's dad. His name is Garrett."

"Right."

"The thing is, though, I didn't meet him at the ballet class for the first time. I actually have known him since I was fifteen."

Joel had closed his eyes.

I decided to keep going and get it all out at once. "Garrett, who you met, Violet's dad, he was my boyfriend. The one I told you about. The one who . . . who broke my heart."

Joel didn't say anything.

I leaned closer. "Joel?"

He was gone. Way down the track on the sleep train.

"Oh, Joel." I whispered and turned off the light. "This is getting way too difficult."

CHAPTER 14

On Monday, I was ready to take Eden to her final ballet class and have an unemotional response when I saw Garrett. If he had the pictures of my mom as promised, I would thank him, talk to the other moms there, and exit as soon as Eden was finished.

I designed the strategy to limit my interaction with him because I didn't want to hear anything that might tug at my heartstrings — no inside jokes from high school, details about his mom, or anything about how his wife was gone all the time.

The other reason I wanted it to be an easy hello/goodbye was because I still hadn't managed to tell Joel about Garrett. At least not when Joel was awake.

He had Tuesday and Wednesday off this week, and our plan was to work on the garden. I wanted to be able to tell him the whole story and conclude it with a tightly sealed "the end" since, with no more classes,

I didn't have a reason to bump into Garrett ever again.

That was the plan. Or so I thought.

But Garrett and Violet never showed up at class.

Eden asked about her friend before the lesson started but was quickly distracted when the teacher put on the music and lined up all her charges. I took a seat next to two other moms and, for the first time, truly watched Eden.

"Is she yours?" the woman next to me asked toward the end of the class. "The one in front with her hair up in a bun?"

"Yes, she's mine."

"She seems like a natural dancer. Has she had a lot of lessons?"

"No, just this class."

"My oldest is fourteen. She showed the same poise and balance when she was this age. She's in a dance company now. It's a lot of work, but she loves it."

I would have thought the woman was trying to advertise or sell me something by the way she sounded so enthusiastic. She wasn't, though. She didn't even tell me the name of the dance company her daughter was with.

I drove home frustrated because the teacher had announced another class was scheduled the following week to make up for the time she had been ill. My closure with Garrett would have to wait another week. Now I wasn't sure if I wanted to tell Joel about Garrett that week or wait until after the final class. I was beginning to wonder if there was anything to even tell him.

Poppy had come over to watch Alex so that I didn't need to take him with me. GiGi was having her hair done; so it was just Poppy and Alex at the house for the hour and twenty minutes that Eden and I had been gone. I stood in the living room and surveyed the chaos.

How is it possible for my son and father-in-law to make such a mess in so short a time?

"Hope you don't mind that I made myself a sandwich," Poppy said.

"No, of course not." The counter was strewn with every possible sandwich ingredient that could be found in the refrigerator and pantry.

"How 'bout if I make one for you?"

"You know what? I'd like that. Thank you." I surveyed the many options and added, "Everything except sriracha, please."

"Comin' right up."

I found it sweet that he wanted to take care of me. I especially appreciated the way he applauded Eden as she showed him all her ballet twirls.

The next morning Joel was the one who had covered the counter with breakfast fixings. I sat on the barstool spoon-feeding Alex applesauce.

"Eden did really well in her class," I told Joel. "One of the other moms told me Eden has natural talent."

Joel pressed the lever on the toaster. "She must get it from your side of the family, then."

"I don't know who that would be. It's definitely not me."

"Are you going to sign her up for another class?" he asked.

"If she still likes it, sure. I wouldn't want to push her too much when she's still so young."

"She's going to be five in September," Joel reminded me.

"Five sounds so old." I reached for the jar of honey in the cupboard, and as soon as the sourdough toast popped up, I spread the honey on top and took a bite.

"Guess you were hungry," Joel said with a laugh.

"This is the only way to eat it. Still warm, slightly crunchy around the edges, and with the honey soaking into all the little holes." I held out the slice for Joel to take a bite.

He chewed slowly, nodding his agreement before swallowing and jutting his chin out, inviting me to offer him another bite.

"Did I tell you that Eden's class meets next Monday for the last time? The teacher just announced it this week."

"Why don't you tell my parents? I'm sure they would like to be there."

"Oh, okay." I felt a little uneasy about them coming and the possibility that I would have to do a bit of explaining about Garrett.

"Do you want me to call them, or will you?" Joel asked.

"I will."

The morning TV show that had kept Eden quietly occupied was ending. I could tell by the familiar theme song that began to play.

"Breakfast." I reached for the remote on the counter and turned off the TV.

Eden let out a big, sad sigh. She always had the same "my life is so tragic" response whenever I disconnected her from anything digital. Her reactions were much more dramatic when she was younger. Both Joel and I had worked hard on the transitions so that we could use TV as well as games on our phones as tools when we needed them but not let her make demands on when, where, and how much screen time she got. I wondered what Alex was going to be like with screens when he was a little older.

I also had wondered many times if other moms had the same challenge. I hadn't ever brought it up with my friends. I think I was embarrassed that my child could burst into tears over being separated from a TV show or when she was engaged with something on my phone.

Thinking of my friends reminded me of the plans for Wednesday movie night. The 7:10 showing had won the vote. As Joel dished up the eggs, I told him about the plans.

"You're going this Wednesday?" he asked. "Tomorrow?"

I nodded.

"How long have you known?"

"A few days. We hadn't settled on the time, though. The movie is at 7:10."

"What movie?" Eden wanted to know. "Are we going to watch a movie?" She began listing her favorites.

"I have that night off," Joel said, ignoring Eden. "Can't you go another night?"

I didn't want to explain to him that it had already taken way too many texts to get all five of us to agree to go on Wednesday.

Instead of replying, I handed Alex his sippy cup.

Apparently, I hadn't tightened the lid all the way. Alex knocked it off his high chair tray, and it fell on the floor, leaving a puddle. It wasn't a big spill, but Joel and I fell into one of our "you're in my space" kitchen dances when we both went to clean it up. I knew he had a thing about being territorial in the kitchen, and having his own space was a big deal for him at work. That was part of the reason it took him so long to find the right chef to hire. He needed someone who could learn his dance steps and fall in at the same pace without stepping on his toes.

Maybe Eden gets more of her dancing skills from her father than he thinks.

We rolled into the usual round of distractions that came when the four of us tried to eat at the same time. The topic of the Wednesday night movie didn't come up again until the next morning. By then, it was no big deal. Joel had invited his parents to come for dinner that night, and he would now have some help with the kids. It made his mom happy, too, because she hadn't come with Poppy on Monday night.

Joel was looking forward to barbecuing on the deck since the weather was so nice. I knew I would be able to slip out easily. All the bases would be covered; it was all good.

Best of all was that he and I spent a good part of the day working in the backyard. The kids got plenty dirty helping us as we prepared a stretch along the fence for our garden. We decided to start small so we could see what grew well in our untried soil. It wasn't a lot of work to break up the earth, mix in the bags of fertilized soil, and mark off the sections. But one of us needed to watch Alex closely while one or both of us answered Eden's endless questions. That meant it was double the work.

Watching Eden's excitement as she pressed the first carrot seeds into the warm dirt made it all worthwhile.

We had just about finished when the typical afternoon clouds moved in and turned the sunlight to a hazy glow in the sky over us. I felt a few misty raindrops on my bare arms and tilted my chin up.

"Do you think it's going to rain, Joel? Look at those clouds over there."

"I hope not. The steaks are marinating, and I planned on grilling for my parents."

Another raindrop came from the ominous, fast-moving clouds, followed by a small army of comrades. I hustled the kids inside and spent the next half hour bathing and dressing them in clean, cozy outfits. By the time they went back downstairs, it was raining steadily, and Joel was staring out the kitchen window.

"Are you still planning to go to the movies tonight?" He looked bummed.

I nodded. "It's not raining that hard, is it?"

"No, it's not the rain. I was just thinking that you might have changed your mind since my parents are coming. You won't be here long enough to have dinner with the family. I'm sure they were looking forward to seeing you too." Joel paused and added, "We haven't seen them since Christmas."

"I've seen them several times. Poppy was here on Monday. And I saw them on Valentine's Day."

"We didn't see them on Valentine's."

"*You* didn't see them. I did. The kids and I went to their house in the afternoon and stayed for dinner. Remember? I told you how your mom made spaghetti for Eden, and she ate some. The kids decorated valentine cookies for them. We made cards for them too."

Joel looked like he was coming out of a bout of amnesia. "So you've seen them a couple of times."

"Yes, that's what I just said."

He looked confused, as if he were just beginning to realize how much life he had missed while being locked in at work.

"Listen," I said. "If it's really a big deal to you that I stay home, I can."

"No. Go. Have fun."

"I'm going upstairs, then, to get ready. You okay?"

"Yeah. I'm fine." He looked over at the kids playing on the floor in the living room. Eden had toppled a basket of toys, and each of them had found something that interested them.

"We should go to the movies sometime," he blurted out. "Just you and me."

I slid up beside him and hoped to lighten his mood by teasing him. "Are you asking me out on a date, Joel Marino?"

He grinned. That was the expression I had been waiting to see.

I smiled back and leaned in to kiss him.

"Let's talk when you get home," he said.

"Yes. Let's. There are a couple of things I've been wanting to talk with you about."

After I showered and got ready, I went downstairs. Joel had country music on. His favorite. I'll never understand why my husband likes that type of music.

The kids were quietly looking at books. Joel prepped mixed vegetables and red potatoes. The sounds and smells in our home made me happy.

"I'm going to leave a little early," I told him quietly so the kids wouldn't hear.

He pulled back and looked at me. "You look great. You sure you're just going to meet your girlfriends?"

I ignored his question. "I'm going to the store. That's why I'm leaving early."

"The grocery store?"

"No, drugstore. I need shampoo and a few other things. Do you need anything?"

"Yeah, the kind of toothpaste I like."

"Do you mean the kind our budding artist likes to paint with on toilet seats?"

Joel smiled.

"It's on my list. Say hi to your parents for me." I kissed him and realized he hadn't showered yet. He was wearing one of his barbecue aprons over the clothes he had gardened in. "Did you want to take a shower? I can wait, if you want."

"You sure?" He untied the back of his apron. "If the timer goes off, check the cake. It's got six more minutes."

"Is that what smells so good? What did you make?"

He was across the room when he answered, "Flourless chocolate amaretto."

My eyes widened, and my mouth watered.

It had been months, possibly years, since he had made that decadent, dense cake that became my favorite after my first taste of it.

"You're trying to keep me here, aren't you?" I called after him playfully.

He didn't answer. Or if he did, he was already up the stairs, and I couldn't hear him.

As I loaded the dishwasher and then cleared some of the clutter off the end of the counter, the doorbell rang.

"GiGi!" Eden cried out, hopping up and running to the door. "Poppy!"

Alex pulled himself up and followed her with his left-right-left-right stride. He echoed her enthusiasm in the same way he had been copying everything she did lately.

I was right behind them and gladly received the hugs from my in-laws along with a potted container of yellow tulips Poppy handed me. "For you, Sunshine," he said. "To brighten this rainy spring evening."

The timer on the oven chimed, and I hurried back into the kitchen to check on Joel's decadent dessert. I pulled the pan from the oven and drew in the rich dark chocolate fragrance. It looked perfect, as always.

Joel Marino, you do not play fair at all.

CHAPTER 15

The rain hit my windshield at an angle, causing the drops to splatter in squiggles. I turned my wipers on high, and when I arrived at the drugstore, I waited a few minutes in the parking lot to see if it would let up. It remained steady, so I made a dash inside with my purse held over my head. The first thing I noticed was a table of umbrellas of all colors and sizes at the front of the store.

Resisting the urge to add another umbrella to the collection in my hall closet, I strode quickly by the display, going up and down the aisles with a plastic basket on my arm. My purse served as my covering once again on my return to the car. I placed the shopping bag on the passenger's seat and thought of how long it would have taken me to shop if both kids were with me.

I pulled my phone from my purse to check the time and saw that I had received a string of text messages. The first was from Tess. She had sent it more than an hour ago, saying she was stuck in Los Angeles on a work project and would miss the movie. Emily had chimed in while I was in the drugstore, saying she wasn't feeling great and was going to stay home.

Christy had added: Can we try for another night? Her text prompted lots of suggestions, and the conclusion was that we would reschedule for next Wednesday, same time, same theater.

I returned home and dropped my rain-splattered purse on the counter along with the shopping bag. "What happened?" Joel rose from the table and came to me as if something were wrong.

"Everyone had to cancel. Not a good night for them."

"Here." He pulled a clean dish towel from the bottom drawer and handed it to me. "Dry off with this. I'm sorry it didn't work out. I know you were looking forward to it."

"It's not a big deal. We're going to try again for next Wednesday."

It struck me that our children made no signs of elation when I came in the way they always did for Joel and their grandparents. I wondered if they had even realized I was gone.

My father-in-law motioned for me to come to the table and sit next to him. Joel set another place, and GiGi helped settle the kids into their places at the table. It felt odd to have everyone doing things for me. And Joel kept gazing at me from across the table for most of the meal.

Dinner was delicious, as it always is when Joel cooks. He had broiled the steaks inside instead of using the barbecue. He also whipped up a delicious garlic aioli sauce and drizzled it over the meat and vegetables. I watched Joel accept the compliments about the meal from his dad and thought of how the two men resembled each other more than ever. Their trademark five o'clock shadows gave their chiseled jawlines and profiles a commanding, no-nonsense look. Joel had been blessed with his mother's distinct, amber-flecked eyes, which added to his man-of-mystery good looks that had captivated me from the first time I saw him.

Joel glanced over at me. I gave him a small smile that I hoped conveyed all that I was thinking about my handsome and alluring husband.

He returned a warm gaze. "While you were out, I told Mom and Dad about our plans to go to Maui."

"We'll be glad to watch the kids," GiGi said.

"Thanks," I replied.

"It's about time the two of you took some time for yourselves," Poppy added. "Time together. That's what makes a marriage last."

I wondered if Joel had mentioned that the trip was to a marriage retreat. What else had he told them? Surely he wouldn't have shared anything personal.

Joel leaned back, looking relaxed, and not at all anxious the way he had when he first told me about the retreat. "I'm really looking forward to it."

"I think it's a wonderful idea for the two of you to get away. The last few years have been very full for both of you," GiGi added.

Joel stood to clear the dishes, and I rose to help. When we were by the sink, I whispered, "Did you tell them it was a marriage conference?"

"No." He leaned close and said, "You seem different."

"Different, how?"

"You were calm when I brought up going to Hawaii."

"Why wouldn't I be?"

"You've gotten upset when I've brought it up before."

"That's because we haven't talked about it much. And it's a marriage retreat."

"So?"

"Let's talk about it later tonight," I said. "Okay?"

He kept looking at me. His eyes seemed to take in my hair, face, sweater. "I haven't seen you like this for a while."

I wasn't sure if he meant that I wasn't tense or that I was wearing makeup, which I hadn't put on in a long time. It had also been a while since I had worn my hair down. I almost always wore it up in a messy bun or twisted into a loose braid. The sweater was old, but I hadn't worn it in more than a year because it was too tight when I was pregnant and was especially curve-accentuating after Alex was born.

Also, I was wearing gold hoop earrings for the first time in ages due to Tess's styling tip. I was a version of myself that my husband had not seen for some time.

Leaning closer, I kissed Joel on his scruffy cheek. "Sorry."

He looked even more perplexed. "For what?"

"You rarely see me in anything other than baggy jeans and sweatshirts."

"You look beautiful tonight."

Joel kissed me, and I pulled back, feeling

a little shy for some reason. The chocolate torte on the stand caught my eye. I saw that Joel had circled it with raspberries.

"Dessert is waiting for us," I said.

Joel, of course, took *dessert* as meaning something else. He put his arm around my waist, pulling me close.

"Yes, it is. As soon as they leave," he murmured in my ear.

I didn't want to break the sweet, flirty moment by clarifying that I was referring to dark chocolate–amaretto happiness, so I didn't move as he kissed my neck and whispered a few more romantic suggestions in my ear.

Before he could completely distract me, I reached over and opened the silverware drawer. I pulled out the dessert forks and whispered, "Save that thought. I'm taking the torte over to the table. Could you bring some plates?"

Joel obliged with a cute grin. He kept up the tantalizing glances and clandestine hints until the kids were in bed and his parents were leaving. We walked them to the door together to say goodnight. As soon as the door closed behind them, Joel took me in his arms and kissed me intensely. He kept kissing me, sliding his hands under my sweater. His warm palm pressed against the small of my back, and I felt every inch of my no-longer-slender-teenager-but-now-very-womanly body warm with desire. Joel knew all the right spots. And I knew his.

All day Thursday I couldn't stop thinking about my husband and our fun, passionate, out-of-the-ordinary night together. I wanted him to come home from work early so we could be together again. I wanted to feel as alive and desirable and deeply satisfied as I had felt when I fell asleep in his arms last night.

The bumpy days of the past year and a half seemed to have evaporated. I couldn't remember what we had argued about on those nights when I had slept alone on the couch. Joel and I were good together. We should never have let anything divide us.

During the long weekend while Joel was at work, I kept busy with projects around the house and felt a contentment returning. I kept thinking of two things Tess had said. The first was being a woman of options. I liked that. It seemed to apply to far more than what outfits I chose to wear or what I made for breakfast. I had the option of crawling back into my lonely cave when I was by myself, or I could stay in the light, so to speak, and bring memories of my mom out into the open.

The second was bringing the sacred to the ordinary. I still wasn't sure what Tess meant by that, but I knew that the project of finding verses to go with the DOEs' words for the year felt like a way of giving them something special.

During the kids' naps and rest times over the weekend, I pulled out my art supplies. The first card I decided to make was for Joel. It was simple, like the ones I used to make for him when we were dating. I painted an ocean scene with a sailboat bobbing on turquoise water. I added a cream curve to the white sail to give it the effect of billowing in the wind. The two figures I added on board were drawn with minimal detail. The woman was leaning back with an arm bent behind her head. The tail of a red scarf fluttered behind her. The Joel figure sat confidently facing the blissful image of me. His legs were stretched out in front of him, and it was clear sailing ahead.

It took me a while to decide on the words I wanted to write inside the card. My first thought was something tantalizing like "Take me" or "I'm all yours" or "Let's sail away together." But I knew he saved all my cards, and I felt funny about our kids possibly coming across them one day when they could read and asking why Mommy wrote what she did. I settled on "Adventures ahead" and smiled to think of all the ways Joel might interpret it.

I left the card on the counter to dry while I went to work on my next project.

For Sierra I lettered the word *wait* along with the last part of Psalm 27:14, "Take heart and wait for the LORD." Then, with a dark blue colored pencil, I went over the word *wait* so that it stood out slightly from the rest of the verse. With the same deep blue, I filled in tiny flowers that were dotted throughout the green vine I had drawn as a border.

On Christy's card with the word *trust,* I wrote a familiar verse from Proverbs 3:5. "Trust in the LORD with all your heart." I used a bright yellow pencil to create a soft haze around the word *trust.* Her vine border was brightened with some yellow touches that were supposed to be butterflies but were so small they could be easily taken as flowers.

For Emily's word, *peace,* I had to search a bit before I found the verse she had mentioned in Proverbs about the ways of wisdom. Surprisingly, it was also in Proverbs 3, where I'd just been looking in my Bible to copy Christy's verse. I used purple to enhance the border around the words, "Her ways are pleasant ways, and all her paths are peace."

The kids were awake, so I put everything out of their reach and spent the rest of Saturday afternoon playing with them in the backyard.

It wasn't until Monday afternoon that I was able to get back to the cards. I hoped to give them to the DOEs on Wednesday when we met again to go to the movies. I had been thinking about Tess and how she said she didn't have a word. The interesting thing was, I had a feeling she did have one but she just didn't know it yet. When she was styling us, she had said that God had filled her life with truth, and it had set her free.

Truth was the word I wrote on her card along with the verse she had referred to from John 8:32, "You will know the truth, and the truth will set you free."

I decided to make a card for my word as well and went back to 1 Corinthians 13. I reread the whole chapter, and as I did, verse 7 caught my attention. "Love never gives up, never loses faith, is always hopeful, and endures through every circumstance."

I made the words fit by writing *Love* at the top and then adding the rest in a free-fall sort of stacked style under the banner word. With a smile, I added tiny red hearts to the vine that ran down the side of the card.

I loved creating art and marking moments like this. Sometimes I felt that I had so little to offer my friends, but this was a simple gift I could always give. A reminder from God's Word. A bit of color. A few curvy flowers. All crafted with love.

Love. My word for the year!

I didn't know if what I was doing was sacred, as Tess had said. I also didn't know if I would end up saving the cards and giving them to each of my friends for their birthdays rather than all at once on Wednesday.

I finished the project just as the kids woke up. Eden was excited about ballet class and eager to slip into her tutu. I unplugged my phone and discovered I had missed a slew of text messages while I was painting. GiGi and Poppy said they weren't able to come to Eden's final class but wanted me to take lots of videos. Christy asked if I wanted to drive to the theater together on Wednesday with her and Emily. And the final text was from Joel, saying that he would be home late and that we needed to talk then.

Fine. We always say that, but we never end up talking.

I texted him back and said I would make cappuccinos when he got home.

We were now running late for dance class, and I was slower than usual because this was the first time I had taken Alex with me. I found myself looking around for Garrett as I pulled Alex out of the car. I wondered if Tiffany would come with him since it was the last class. I wondered what she looked like and if he looked at her the way he used to look at me when we were so young. I really hoped that, in seeing them together, it would be evident that she was the best part of his life and that they would always be together. I wanted to know that he ended up with someone who loved him as much as I loved Joel.

Eden scampered off to join the other ballerinas. Alex was surprisingly clingy when we entered the studio and wanted me to hold him. It made sense, since this was all new to him. I took a seat at the end of the row of chairs in case I needed to get up with Alex. I settled him on my lap with the diaper bag within easy reach so that I could pull out snacks, toys, and books to keep him entertained for the next hour. Another mom sat beside me. I smiled, said hello, and looked around. There was no sign of Garrett or Violet.

I managed to hold up my phone in the open space between the two people seated in front of me and recorded Eden's performance as promised. Alex remained on my lap, content with his snacks. The dance was as cute as could be with the six little ballerinas in their tutus.

Eden took a bonus twirl as the music came to an end and concluded her front-row performance with a curtsy. She was the only one of the dancers who remembered to do that. When the audience clapped, she rewarded them with curtsy after curtsy until their soft chuckles turned into friendly laughter.

I don't know if she realized she was the little diva they were laughing at, but I'm glad I caught it all on my phone.

The assistant scooted the dancers to the side so their instructor could say a few words to the parents about the next class and other class options offered at the studios. We concluded with another round of grateful applause, and Eden came dashing over to me, beaming.

"Did you see me, Mommy?"

"Yes, I did, darling." I leaned over and kissed her forehead. "You were wonderful. I love the way you dance with all your heart."

"Thank you." She granted me another one

of her curtsies.

I gave her a big smile. "Did you like dancing for everyone?"

"Yes!" Eden twirled and twirled again. She definitely had better balance than any of the other Tinkerbells who had just performed.

"Come sit here next to me for a minute. I need to do something." I didn't tell her I was sending the video of her to GiGi and Poppy because she would want to see it, and then Alex would want equal access to the screen. It only took me a few seconds to send it to them and Joel.

With my purse and the diaper bag in one hand, Alex on my hip, and Eden skipping along next to me, we exited the studio.

"Jennie?" Garrett strode toward the three of us, waving a large envelope.

I stopped, let go of the diaper bag, and reached for Eden's arm so she wouldn't scamper into the parking lot. My heart did an embarrassing flutter. I thought I was way past this.

"Glad I caught you!" Garrett said, approaching me. "I don't have your number, and I don't think my messages have been getting to you."

"I haven't been checking."

He was wearing a New York Yankees baseball cap. I remembered how Garrett's big dream in high school was to go to one of their games and catch a fly ball.

"This must be your son." He grinned at Alex and leaned in closer. "How you doin', little man?"

"His name is Alex," Eden said.

Garrett lowered himself to look Eden in the eye. "Did you have fun dancing for everyone, Eden?"

She nodded and repeated her applause-worthy curtsy while holding my hand. It didn't appear that she remembered Violet or that Garrett was Violet's dad. Lifting my hand above her head, she continued to hold on as she did three ambitious spins.

"Very nice," Garrett said with a smile. He looked up at me, still appearing a bit flustered, as if he had raced to get here. "Tiffany went to see her grandmother and took Violet with her. They didn't make it back in time for class."

Eden stopped twirling when she heard Violet's name. "Where's By-let?"

"She's with her mom," Garrett said.

"I want By-let to come to my house."

Garrett and I exchanged awkward glances. He held out the envelope. "I wanted to make sure you got these."

"Thanks." I adjusted Alex, who was squirming, trying to get down. I tried to reach for the envelope without compromising my grip on him.

"Here. Let me." Garrett reached out his hands, offering to take Alex. I pulled back, but my son went to Garrett in an instant. For a moment we had a small tug of war until I told myself I was being too protective, and I let Garrett take him. It became immediately clear that all Alex wanted was the baseball cap. Garrett let him try to reach for the bill and attempt to pull it off.

I tried to remember if I had ever seen my husband in a baseball cap.

"Let me grab the bag too," Garrett said. "Where did you park?"

I nodded to the left and had a flashback to all the times Garrett had walked me to my car in the parking lot at Washington High. We had a little routine every day. I always got in, rolled down the window, and positioned my face just right, looking up at him. He always rested his left forearm against my blue Honda, bent down, kissed me, and then pounded two times on the roof before I cruised off to my job at the arts and crafts store at the mall. I remembered the two thumps of his fist were his way of saying, "Love you."

Here we were, fifteen years later, and Garrett was once again walking me to my car. Only this time he was carrying my son in one brawny arm and my diaper bag and an envelope of photos of my mom in the other.

This does not feel right.

The moment seemed too easy, familiar, and friendly.

"Mommy, are we going to By-let's house?"

"No, Eden."

"Can she come to my house?"

"Not today, honey."

"Pleeeeease?"

"Maybe another day," Garrett told Eden in his dad voice. "I know Violet would like that too."

I kept my head lowered as I opened the door and strapped Eden in her car seat.

No. No, no, no, no. We are not setting up playdates. We are not going to do family barbecues with our spouses. This is it. This is our last time.

I glanced across the back seat as Garrett was expertly settling Alex into his car seat. Garrett caught my gaze. His expression looked serious. Or maybe it was a sort of sadness. It felt as if we had entered an alternate universe for that sliver of a moment where two beautiful children, a boy and a girl, bridged the landscape between Garrett and me.

But these are my children. Joel's and mine. Our children. Not Garrett's and my children. These are not the children I once dreamed I would have with Garrett.

My throat tightened as I closed Eden's door and climbed into the driver's seat. I fastened the seat belt and glanced over to see that Garrett had put the diaper bag and the envelope on the passenger's seat. Looking to the left, I already knew that he would be standing there. I started the engine and rolled down the window, turning my head just enough but keeping my shoulders facing forward. My hands gripped the steering wheel at ten and two, just like we had learned when he and I took driver's training together.

Garrett rested his forearm above my window. He leaned down, but not too close. For a moment, neither of us spoke. I knew he was remembering. He had to be. This moment was far too familiar. The years seemed to be folding in for both of us.

I need to go. Now.

"Listen," he said. "I put my card in there."

I watched his eyes, reading the deeper meaning in his tone.

With a half-grin that revealed his nervousness, he added, "You never know when you might need a website."

I paused before saying, "I don't think I will." My voice was soft, but I hoped he caught the intended double meaning. To be certain, I added, "I'm sure that I won't."

"Okay." He pulled back. "Okay."

"Thanks again for the pictures."

"Sure." He raised his left hand in a farewell sort of gesture, keeping his expression reigned in tightly.

"Bye, Garrett."

"Bye, Jennie."

I rolled up my window and looked straight ahead. Just before my foot eased onto the gas pedal, I heard it.

One, then two fist pounds on the roof of my car.

An echo from a place that no longer existed. A message from half a lifetime ago. A gesture from a person I now knew I must never see again. Because if I let him, I was sure that Garrett was willing to once again occupy as much of my heart and life as I would relinquish to him.

CHAPTER 16

I waited up for Joel that night. I knew this was the night we would finally talk about Garrett. I would tell Joel everything and assure him, now that ballet class was over, I would never see Garrett again.

The envelope from Garrett was waiting on the coffee table, unopened. I decided I would open it after I had talked to Joel and told him how the progression with Garrett had unfolded. I wanted to have Joel with me when I looked at the photos of my mom. It was as if the "evidence" inside that envelope would prove my innocence.

More than that, I wanted Joel to view the photos with me because I wanted to share a new memory of my mom with him. Especially if they were pictures I hadn't seen before. I needed to feel that Joel was more connected to memories of my mom.

A little after nine o'clock I started a movie I had recorded months ago. I was only five minutes into it when I heard a key unlocking the front door. I pressed mute and I went to greet Joel in the entryway with a warm smile.

He looked absolutely beat.

"Hi." I kissed him. "Long day for you."

"Yeah." He kept walking, heading for the kitchen. "Do we have anything for a headache in here?" He opened the cupboard where we kept vitamins and a variety of protein powder shake mixes. He found what he was looking for and poured a glass of water to down the pills before leaning against the counter with the half-full glass in his hand.

I stood a good five feet away, giving him space the way he liked in the kitchen. I wanted to throw my arms around him and ask a dozen questions. But with Joel I knew it was best to wait until he wanted to speak.

He looked over at the movie on the TV. "We were going to watch that together, weren't we?"

"We still can. I'll save it."

He took another long drink of water. *Something is wrong.*

"How are you doing?" I asked cautiously.

"Vincent quit."

"What?" I stared at Joel in disbelief. "Why?"

239

He shrugged and drank the rest of the water. I took his action to mean he had lots to say on the subject but was choosing not to start a conversation that would drain him of the teaspoon of energy left in him.

We stood in silent agony as my mind whirled with the ramifications of this news. Vincent was supposed to be the answer, the relief after all the months of Joel working seventy-hour weeks. What had gone wrong? Vincent was the reason Joel and I were starting to get close again and our little family could go to the beach and plant a garden. Without Vincent I pictured a repeat of the last year of our lives, and as I did, the tears came.

"Joel, I'm so sorry."

He stared at me, as if he couldn't understand why I was the one crying. He looked vacant, drained. I felt that I was looking into the face of his father.

"I've gotta go to bed."

I nodded my understanding. "Can I get you anything?"

"No." Joel came closer and reached for my hand. He held it for a moment, gazing at me and forcing the slightest of smiles.

"You're beautiful."

I felt myself blushing as I returned a smile. "I love you, Joel. You'll get through this."

"I know. We will. Let's talk about it later."

"Okay."

"We have a lot to figure out."

I nodded and kept smiling as Joel let go of my hand and trudged out of the kitchen. His footsteps on the stairs sounded as if he were carrying a weight that was far too heavy for him to bear.

I stood in the kitchen motionless. The only thing I knew to do was pray. I prayed for Joel, for our kids, for the restaurant, for a replacement for Vincent, for wisdom, for guidance, and for myself. I prayed that I would be courageous and that I would know how to love my husband through all this.

When I looked up, the movie was still going. I went over to the couch to pick up the remote and save the recording before turning off the TV. I noticed the envelope still waiting on the coffee table. I sat down and stared at it. My earlier plan of opening it with Joel seemed like a bad idea.

Why did I think I needed to create a ceremony over this? I'm always envisioning events, aren't I?

With swift, decisive motions, I reached for the mailer, tore it open, and shook it until seven photos and Garrett's business card floated into my lap. I started with the photos. Five of them I had seen before and

241

probably had copies of. The last two I hadn't seen. One was of my mom in a beach chair holding a baby. Garrett's mom was in the beach chair next to her. Both were wearing sunglasses, and Garrett's mom had on a white visor with the brand name of a golf ball company across the band. My guess was that it was taken about ten years ago.

I didn't know who the baby was. It was wearing a denim baby-style beach hat with a strap under its chin and a onesie with an appliquéd yellow giraffe on it. What captured my attention and made me sit and stare was the way my mom was holding the baby. It was so tender, a cuddle pose with my mom's chin resting on the baby's hat-covered head. It was such an accurate image of the way my mom loved people. Both her arms encircled the little one on her lap. Her shoulders were curved in and her smile was contagious. She was the most snuggly, protective, gentle, and caring woman in the world. She gathered fragile souls under her wings with ease and made them feel loved.

Oh, Mom, you never got to hold my babies.

A sob burst out of my chest, and I covered my mouth to muffle the messy sounds. I felt as if a grenade of loss and longing had exploded inside, and it took me a moment to catch my breath. I reached for the box of tissues and dried my tears with one hand while still clinging to the photo in the other. As soon as I felt my equilibrium return, I stared at the image once more.

I miss you so much, Mama. I wish so badly that my children could have known you. I wish you could have gathered them in your arms the way only you could do. I wish you were here. I miss you so, so much.

The tears stopped. My heart felt strangely calm. As I continued to stare at the photo, I felt the familiar sense of loss, but I felt something new as well. It was as if I were being sheltered, covered, encircled by a powerful feeling of comfort. My deep and unchanging love for my mom seemed to have entered a new realm within all the overlapping stages of grief. I wouldn't call it acceptance, but it was the closest I had ever gotten to feeling settled in my spirit.

I smiled at my mom's image in the photo. I wondered what she looked like now in her new, heavenly body. She wasn't really gone. Her spirit was eternal; I believed that mystery more than ever. I would see her again.

Bolstered in this unexpected way, I picked up the last photo. It looked like it had been taken on the same day at the beach. My mom and Garrett's mom were standing together on a beach blanket. Both were wearing billowing cover-ups that were filled to a Liberty-Bell shape and size thanks to the strong ocean breeze. They were holding on to each other and laughing.

The way they were posed in their cotton cover-ups reminded me of the way Eden and Violet looked when they hugged in their tutus.

I stared across the room, focusing my narrowed, blurry vision on the kitchen window where all was dark outside. What would these women have thought if they saw their granddaughters reenacting the "friends forever" hug, with the big poofs billowing out?

Would there be more of a chance of a relationship between Eden and Violet if their grandmas were still alive?

My eyes returned to the photo, and that's when I noticed my mom's toenails.

Oh My, Cherry Pie red. I need to get a pedicure. I need to walk around with Oh My, Cherry Pie red toenails.

With what almost sounded like a contented sigh, I took the photos with me upstairs. I quietly slid them into the drawer of my end table. All I wanted to do was slip into bed beside my slumbering husband and fall asleep praying for him.

The prayers for Joel continued all day Tuesday and Wednesday. Even though they were supposed to be his days off, he had to go to the restaurant. I remained in the dark about what had happened with Vincent as well as all the other details I was curious to know. All Joel had said was that he had interviews already lined up and that he was determined to fix this.

He texted me on Wednesday morning to say that he had just interviewed a replacement, and he was hopeful. I texted back that I was praying for him and that I loved him.

That afternoon Joel's parents came over to watch the kids so I could go to the movies with the Haven Makers. Poppy had a lot of questions for me about Joel and the state of the restaurant. My reply to almost all of them was, "Good question. I don't know."

"We think something needs to change," GiGi said. "Have you and Joel discussed the possibility of his leaving the Blue Ginger and no longer being a part owner as well as chef? It's turned into two full-time jobs. That's too much for anyone, especially a perfectionist like Joel."

"We have a lot to talk about," I said. "As soon as he gets some time off, I'm sure we'll look at all the options and try to figure out the best way to go."

"You seem remarkably calm, Jennalyn," my mother-in-law said.

"I do feel a little more relaxed knowing that he interviewed someone this morning. But believe me, I've been riding the roller coaster for days. Months, actually. No, make that a year or more."

She was holding Alex and walked over to the kitchen sink to wash something off his hands. I knew where my husband's leaning toward perfection came from. His parents were great models of how to live an energetic, productive, do-it-all life and do it in an orderly, tidy way. I knew I would never match their level in all those areas, but the good thing was that I rarely felt inferior to any of the highly motivated Marinos. I felt more reserved and private about the way I dealt with things. I think that frustrated them sometimes. My choice not to discover the gender of our second child or to reveal our name options to the clan was something none of them understood.

"You keep us updated, okay?" Poppy said.

"And if there's anything we can do for you," GiGi added, "anything at all, you let us know."

"I will. Thank you. It's helping a lot for you to be here tonight so I can spend some time with my friends."

"We're happy to do it." Poppy opened the dishwasher to unload it.

"Those haven't been washed yet," I told him.

"You need one of those magnets," he said. "We have one. It says 'clean' on one side and 'dirty' on the other. We'll get you one."

"Great. Thanks." I slid over to where Eden was seated at the counter, eagerly turning the pages in a new coloring book GiGi had brought her. I gave my little girl a kiss and said, "Have fun with Poppy and GiGi, and do what they tell you."

"I will. Bye, Mommy."

Alex seemed to catch on that I was leaving. He reached out his freshly washed hands and said, "Mama. Mama."

"Someone is learning new words!" Poppy made a funny face, distracting Alex long enough for me to make an exit. Just before I opened the front door, I heard my father-in-law say, "Now say 'Poppy.' You can do it. Paaa-pee."

The night was beautiful and clear. I drove to the theater thinking about how blessed I was to have such great in-laws and to live only ten minutes from them. The Bible verse in Job about how "The LORD gave, and the LORD has taken away" flipped itself in my thoughts.

"The Lord takes away, and the Lord has given," I said to myself. I pulled out of our driveway thinking how God had taken away my mother, but He had given me GiGi and Poppy.

It wasn't nearly the same by any means. However, having them in our lives softened the pain of the loss and added a new relationship that I hadn't experienced with anyone else. GiGi never felt like a substitute mother to me. She was more like a combination of a special aunt and a favorite teacher.

I was grateful. I didn't express that often enough.

I want to do a better job of letting them both know how much they mean to me.

That thought initiated ideas on the ways I wanted to do a better job of being intentional about showing love to others. The list was growing when I parked and made my way to the entrance of the large movie theater.

Sierra was in the lobby, waving at me. Emily was there, too, and as soon as I came in, I saw Christy headed our way from the restrooms.

We did our usual round of hugs, and Sierra pulled out her phone. "Has anyone heard from Tess? Maybe we should go in and save her a seat."

"We're early," Emily noted. "Let's wait for her here. We have time."

"Did we ever decide if we want to go somewhere after the movie?" I asked.

No one answered because we saw Christy waving. "There's Tess."

Tess looked stunning, as usual. I couldn't tell if she was wearing a long skirt with a fold down the center or if they were wide pants. She had on a crisp white blouse, and a long gaucho-style coat completed the outfit. She strode toward us looking like a model.

"I'm so upset." Tess hugged each of us. "I was determined to be the first one here this time. I allowed extra time for traffic, but it still took me almost an hour. One of these times I will be early. Just wait. You'll all be shocked, I know."

"Don't worry," Emily said. "We've only been here a few minutes."

"Shame off, grace on." Christy seemed to still be admiring Tess's outfit. "I love this."

"Thanks."

Something or someone behind Tess distracted Christy's attention. She tilted her head, and her mouth opened, but no words came out.

A tall, dark-haired, very handsome guy

was coming toward us. He seemed to recognize Christy. His smile was irresistible, and he looked vaguely familiar, but I wasn't sure why. I noticed that Christy seemed stunned to see him.

He was only a few feet away when Tess turned her head to see what Christy was looking at. As soon as the guy saw Tess, he stopped.

Tess froze in place.

That's when I knew. *It's Guy. He's Tess's "Guy." And he knows Christy.*

Christy found her voice and said the name that Tess never had shared with us. "Rick Doyle!?"

CHAPTER 17

When Christy said Rick's name, Sierra spun around and made it clear that she knew him too. Sierra gave him a hug. He then leaned over and gave Christy an awkward, sort of nontouching Hollywood-kiss-on-the-cheek gesture.

Before he could greet Tess with any kind of familiarity, she mumbled "Excuse me" and turned with a quick flip of her long coat. I watched as she took brisk strides toward the bathroom.

Sierra introduced Emily and me to Rick, saying, "You guys have seen the show *Diner Do-Overs,* haven't you?"

"That's why you look familiar," Emily said. "I loved the episode where you helped that couple who had a daughter who needed an operation."

"Our most popular episode." Rick nodded, turning his head to watch as Tess disappeared inside the restroom.

"Is that the one where you pulled up the floorboards?" Sierra asked. "And then you found the old cashboxes with all the money?"

Rick nodded again.

"Did the producer plant the money?" Sierra speculated. "They set it up, didn't they? Since the little girl needed the operation."

"No, it was real."

"That's amazing. I was so sad when your show was cancelled."

When Rick didn't reply, Sierra tried to follow his gaze. "Is Nicole here?"

"No." Rick turned his attention back to Sierra. "She's at her mom's."

"Are you guys visiting?" Christy asked. "Or working? Or . . ."

"I live here now."

Christy's expression suggested to me that she was putting the pieces together and coming to the same conclusion I already had reached when I saw Rick's reaction to Tess.

"I'll tell Todd I saw you," Christy said. "If you have any free time, I'm sure he would like to see you. We're in the same place; so just stop by or let us know if you're free for dinner sometime."

"Thanks. I should get going." Rick nodded at each of us, repeating our names like a charmer. "Enjoy your movie." He gave us an open-palm wave as he walked toward the concession line.

Sierra returned to her troop leader voice. "That was a surprise. A blast from the past, right, Christy?"

She nodded but didn't say anything.

"How do you guys know each other?" I asked.

"We all went to the same college and . . ." Sierra looked around. "Where's Tess?"

"Restroom," Emily said.

"Good idea. I'll be right back," Sierra said. "Do you guys want to save us seats?"

Reaching over and resting my hand on Sierra's arm, I said, "I have an idea."

"Can it wait till I get back from the bathroom?"

"Actually, I think we should all go to the bathroom," I said.

"I'm okay," Emily said.

"For Tess," I said quietly. "I think we should all go check on her."

Emily looked confused but came along. I caught a last glimpse of Rick in the concession line. Some fans apparently recognized him and were posing with him for pictures.

Reaching for Sierra's arm again, I pulled her to the side right before we entered the restroom. "Sierra, I think he's the man Tess told us about. That's why she left so suddenly."

Sierra glanced at him and back at me. Her eyes widened. "You think Rick is 'Guy'?"

"I don't know for sure, but I think so. I wanted you to know what I was thinking before any of us said anything to Tess."

Sierra's expression softened. "Oh, wow. It makes sense. Especially when he said Nicole was at her mom's. It sounded odd the way he said it."

"I thought so too."

"You know what?" Sierra said. "We can go. We don't need to see the movie if she feels uncomfortable."

"Knowing Tess, she'll probably say she's fine. But I was thinking maybe we could all find a little haven where we can talk."

"That's a great idea, Jennalyn. I mean, if Rick is Guy, this is significant." Sierra leaned in. "Christy dated him in high school."

Now I was the one who was stunned. "She did?"

Sierra nodded. "He and Todd ended up being roommates in college and then Rick ran a café near Rancho Corona University." Lowering her voice, Sierra said, "Katie worked at the café and seriously dated Rick during her senior year at Rancho Corona."

"Are you making this up?"

"No!"

"That's a lot of overlapping relationships," I said.

"I know. It didn't seem strange back then because we were all in a small circle of friends. But it's true that Rick got around. Katie used to call him 'Slick Rick' before she fell for him." Sierra pointed to the women's restroom door. "I think we should get Tess outta here."

We found Tess, Christy, and Emily standing in the corner by the last sink. It appeared that Christy had just brought Tess and Emily up to speed on her high school connection with Rick. They both appeared as incredulous as I had been when Sierra told me.

"How long did you date him?" Emily asked Christy in a hushed voice.

"Just a few months. During my junior year."

I suddenly felt uncomfortable. Not just for Tess but also for Christy. I knew what it felt like when I had the unexpected encounter with Garrett. Even though Christy had been gracious about inviting Rick to stop by and now seemed to be downplaying her dating relationship with him, I recognized the flicker of surprise in her expression when she saw him.

"Do you guys want to skip the movie and go somewhere to talk?" I suggested.

"Yes," Christy said. "I like that idea."

"We don't have to leave." Tess sounded annoyed.

"I know we don't have to," I said. "But since we're women of options, I would prefer the option of going somewhere to talk."

Sierra and Emily agreed. We opted for a nearby Mexican restaurant that had large private booths. I was glad we were doing this. It felt more like we were being "us." We weren't the shopping or moviegoing kind of friends. We were talkers. Tonight we had several items to discuss.

Tess ended up in the center of the booth, and we slid in beside her, two on each side. As soon as we were settled, she said, "Look, I appreciate the whole solidarity sisters' gesture, but we really didn't have to leave. We could have gone to the movie. It was not a big deal for me to see him."

"It didn't seem that way when you bolted to the bathroom," Sierra said.

"I just preferred not to have a conversation with him right then." Tess looked down at the menu.

The waiter arrived with two baskets of warm tortilla chips and a bowl of salsa.

"Could we get some guacamole?" I asked. "And a pitcher of your house lemonade?" I looked at the others. "What does everyone else want?"

We ended up ordering an assortment of appetizers and a few items from the dessert menu, including flan and churros with hot chocolate dipping sauce.

As soon as the waiter left, Christy said, "Tess, I have to say something. Todd and Rick are pretty good friends. I knew that Rick and Nicole weren't doing well since their show was cancelled because Todd told me he had reached out to Rick. They've talked a few times. I don't know how recently, or what they discussed, but I wanted you to know that."

"I obviously had no idea you guys were connected," Tess said.

Christy looked concerned. "You said before that you were one of the only people he could talk to. That's just not the truth."

Tess nodded. She stared at her hands and repeated Christy's last word. "Truth."

I felt a little zing, knowing I had written that on a card as her word for the year. The cards for the DOEs were in my purse. I was glad I had brought them. Maybe tonight was going to be a good time to give them to everyone.

Tess looked at Christy. "Thanks for letting me know."

"This might not have anything to do with anything," Sierra said, "but do you think Rick knew you were going to be at the theater tonight?"

"No. How could he?"

"I don't know. Technology is crazy. Maybe you have something connected on your phone that links to his phone. It's so easy to track people and get personal information."

"He's not stalking me, if that's what you're suggesting."

Our young waiter arrived with the pitcher of lemonade and filled our glasses.

"Can we talk about something else?" Tess reached for her glass, her crystal blue eyes peering at us as she took a sip and lowered her glass. "It's still kind of freaking me out that Christy and Sierra know him."

We all reached for our lemonades and caught each other's glances around the table as if trying to see who was going to speak up first.

"I wanted to tell you earlier, Tess, that your outfit is really adorable." Emily's calm voice had an immediate normalizing effect on us.

"Thanks. Oh! And that reminds me. I have something for each of you. They're in my car, so remind me that we need to go to my car first when we leave." Tess reached for a tortilla chip and dipped the corner of the triangle into the bowl of salsa.

"I have something for everyone too," I said.

Emily gave me an expectant look as I reached into my purse and pulled out the four handmade envelopes that I'd embellished with the names of each of the DOEs.

"I hope this is what I think it is," Emily said.

"What do you think it is?" I asked.

"Is it one of your beautiful invitations for our spring picnic?"

Sierra looked up. "Did we decide on a time and place yet? Because I know the perfect cove at the beach where we could set up our soiree."

"I don't think we've decided yet," I said. "At least, not that I know of. This is something different. Go ahead; open them."

Christy was the first to look at hers. "I love it! Thank you, Jennalyn!"

"I still have the one you made the first time we met," Emily said. "Thank you. I'm going to frame this one too."

"It's perfect," Sierra said.

I caught Tess's eye and said, "I know you said you didn't have a word for the year, but I think you do. You said it again tonight."

Tess held up her card and read the verse aloud. " 'You will know the truth, and the truth will set you free.' " She looked at me incredulously. "How did you know?"

I shrugged. "Would it sound weird if I said that God's Spirit whispered it to me?"

Tess looked at us with tears in her eyes.

"Tess, what is it?" Christy asked.

"I need to say something." Her expression made her look young and vulnerable.

"You guys know how much I value truth. When I was going through counseling, truth had to become the new foundation for my life. No more lies. That's what my whole childhood was about. My counselor told me I was an expert at giving guarded confessions. I learned from the best, you know. My mom was famous for her partial disclosures. She only told people enough details to make herself look good. I don't want to live that way."

Tess sat up straighter. "I know I asked if we could change the subject, but I need to tell you the truth. I made it sound like I hadn't spent much time with Rick. It's true. I didn't. We only met face to face a few times. But we talked on the phone. A lot."

She caught my eye, and I gave her an encouraging smile. I was glad she was telling the others.

"Many of our conversations lasted for hours. I told him so much about my life. He told me more than I should have heard about his marriage, career, his family, and the things he struggles with. We both cried a couple of times, and we had our inside jokes. It was addicting to have someone phone me all the time. Someone who was coming to know me well. I never had a relationship with a guy in which I felt so close so fast."

Tess's warm-toned skin took on a red tint across her cheeks and nose as she looked down. "I felt like I was falling in love with him."

She reached for one of the unused napkins at the center of the table. "Don't take this literally, but at times I felt like we were having an affair. We were never involved physically at all. A few hugs. He kissed me once on the cheek when we first met. That was it."

She shook her head as if she were embarrassed. "This is hard for me to admit. I recorded all the seasons of his show, and I watched them all the time. I found myself thinking about what it would be like to fall asleep next to him. It got so bad I had to delete them. Thankfully I was able to close that door of possibility in my mind and bolt it shut.

"You guys gave me the boost of courage I needed to walk away emotionally. I don't think you realize how much I valued your opinions. None of my other friends that I told said the things you did. They suggested that I convince him to run away with me, and that I should do whatever made me happy."

"Well, I'm glad you didn't run away with him," Christy said.

"So am I." Tess looked up. "But since I'm being truthful, I'm telling you, it could have happened."

Her hands had formed into fists, the right one clenching the crumpled napkin. She rested them on top of the table and drew in a deep breath. "I was doing so well. Then he appears out of thin air at the theater tonight."

"Of all the gin joints . . ." Sierra's best Bogart impression fell flat.

Emily gently leaned her head on Tess's shoulder for a moment, her familiar tender gesture of empathy. "Thank you for being honest with us."

Christy reached over to cover Tess's tightened fist with her hand. In a soothing voice she said, "You're doing well, Tess. It's a lot for you to process."

"You know that we're here for you, don't you?" I asked.

Tess's shoulders relaxed. She nodded.

"Thanks for letting us in on what you're going through," Christy added.

"Being single, I sometimes struggle with these emotional longings and desires that I can't do anything about," Tess added. "Not really. Not in a fulfilling way."

Christy spoke up. "We're all vulnerable emotionally. I could fall into an emotional affair just as easily as you did."

"An emotional affair?" Tess countered. "Is that what you would call it?"

Christy nodded.

"But we never . . ." Tess seemed to be searching for the right word.

"Gave yourselves to each other?" Christy suggested.

"Yes. We never even kissed." Tess shifted her position in the booth so she could face Christy. "I know I said I felt like we were having an affair, but I meant that in reference to being secret about our long conversations. It wasn't as if we were planning to go off somewhere to be alone so we could give ourselves to each other, as you put it."

"But you did give your heart." Christy's words came out carefully and tenderly.

Tess kept looking at Christy, blinking slowly.

"You gave your mind and your emotions. You gave your stories and your opinions and your advice. You let him know you. That's why he looked at you the way he did tonight. He knows core essence pieces that make you, you. I mean, we all get that giving ourselves in love to someone is much more than skin on skin."

It took Tess and the rest of us a moment to absorb what Christy said.

"You're right, Christy." Tess leaned back. "Emotionally I was all in, even though I knew I shouldn't be." She pressed her lips together and let out a long, slow breath through her nose.

"It feels so freeing to share this and to no longer hide any of it from all of you," Tess said. "I wish I'd opened up sooner."

My sense of discomfort had been rising while Christy talked. I was comparing Tess's clandestine conversations with Rick to the hidden communication I had carried on with Garrett. She had been brave and open in telling the truth. I felt like a coward. By avoiding the conversation with Joel for so many weeks and not sharing any of the emotional struggle with my friends, I had put myself in a prison of isolation. My heart wasn't free.

"I need to slide out for a minute." I nodded to the empty pitcher of lemonade. "Sorry for the bad timing."

CHAPTER 18

I felt a little sick to my stomach. I wanted to blame it on the combination of the salsa and lemonade. But I knew I felt uncomfortably convicted that Joel didn't know about Garrett.

As I locked the stall door, I wondered if Joel was still at work.

What if I left now and waited for him at the Blue Ginger? Maybe he and I could sit in the car somewhere and talk. I need to tell him the truth, the way Tess is doing with us. I need the truth to set me free of any entanglements. I need to feel connected with Joel.

I began to romanticize how meeting Joel at work would be like when we were dating. We could find a drive-through and order onion rings with packets of both mayonnaise and mustard. We would make a mess, but we wouldn't care because we would be driving up the coast highway with the moon over us and Joel's annoying country music turned as low as I could convince him.

We would pull over at Huntington Beach, and we would talk. I would tell him everything. He would open up his heart to me, and we both would understand what the other was feeling. We would kiss. Then we would drive home feeling like we were "us" again.

Someone entered the restroom, startling my thoughts back to reality. I knew conversations, particularly this one, couldn't be that easy with Joel anymore. If I tried to talk to him tonight, he would be too tired and too stressed.

"Jennalyn?"

I stepped out of the stall and saw Christy waiting by the sink. She smiled and asked if I was all right. I nodded and washed my hands. I could have said something more to her. I could have told her what was going on in my head and heart right then. But I didn't. Instead I asked how she was doing.

"Me? I'm good. Why?"

"I wondered if it was difficult for you to run into your old high school boyfriend."

"It was odd. Kind of uncomfortable. Mostly I felt sad. I didn't realize he was living here alone. I thought he and Nicole were still in New York with their daughter, Maisey."

"Do you know his wife well?"

"Not really. Katie and Nicole were close because they were both resident assistants during college their senior year. Todd and I were already married by then, so I didn't spend much time with them."

I tossed my crumpled paper towel into the trash and felt a restlessness to return to the table.

Christy's expression looked concerned. "My heart goes out to Rick and Nicole. I'm sure they had a lot of pressure on them from the TV show."

"I can't imagine what that would be like."

Christy's gaze rested on me. Her expression remained concerned. She didn't say anything. Neither of us moved.

"Christy?"

"Yes?"

"I ran into my high school boyfriend in January."

It was one of those moments when I heard myself say what I was really thinking, and then I stopped and looked around because I was sure someone else said it and not me.

Christy's eyes showed how unexpected my declaration was. "The one you dated for a year?"

I nodded. "Two years."

"When did you see him?"

"At Eden's ballet class. His daughter was taking lessons too."

"Was it the first time you had seen him since high school?"

I nodded.

"How did you feel?"

I didn't have an answer for her. Not a simple one, at least. Nothing I wanted to say aloud. Much of what I felt was linked to my mom, and I realized then that I hadn't completely separated the complex feelings yet in my own heart and mind.

"He apologized to me for how he ended the relationship."

I found it easier to offer Christy a report than an answer about my feelings. I wanted to wrap up my unexpected confession with a quick, positive summary. "I appreciated it. I had forgiven him years ago, though."

Christy seemed to study my expression. "Was he at the class every week? Or did you only see him the one time?"

"He was there off and on. At the last class he gave me some photos he had of my mom."

"Of your mom? That seems odd," Christy said.

"His mom recently passed away, and that's how he came across them. They were of our moms together at the beach." I swallowed and forced a smile. "I'm glad he gave them to me."

"How was it? Seeing him and being around him?"

I shrugged, trying to minimize the topic since Christy clearly wanted to explore it more deeply. "It was okay. A couple of the conversations were sort of clumsy."

"So, you had several conversations with him?"

I nodded. "But now that the classes are over, I don't expect to see him again."

"What did Joel say when you told him?"

"I haven't really talked to him about it. Not that there's anything to tell."

Christy tilted her head as if she wasn't convinced.

"You know how Joel has been so busy at work."

"You're going to tell him, though, aren't you?"

"Yes. Absolutely."

"Jennalyn, I think you need to tell him soon." Christy still looked concerned. "What if Joel had seen an old girlfriend a number of times and the two of them had a serious conversation? You would want to know, wouldn't you?"

I hadn't thought of it that way before. If the tables were turned, I would be hurt as well as suspicious if Joel hadn't told me right away. I felt my heart pounding faster and scrambled to justify the circumstances.

"Joel and Garrett met at the first class, but I wasn't there. They talked to each other as if they were just two dedicated dads." I laughed nervously.

"Jennalyn . . ." Christy's expression seemed as intense as it was when she said she was worried about Rick and Nicole. "Relationships in all stages of life are complicated. Emotional connections are hard to break. You need to tell Joel."

"I know," I said quickly.

"These things can turn into big misunderstandings. You don't want Joel caught off guard if the two of you happen to run into Garrett."

"You're right."

"Just promise me you'll talk to him soon," Christy said. "I have a nervous feeling about this."

I appreciated that Christy was taking my personal issues to heart, but it made me uncomfortable. I had told her very little, and yet she seemed to be right in the center of everything I had been going through and processing for the past month and a half.

"Don't be nervous for me." I tried to sound lighthearted. "I honestly don't think it's going to be a big deal. There's not much to say."

"Maybe not." Christy tried to offer me a smile, but it was a weak one. "Whatever there is to say, it needs to be said. You and I are both experienced at holding our feelings in for a long time and not sorting out what's true and what's a trap."

I was finding it difficult to keep my expression clear and not leak any of my complex feelings or details about the midnight conversations with Garrett. Christy's approach was gentle as always. It was clear, though, that she had picked up hints of my struggles.

She reached over and gave my arm a squeeze. "I'm always available if you ever want to talk. You know that."

"Yes. I do."

We headed back to the table, two introverts who had communicated volumes with a handful of sentences and a lot of unspoken, friend-to-friend, heart-to-heart understanding.

I felt some relief from having blurted out the truth about seeing Garrett and hearing Christy's concerned counsel. In a way, the pressure valve of my secret was released. Now all I needed to do was tell Joel.

For a moment, I wondered if what I had

shared with Christy would be considered a partial disclosure, like Tess had talked about.

But my situation with Garrett is nothing like Tess's with Rick. I'm probably making too big a deal out of this. It's over. Once I talk with Joel, it will be done. Done and gone from my life. Not a big deal.

"We learned something interesting about Christy while you two were gone," Emily told me when I slid into the booth. "Did you know that Christy was a cheerleader in high school?"

I must have looked as surprised as Tess and Emily had been. I never would have pictured our reserved, not necessarily athletic Christy as a high school cheerleader.

Christy's face turned crimson. "No, not true! I tried out. But, no, I was never a cheerleader."

"Oh, I thought you were. It is true, isn't it, that Rick was the one who convinced you to try out?" Sierra asked.

Christy nodded. "Rick can be convincing."

Tess raised her glass as if silently adding her agreement. I noticed that Tess was smiling. It was good to see.

I somehow felt emotionally attached to Tess's airy demeanor and tossed out what felt like a good conclusion to our evening of complex conversations.

"We really are all just a bunch of Daughters of Eve, aren't we?"

"Because we're so vulnerable?" Emily asked.

"And naive?" Christy added. I glanced at Emily and Christy, pushing back the thought that both added those descriptors because that's how they saw me.

Tess, however, took the comments as meant for her. "I was thinking about that as we were talking tonight. Nothing is or was perfect. For me, for Eve, for all of us. Paradise lost and all that. Eve had to start over and so do I. I need to step away from Rick and all his issues to let my heart be free so I can start over."

"I'm really glad you see it that way, Tess," Christy said.

"Eve kept going, though," Sierra said. "She didn't stop giving and loving."

"I'm not about to stop being open to love, if that's what you're saying. I want a man who is able to be all-in because that's how I'm going to be when it's the right man and the right time." Tess looked centered. Confident. I wanted to get to that place too.

I motioned for the waiter to bring our check. Even if the others wanted to keep talking, I felt a nudge to go home.

"We paid already," Tess said. "The three of us covered the check this time."

"Thanks," I said.

Christy reached for her purse. "Should we leave the tip?"

"No, we got that too."

"We'll cover it next time," I said.

"Next time will be our picnic, right?" Sierra asked.

"We need to decide where we're going to set it up," I said. "Once we decide that, I would be happy to do everything else."

"I'm still voting for the beach," Sierra said. "I know this perfect little cove near Corona del Mar."

"Then let's have it at the beach," Tess said. "Does everyone agree?"

The yeses were unanimous as the others slid out of the booth and we headed for the front. The manager had locked the door already and was waiting for us with the keys to let us out.

"Thank you," we all said in a variety of tones and with a muffled ripple of laughter.

"I've never closed down a restaurant before," Christy said, as we headed to the parking lot.

"First time for everything," Tess linked her arm in mine and Emily's. Christy and Sierra came alongside, as if we were reenacting the scene of Dorothy and her companions dancing down the yellow brick road to Oz. The five of us strode arm in arm, in measured step, toward our cars.

"What a clear night," Tess said.

"Stop!" Sierra ordered. "Look up!"

We stopped, arms linked. The gleaming full moon gazed down on us, and we gazed right back.

"I don't want to ever lose any of you," Tess said in a low voice. "You're the closest friends I've ever had."

I felt unsettled. I hadn't been completely open and honest with Christy or any of the other DOEs the way Tess had been. I felt like I was in hiding. But I still agreed along with the others that I was right there with them, friends forever. Heart to heart.

It was just that my heart was a little encumbered right now.

"This way." Tess pulled us toward her car. "Did you forget that I brought presents?"

"Is this going to be a thing for us?" Emily asked. "First the cute mugs from Sierra, then the handmade cards from Jennalyn. I'm really bad at coming up with ideas for gifts."

"I'll make it easy. Think of my presents to all of you tonight as your birthday gifts for the year." Tess opened the back of her car and lifted the cover that hid the treasures beneath.

"Jennalyn." Tess handed me the expensive black boatneck top she had held up to me in her studio. "This is for you."

"Tess!"

The bounty continued as she handed out the clothing she had suggested for us at her home. Sierra burst into tears when Tess handed her the cocoa-brown leather jacket.

"It's too much," Sierra tried to hand it back.

"No, no, no!" Tess held up her hand. "You never protest when a sister gives you a gift. You say thank you, you give her a little kiss on the cheek, and then you wear it like you deserve to look as gorgeous on the outside as you are on the inside."

We all cried a little, laughed a little, and gave Tess the prescribed kiss on the cheek.

As I drove home under the full moon, I wondered how different my life might have been if I had had friends like my sweet haven makers when I was in high school. I realized why I didn't pursue close friend-ships then. From the end of my sophomore year until five weeks after graduation, all my free time had been spent with Garrett.

After unlocking the front door, I entered quietly, surprised to see that the light was on in the living room and a low murmur was coming from the TV. Joel was asleep on the sofa with his phone on the coffee table. I tried to decide if I should wake him or turn off the TV and lights and let him sleep. I whispered his name twice. He gave no indication that he heard me.

At that moment I didn't feel convinced that I should try harder to wake him. Tonight wasn't the right time to have a deep heartfelt conversation with him.

I tossed a throw blanket over him and headed upstairs as quietly as I could. I set the alarm for 5:30 a.m. since that was the time Joel usually got up if he was planning to go to work for early prep.

My sleep was deep, which made the alarm even more jolting when it went off. I found Joel still asleep on the couch, snoring like a cartoon character who was only pretending to be zoned out.

"Joel." I shook his shoulder gently. "Joel."

He readjusted his position but didn't open his eyes.

"Hey, Joel. Joel, wake up."

He squinted at me, and I smiled as sweetly as I could. "It's five thirty. I didn't know if you had to get up."

"What day is it?"

"Thursday."

"I'm going in at eight."

"Okay, I just wanted to make sure. I'll let you sleep some more."

"Okay."

I yawned and started back upstairs, hoping my side of the bed was still warm. The house was chilly.

"Hey," Joel called out. "Wait. Come back."

I yawned again and went back, my arms folded across my chest as I tried to warm up.

"Come here." Joel scooted as far back as he could on his side and lifted the throw, inviting me to cuddle.

"You sure we'll fit?"

"We used to. Come on."

I slid in and felt the luxury of his warm arms covering me, his warm breath on my neck.

"We've still got it," he murmured. "Just like all the good old times."

I smiled and nestled into a spooning position, transported back to memories of our best make-out sessions on the old couch at our first apartment.

"I waited up for you," Joel said. "When did you get home?"

"Late. I tried to wake you."

He kissed the side of my neck. I turned my head so we could give each other a proper kiss.

"Cumin?" Joel asked. "When did you have Mexican food?"

"How can you always pick out flavors like that? I brushed my teeth."

"It's your lips. Come here. I'll tell you what else you had." He kissed me again. "Salsa and tortilla chips. Wait." Another lingering kiss. "Corn, not flour. And . . ." He kissed me again. "Lemonade. Definitely lemonade."

I twisted around until I could face him. "You cannot tell that by my lips."

The dim glow from the light above the stove revealed that Joel's eyes were still only half opened. He grinned. "I checked the car app when my parents left since you had my car last night. I saw you were parked at Alejandro's. They've always been heavy-handed with the cumin. And I know you like their lemonade."

I pinched him.

He playfully pinched me back, and a tussle broke out under the blanket. We could have moved upstairs to the bedroom. But I think it made us both feel like newlyweds to shift and twist and find each other on the sofa.

Later that morning, when the kids were watching their usual morning educational show and Joel and I were both showered and dressed, he looked over at me while making coffee, and he winked.

I grinned. It's funny, but the first thing I thought was, *We don't need a marriage conference. We just need a nice long vacation.* It wasn't the first time I'd thought it, but this time I was reminded of Christy's comment about how love is more than skin on skin. It's giving ourselves to each other in every way.

The night before, during the conversation with Christy, I had felt such conviction that I needed to have a tell-all conversation with Joel. This morning, when everything felt better than ever and on track, I wondered what such a purging would accomplish.

Maybe I've been relating too much to Tess's issues and projecting them onto myself. I think I've been more conflicted than convicted.

A few weeks ago I had felt so out of sorts because Joel didn't remember what my usual order was from China Palace. This morning he made it clear that he knew that I preferred corn to flour tortillas and that I liked Alejandro's lemonade. Food was such a portal to my husband's heart. His love language.

Joel really does know me. He does! I've been making too big of a deal out of every-

thing, including Garrett. We need to just move forward.

"Hey," Joel said. "My dad's birthday is this weekend, remember?"

"Yes."

Joel poured his coffee into his favorite thermos. "I reserved the back room at the Blue Ginger, so we're all set for four o'clock on Sunday. Mom wanted an early dinner instead of lunch."

"Will you have a replacement by then?"

"Probably not. If I do, I'll still be training him. I have two more interviews today." Joel checked the time. "I'll be able to pop in and out."

"Any ideas for a gift?"

"You know Poppy. Having the family together is the only thing he wants every year. If you make him a card and have Eden draw a picture for him, he'll be happy." Joel leaned in and kissed me on the cheek. "Love you."

"When will you be home?"

"Not sure." He went over to the kids and gave them big hugs and kisses.

"Daddy, can we go to the park today?" Eden clung to Joel. Her bed-head hair hung down her back. I was glad that I'd made an appointment last week for a haircut that afternoon. It was becoming nearly impossible to brush out the tangles without Eden ending up in tears.

"Maybe Mommy can take you," Joel said.

"I want you, Daddy. I need you to take me to the park." Eden gave him a pathetic little-girl pout. "Pleeeeease."

Joel turned to me, looking for a little backup.

"Eden, we already have special plans for today."

"What special plans?"

"You get to have your hair cut this afternoon." I tried to make it sound as exciting as possible.

The TV distracted her, and she answered the question the character was asking the audience. "E!" she shouted. "Like Eden!"

Joel gave me a surprised look as if we were raising a child genius. I saw it as one more touchpoint where he was so disconnected from our kids, he didn't know what was normal for their developmental stages.

I followed him to the door. He gave me another kiss. "Have fun at the park with the kids."

He was out the door before I had a chance to correct him and say that we were going for a haircut, not to the park.

CHAPTER 19

Eden and Alex were wild all morning. Wild! I couldn't figure out what had set them in motion or why they were getting into everything. I put aside my list of things to do, packed them up, and took them to the park.

Bad idea. They were wild at the park too. I felt like a terrible mother when Eden refused to share the sand shovel and bucket with her brother and a little tyke who wanted to play with them.

The jaunt was cut short, and I considered canceling the haircut for that afternoon. Anything to avoid taking our circus on the road and subjecting others to the minute-by-minute meltdowns of one or the other.

We ended up going for the haircut after very short naps, and I couldn't believe it. My children were golden. "Little angels" the hairstylist called them. Eden sat in a barber chair shaped like a red race car. Alex took his turn in the chair, and the stylist gave his thin hair a little gel and a cute part down the side. Alex loved turning the steering wheel and pushing all the buttons. They looked so cute and were rewarded with fruit-sweetened lollipops. Eden asked if we could come back every day.

I decided to stop at GiGi and Poppy's on the way home so they could see my two little radiant sunbeams, who no longer looked like two little waifs.

"Stay for dinner," GiGi said.

"No, that's okay," I said. "I just wanted to say hi and thank you again for watching the kids last night."

"Of course. Anytime."

Poppy already had both kids beside him and was reading them a book, which was his favorite thing to do right when they arrived. It always calmed them, and Poppy used all his funny voices, which they loved.

"Why don't you leave the kids here for the night?" GiGi suggested. "We have everything they need. You and Joel could have an evening alone. Wouldn't that be nice for the two of you?"

"It would be wonderful. I don't know when Joel is coming home, though."

"Call him. Tell him the two of you have the whole night to yourselves."

I had a feeling my mother-in-law was

concerned because she recently had come to understand how much Joel was working and how little we saw of each other. Or it could have been that she noticed my yawning after my late night and was trying to send me home for a nap. Either way, I accepted her invitation and told the kids that GiGi and Poppy had a surprise: they wanted Eden and Alex to sleep at their house that night.

"And have pancakes in the morning," GiGi said. "Won't that be fun?"

Eden was elated. "Bunny pancakes? Can you make the bunny pancakes?"

"For you, yes. We'll make bunny pancakes for breakfast."

Alex took his cue from Eden, and when I left, the two of them were hopping and jiving in the living room as Poppy watched, grinning ear to ear.

Who gets to have in-laws like these two?

I checked my phone before driving home and saw that I had a text from Christy. She asked if I wanted to meet at the park that afternoon for a playdate.

Can't meet today. How about Saturday?

Christy replied with an "okay" emoji and 10:00?

I typed yes and added a clapping-hands emoji. I was so glad she had initiated a play-

286

date. Hopefully my children would behave differently at the park if Hana and Cole were there. Even if they didn't, at least I knew that Christy would understand.

Joel was already home when I returned. He was once again stretched out, sound asleep on the sofa. His schedule had been so unpredictable that I didn't expect him to be there.

Poor guy.

I covered him with a blanket and left a note on the coffee table before tiptoeing upstairs to snatch a nap in our comfy bed. I was bone-tired and knew that I had the freedom to sleep with no interruption from the kids. I settled into my favorite position on my right side and felt sleep close in on me with a mental and emotional heaviness.

I heard Joel come into the bedroom sometime later. I woke, and for that brief twilight intersection between conscious and subconscious, I realized I had been in the middle of a vivid dream, and I remembered all of it. I was dreaming about Garrett.

We were at the park with our kids, sitting close on the bench, and he had his arm around me. He was offering me a drink of his soda, and I was reaching for the cup, ready to share like we did in high school.

My heart raced. *What was he doing in my dream?*

I sat up and, realizing it was getting dark, turned on the bedside lamp. I tried to focus my eyes to see the time.

"Hi," Joel said softly.

"Hi, Joel. Hi." I felt odd, but I had to say his name aloud to bring myself back. To remind my confused thoughts of who I was and where I was. "What time is it?"

Joel bent down and kissed me on the forehead. "Time to give your husband a kiss."

I played along and gave him a half-hearted kiss, still trying to move past the adrenaline burst and feel centered again. "Did you see my note about the kids staying at your parents?"

"Yeah. What was that all about?" He slid into bed next to me and propped the extra pillows behind his back. Leaning over, he turned on the lamp on his nightstand.

"They said they wanted the kids to stay. I think your mom is worried that we don't see each other enough."

"We don't," Joel said.

"No, we don't." I sat up and faced him, crossing my legs and stretching my arms over my head, trying to pull myself into the waking present. "You came home earlier than I thought you would."

"Thursdays are usually the slowest nights, you know."

At that moment I couldn't have told you what night of the week it was. I still felt out of sync.

"I felt good about the staff and how everything was looking, so I left. They haven't called me yet, so no news is good news."

"Did you hire a new chef?"

"Not yet. One more interview tomorrow." Joel shook his head. "You'll never guess who this last guy is. He called today and convinced me to interview him."

"Who is it?"

"Vincent. He said he wants another chance."

"That's odd. Why did he resign? I don't think you ever told me."

"I never told you because he never gave a reason. I agreed to interview him tomorrow because I want to find out what happened." Joel reached over and brushed my hair from the side of my face. "You never told me how the movie was last night."

"We didn't go. We ended up at the Mexican restaurant talking all night."

"Why? Were you late for the movie?"

"No." I gave Joel an abbreviated version

of how Tess saw a guy she had sort of gone out with, how it was complicated, and that we left so we could talk. I'm not sure why, but I added that Christy and Sierra knew the guy and that Christy had gone out with him in high school.

"Strange coincidence," Joel said.

"I know." Adjusting my position and watching Joel's expression carefully, I attempted the icebreaker declaration that I had avoided for far too long. The moment had come. I wanted the truth to set me free in my thoughts and in my emotions.

"I had a strange coincidence too."

Joel waited, his arms bent and his hands behind his head.

"I ran into the guy I used to date in high school too."

"Last night?"

"No. In January. You met him, too, actually."

"I did? When?"

"At Eden's first ballet class. He was there with his daughter, Violet."

Joel lowered his arms and leaned forward. "That guy was your high school boyfriend?"

I nodded.

"Was he there all the other weeks?"

I nodded again, keeping my expression cool.

Even in the soft light of our bedroom, I could see that Joel's expression had darkened. "Why are you just now telling me?"

I froze up. "It's not a big deal. Just a coincidence. Christy saw a guy she dated in high school; I saw the guy I dated in high school. I wanted you to know. That's all."

You're minimizing. Tell him. Tell him everything. Don't pull back.

"But you saw him every week," Joel said.

"Not every week." I felt like I was walking into a trap of my own making.

"Did you meet his wife?"

"No, she didn't come with him."

Joel studied me, looking suspicious. "That guy messed with your head back then. I don't want him messing with you now."

"He apologized for that, actually," I said.

"When?"

"The first time I saw him. He said he had been wanting to apologize for a long time. I think it was sincere. I told him I forgave him."

Joel scrutinized my expression. "Where did you go to have this deep conversation?"

"Just outside. In front of the studio."

"You left Eden inside alone so you could have a clear-the-air talk with a guy who doesn't deserve even a second look from you. Jennalyn, what were you thinking?"

291

I wanted to lash out at Joel for talking to me the way he did, but if he was this tense already, what would he say if I told him about the deeper conversations I had with Garrett?

Joel's body language made it clear that he was mad. Really mad. "Aren't you going to say anything?"

"You don't have to get angry at me. It's not a big deal!" I felt like bursting into tears to relieve the emotional pressure. I was being a coward. I knew it. I wasn't willing to tell Joel everything. Not under these circumstances. I wanted him to be patient and listen so he could understand. Of course, he couldn't understand unless I gave him the whole story.

There was no way I was willing to step into that minefield right now.

"What's going on with you, Jennalyn?" He climbed out of bed and paced. "You're off having a reconciliation session with this jerk, in January, months ago, and you don't think it's important enough to tell me? What else aren't you telling me? Are you seeing him?"

"No, of course not! How can you say that?"

"Because all the signs have been there."

"What signs?"

"You've been different. Your hair, the

makeup, you've lost weight. You're not in the funk you were in at Christmas. You could be leading a double life with him, and I would never know."

"Joel!"

"Are you having playdates with him?"

"Joel, stop! Just stop! This is crazy! I'm not seeing him, and I'll never see him again!" I was on my feet, facing him and feeling the fire in my veins.

"Then why did you even bring it up?"

"I wanted to tell you." My voice quivered, and I hated myself for being so wobbly.

"Then why didn't you just tell me back in January?"

"Because!"

"Because why?"

"Because you're never home!"

It was the worst line that could have slipped out of my mouth. He marched past me, slammed the bedroom door, and stomped down the stairs. I stumbled back to the bed and folded at the waist.

What have I done?

CHAPTER 20

"It was the worst argument we've ever had," I told Christy on Saturday when we met up for our morning at the park.

I almost cancelled meeting her because I was still so emotionally spent. But now I was there, sitting on the bench, watching our kids playing together nicely. I was glad I had come.

I hadn't told Christy what the argument was about. All I said was that Joel and I had a whole night to ourselves since the kids were at Poppy and GiGi's, but all we did was fight.

"How did things turn out for you guys? Were you able to talk it through?" she asked.

"No, not really. We called a truce and finally went to bed with our backs to each other. Nothing was resolved. I didn't get to really open up and tell him everything I wanted to talk about. It was so frustrating."

"I hate those kinds of nights." Christy

looked at me closely. She had sunglasses on, so if her eyes were giving any hints about what she was thinking, I couldn't tell.

I looked around to make sure no one was close enough to hear us.

"We just fell back into our normal routine. That's what we do. He says he isn't mad. I say I'm fine. We go on."

"Are you fine?" Christy asked.

"No."

"What's going on?"

"I need to get something off my heart. I don't know if this is the best time or place, but I would really love it if I could talk to you about all of this, Christy."

"Of course."

I suddenly wasn't sure where to start and felt self-conscious. "You asked me to promise you that I would tell Joel about seeing my high school boyfriend."

"Was that what the argument was about?" Christy asked. "Did you tell Joel about seeing . . . should I call him 'Guy'?"

I realized I hadn't told Christy his name, so it made sense for her to assign the same man-of-mystery label to Garrett that we had given to Tess's Guy. In that moment, I hated that I had a Guy in my life.

"His name is Garrett," I said softly. "There's more than what I told you at

Alejandro's. Garrett reached out to me online, and we ended up chatting through a game app. I know it sounds stupid, but I kept it a secret."

It took Christy a moment before she asked the next question. "What did you and Garrett talk about?"

"He and I both lost our mothers, like I mentioned before when I said he gave me the photos. Our moms were friends. Garrett and I started messaging about our moms and how hard it was to lose them. It was helpful to me at the time. I liked that he brought back good memories of my mother."

Christy's eyes were still hidden behind her sunglasses, but her lips were in a soft expression that made me feel like I was being seen on the inside, so I went deeper.

"But then he told me a lot about his marriage, and I could tell that he wasn't very happy."

"That's a dangerous place for you to step into," Christy said.

"I know."

I told Christy about the cave I had crawled into when I was alone, and how my mom and Garrett were in there with me, which messed with my emotions. I told her about the unexpected dream I had about Garrett on Thursday before the argument with Joel.

"And you were sitting on this bench with him in your dream?" Christy asked.

I looked around and realized, yes, this was the bench.

"We can move over to that other bench if you want," she said.

"No, it's fine. It doesn't bother me. Honestly. I know the dream was just a mushed together mess of thoughts and emotions in my subconscious. The timing of it was terrible. It kind of repulses me now when I think about it."

"How much of this have you told Joel?"

"None of it. Only that I saw Garrett and that he apologized to me."

"Didn't Joel ask any questions after you both had mellowed out?"

"No, he's been focused on work. Yesterday I hoped we could talk, but all he wanted to do was tell me that he had hired Vincent back. Vincent had given him an earful about all that was wrong with the way things were set up at the Blue Ginger."

"Vincent criticized him, and Joel hired him back?"

"Joel said Vincent was right; big changes need to be made. Joel is super optimistic. I hope he's right about this being the change he's been working toward."

Alex had toddled over to me and patted my legs with his sandy hands. I dug into the diaper bag and pulled out a wet washcloth in a zipped-up plastic bag so I could wipe his hands and mouth.

"That's a good idea." Christy nodded at the DIY baby wipe.

"I got the idea from Sierra. It saves on all those disposable ones I used to buy by the case."

"I'm right there with ya."

"It only works if you remember to remove it from the diaper bag after every outing. I pulled one out last summer that had been hidden in the bottom of the bag for weeks. I had to throw it away. It looked like a lab culture of some highly contagious virus."

Christy grinned. "Perfect analogy."

I turned to read her face. I wasn't sure what she meant.

"That's why you need to get everything out and tell Joel. If you keep this in the dark or only do the . . . What did Tess call it?"

"A guarded confession?"

"I think she called it a partial disclosure," Christy said. "You need to get everything out in the open with Joel, no matter how messy it is or how angry he gets."

"I understand."

"There wasn't anything physical between

you and Garrett, was there?"

"No!"

"I'm not accusing. I'm just asking," Christy said. "You don't need to share any of the details with me unless you want to. All that really matters is that everything is explained and resolved with Joel."

"I know. You're right."

Alex was on my lap, resting his cheek on my chest as sweet as could be. I stroked his hair and kissed him on the top of his head. He popped up and looked at me with a big drooling smile.

"How many teeth do you have now, Alex?" Christy leaned closer. "Look at you! You're getting to be such a big boy. Come here. I have to get some cuddles in before you're too big and won't want your Auntie Christy giving you squeezes."

Alex went to Christy eagerly and played along with her game of peekaboo. He rewarded her with his best belly laugh, and she gave him a big squeeze.

I felt different. Slightly relieved. Slightly more burdened. Christy had been understanding and accepting of everything I had told her. It made me wish I had talked to her about Garrett from the start.

The reason I felt more burdened now was because I knew I couldn't leave this closed up in the bottom of the diaper bag, so to speak. I needed to tell Joel everything, and I didn't know how I was going to do that.

Alex wiggled out of Christy's arms and went back to where the big kids were playing on the slide. Christy and I watched as seven-year-old Hana, who had gladly taken on the nanny role for all three of the littler ones, picked up Alex and safely placed him into the baby swing. She pushed him slowly and sang a cute song for him.

"She's become a little songbird, hasn't she?" I asked.

Christy nodded. "Just like her daddy. I love it when the two of them sing together. Music is a gift I don't share, so I enjoy seeing it grow between them."

We pulled out our water bottles and sat quietly for a moment.

"Can I tell you something?" Christy asked.

"Of course." I expected Christy to have some advice that might be hard to hear.

Instead, she told me about a situation with her and Todd that occurred a few years ago. He had come home one day from the high school where he teaches and told her a teenage girl in his class had caught his attention.

"What does that mean?" I asked.

"He meant that he was attracted to her."

"He told you that?"

Christy nodded. "It's something Todd and I decided to do to dismantle any fantasies we might hide from each other about another person. Attraction happens. So we decided to be transparent and honest and tell each other when it happened."

"I can't see how that would help," I said.

"It might not help every couple. For us, it's like defusing something that could be a bomb. When we speak about it openly to each other, it brings the attraction into the light. And it helps us trust each other more." Christy stopped and grinned. "Hey, there's my word again: *trust.*"

"I've never heard of anyone doing something like that. I don't know how I would feel if Joel told me he was attracted to someone else, like a waitress at work."

"You would probably do what I've learned to do. You listen as unemotionally as possible; you don't react. You thank him for being honest and ask him later how he's doing with his feelings. It gives him the freedom to keep talking about everything that's going on inside him. I think it defuses the allure. Does that make sense? When it's all out in the open, the temptation doesn't have power the way it does when it's hidden."

"It sounds wise," I said. "I just don't know

if Joel and I could communicate on that level. Especially after the way things went the other night."

"You can get there. If we could, anybody can." Christy offered me a comforting smile. "The secret is that you can't give up if the first attempt fails. Marriages are organic. They take time to grow."

I thought about all the ways our little backyard garden had reminded me of our marriage. "And they need watering and weeding, and the bugs need to be destroyed."

"Exactly."

"We really do need the marriage conference next month. I hope it works out for all four of us to go."

"Me too." Christy looked over at the kids. "Hana, help your brother, please." She hopped up to comfort Cole, who had come down the slide and landed with a bump that made him burst out in a wail.

At that point, Christy and I were back into full-time mom patrol, and our conversation went on hold. The good thing was that the kids were having a great time.

They were having such fun together, so Christy suggested that we all go to her house for lunch. "Todd is working for Aunt Marti today, so we can put the kids down for naps after lunch, if you want, and talk some more."

"What's he doing?"

"She hired him to paint their living room. She changes the color every few years. This time she's going with a custom mix that she says has more sunlight tones in it. The neutral shade she had for the last two years apparently had too much gray and made the living room drab on dark days."

"I don't remember it appearing drab the last time we were there."

"I don't either. But she's good with colors and loves to decorate, as you know, so Todd is happy to let her pay him for the work. He's determined to have all the money for Maui saved up before we go."

"Do you ever tell Todd thank you for working so hard?"

Christy thought a minute. "I don't know. Maybe sometimes."

"I was thinking earlier that I need to let Joel know how much I appreciate all that he does to provide for us."

"Thanks for the reminder. I'm going to tell Todd tonight."

Just then we had a tumble, followed by tears, and we knew we should pack up and head over to Christy's. Lunch was easy, and it wasn't too difficult to settle the little kids into their naps. The key was putting each of them in a separate room. Hana was content to turn her room over to Eden. Alex settled into the Pack 'n Play in the downstairs guest room. Hana, who reminded me that she never took naps anymore, was content to take her book up to Christy and Todd's bedroom and have their big bed all to herself for an hour of reading.

Christy poured us glasses of mint iced tea with lots of ice. "Do you want to try my newest favorite? I add just a little pomegranate juice. It's so good."

I gave it a try and agreed. "This is really refreshing. I should tell Joel. He's always looking for more mocktails to add to the menu. This would be good."

"Add a sprig of mint, and it can be a springtime special," Christy suggested. "Do you want to sit outside on the deck or in the living room?"

"Let's stay inside in case Alex wakes up."

Christy moved some toys, shifted a mound of unfolded bath towels back to the laundry basket, and slid it to the corner of the room with her foot. We sat on opposite ends of the sofa, facing each other. I liked the way Christy seemed comfortable to invite me into the middle of her daily clutter and not feel like she had to clean up or impress me.

I mentioned that to her one time, and she said she had relaxed a lot about making sure her house was always picked up. She decided the trail of toys on the floor and dishes in the sink were "evidence of life." I always remembered that when I looked at a magazine image of a perfectly decorated living room. The photos seemed to be missing any evidence-of-life touches that make a house a home.

We talked more about plans for Maui, Christy's latest order for decorative pillows, food possibilities for our haven makers' picnic, and whether we should go together for haircuts the way we had several years ago when we both needed to feel renewed.

"I like the idea of going together for haircuts before we leave for Maui." Christy's expression clouded. "Although that means I'll have to save up even more if we go to the place we went to last time. I remember it was pretty expensive."

"We can find another place," I said. "Or how about if you let me treat you for your birthday?"

"My birthday isn't until July."

"So? I want to beat the rush this year and celebrate you early. After all, Tess set the standard for all of us this year."

Christy laughed.

I grinned and tried to convince her. "Let me do this for you, Christy. I never know what to give you. I'm terrible at coming up with meaningful gifts the way you do. Please. Let this be my meaningful gift for you this year."

She hesitated for a moment. "Thank you. I'd like that a lot." Christy reached for her iced mint tea and said, "Tell me one of your memories of your mom. I want to hear more about her."

I was surprised at her request and wasn't sure where to start. I couldn't remember anyone asking me to share a memory about her. Except Garrett.

Christy helped to get me started by saying, "I know she liked red toenails. You told me that at Tess's."

I didn't remember mentioning that to Christy, but the image of Mom's red toenails made me see her immediately in my mind's eye.

"Oh My, Cherry Pie," I said with a shy grin. "That was her favorite."

"She liked cherry pie?" Christy asked.

"That was the name of her nail polish. But I should add that my mother did not simply like cherry pie; she loved cherry pie. That's what she wanted instead of birthday cake or Christmas cookies or any other special dessert. She thought cherry pie was the greatest gift God ever gave to the culinary world."

Christy laughed. "Did your husband agree with that?"

"She let Joel know how she felt about cherry pie. He always laughed, but one time he said, 'I think you love cherry pie more than life itself.' " I choked up repeating the story.

Christy gave me a sympathetic look. "Jennalyn . . ."

I knew Christy was giving me an out. A chance to talk about something else, but I wanted to keep going and tell the story. I wanted her to know this.

"When Joel said that to her, she told him that long after she was gone from this earth, there would still be cherry pie. She said that cherry pie would remind the next generation of all the sweetness in the world."

Christy had tears in her eyes too. "I love that."

"I do too. Thanks for helping me to remember, Christy."

CHAPTER 21

It felt so good to tell the cherry pie story for the first time since Mom had passed away. More memories came fluttering into my thoughts.

"My mom loved words and phrases that had double meanings. It was part of her unassuming sense of humor. I can't think of any right now. I wish I could. When I do, I think I should write them down so I can tell my kids one day."

"That's a great idea," Christy said.

"Oh, I just thought of one! Hana would love this joke. My dad asked one day what time my mom was going to the dentist and she said, 'Tooth-hurtie.' " I waited to see if Christy got it.

She thought a moment and then grinned. "Oh! Two thirty. You're right. Hana is going to love that one."

"My mom could always make me laugh. Always. She embarrassed me plenty of times by things she said that were just plain silly. She would crack herself up over a ridiculous pun. Then she would look you in the eye and deliver a javelin of truth. I don't know how she did it."

"I love that you're telling me all this, Jennalyn."

"You know what's interesting? I hadn't thought of this before. I haven't had a piece of cherry pie or a pedicure since she died."

Christy raised her eyebrows. "Is it just too close to the memory of her?"

"Probably. I don't know. Joel wanted to make me a cherry pie once right after Eden was born, and I burst into tears. He hasn't offered to make one since."

"What about the pedicures?"

"My mom used to take me with her to the nail salon starting when I was eight. We always went the first Saturday morning of the month. Same place. Same massage chairs. Same women working there."

"What color did you get?" Christy asked.

"It was different every time. One time I went on a peach streak; another time I had each toenail painted a different color. I think I was ten when I did that. My mom called it my rainbow pedicure."

I smiled, remembering my mermaid phase, and told Christy about how I had tried four different blues before finding the perfect shade.

"One year, for the Fourth of July, I did red, white, and blue, and my mom paid extra to have a few little stars added on my big toe. We went on vacation to Lake Tahoe the next day, and I was so mad because . . ." I paused. The memories had collided.

My instinct was to pull back and not tell Christy what happened next. Then I realized this was my chance to try a new option instead of hiding. I could bring the memory out and into the light, the way Christy had talked about earlier at the park.

"I was mad because our family was on vacation with another family. We hardly knew them, and I didn't want them to be there. The first day, down at the water, their son, Garrett, tried to push me off the dock."

"Garrett?" Christy repeated.

I nodded. "Yes, Garrett. That's how we met. I twisted my ankle, and two of the stars came off my big toe." I chuckled. Telling the account to Christy diffused a bit of the heartache I had been carrying around since January, when the memories of Garrett had only been examined in the dark.

"I think I was more upset about the stars than the wrapped ankle and having to hobble around the rest of our vacation."

Christy sipped her tea-and-juice elixir and kept looking at me. When I didn't offer up any more stories she said, "You don't have to tell me if you don't want to, but I'm curious. How did your relationship with Garrett end?"

I thought a moment and decided that I didn't mind telling her. In fact, I wanted Christy to know. I wanted someone other than Mom to know this part of my life. All Joel knew was that Garrett had been the one to end the relationship and that I had been hurt by him.

"Garrett got a summer job at a kids' sports camp right after we graduated from high school. He met a girl there. JoyAnna. They worked side by side every day, and he had 'planning meetings' with her a couple of nights a week."

Christy raised an eyebrow when I said "planning meetings" and repeated the name "JoyAnna" as if she were about to add a boo-hiss.

"I was clueless. I thought all our secret plans were in motion. He had an athletic scholarship to a little college in Idaho. I had secretly enrolled at a community college near his school. We were going to marry and then tell our parents because we knew they would tell us we were too young."

"You guys had it all planned?"

"We did. Or at least, I thought we did. The thing was, it was all a secret. Our secret. So when he met JoyAnna and decided he wanted to date her, it seemed to everyone else that our high school relationship had simply run its course, and we had agreed to see other people."

Christy shook her head.

"I was the only one who knew that he had planned a future with me. That is, until I finally told my mom." I leaned back.

Christy looked hurt, as if she were feeling the pain of the betrayal that I had gone through. "I'm so sorry that happened to you, Jennalyn."

"The unexpected gift that came out of it was that my mom and I grew really close during that time. I had kept so much hidden from her. I thought I was being loyal to my future husband, but I discovered I had shut out all other relationships to keep the secrets. Once I opened up to her, Mom became my best friend."

I told Christy about watching the movie *Emma* with my mom, and how she had initiated the memento-burning party for the two of us at the beach and how that's when I forgave Garrett.

Tears came to my eyes. They were familiar

tears. Silent, flowing out of my heart without a sound. I wasn't embarrassed or ashamed to cry in front of Christy. She made it clear that the tears didn't frighten her, nor did she seem to feel the need to stop them. She simply entered the moment with me.

"I love that your mom did that memento-burning party with you at the beach," Christy said. "What a tangible sort of wild way for her to enter into your heartache to help to start the healing process with forgiveness."

"I told you: she was savvy. She knew how to go to the heart of things. I'm so glad Mom walked me through the process of forgiveness because that's how I was able to heal and be free. My heart was available and uncluttered when I met Joel."

"I like that: 'available and uncluttered.' An uncluttered heart. I'm going to remember that."

In the same way that the toys and dishes were evidence of life in Christy's world, memories of my mom were evidence of her life. Instead of putting away those memories and trying to make my life look organized and tidy, I decided that I didn't mind if those mismatched pieces of evidence were strewn throughout my days. I didn't want to ever burn, bury, or hide memorabilia related to Mom.

"I can tell that the friendship you and your mom had was extraordinary. I hope you and I can have that with our daughters."

I agreed. Then, to my deep joy, Christy added words that took away any insecurity the twelve-year-old in me had once held on to about my place on her friendship scale.

"And, Jennalyn, I hope that same kind of extraordinariness will always be in our friendship too."

I nodded and dried the last of my spontaneous waterfall tears.

"You know what I was just thinking," Christy said. "I'm guessing it won't be long before your girly-girl will want to pick up the tradition with you and have a standing date on the first Saturday of every month to have a pedicure."

"Are you kidding? Eden would be over the moon if I took her for a pedicure. You should have seen her when she got her hair cut! She would be all about the pink. Lots of pink."

"Hana would probably want green. That's her favorite color lately. We should take both our girls some time."

"Yes, let's do that. How fun!"

We heard a door open upstairs and timid footsteps coming down the stairs. Hana stopped where the staircase opened to the living room. She leaned forward and smiled at us.

"I think it's been an hour," she said. Her shoulder-length blond hair had escaped her ponytail on one side, creating a lopsided pouf. She was wearing an overly baggy navy blue hoodie with the faded words *Rancho Corona University* across the front.

"Come join us." Christy held out her arms, welcoming her daughter.

Hana shuffled over, with the sweatshirt's sleeves hanging past her knees. She planted her skinny little self onto the sofa between us, and Christy put her arm around her.

"I used to wear your daddy's sweatshirts too," Christy said.

"It's cold in your room," Hana said. "I wanted to warm up."

"I'll warm you up." Christy cuddled her close and kissed her on the top of her head. "How was your book?"

"Good."

"What part are you at?"

I stood and pointed to the downstairs bathroom so that Christy would know why I was leaving. It was fun to hear Hana tell her mom about a book that Christy apparently had read when she was young. Watching the way Christy mothered Hana was a small gift. If it was Eden, the first thing I probably would have done when she came to the couch was fuss with her hair. That would have undoubtedly made her self-conscious. Christy's ease in folding her daughter into her everyday moments was so much like the way my mother used to treat me. I could learn a lot from Christy.

When my kids and I reached home, Eden convinced me to make waffles for dinner. She had heard Hana talking about having waffles that morning before they went to the park. I'm not sure Eden had eaten enough waffles in her short life to remember what they were.

All I cared about was that she wasn't requesting cheese.

She helped to make the waffles on our rarely used electric waffle maker. I put a slice of strawberry on each cooked square and added a small dollop of peanut butter on the center in one of my never-ending efforts to introduce her to a new protein food source.

Eden ate the entire waffle, peanut butter, strawberries, and all. I did a little dance on the kitchen floor, imitating the way Eden liked to twirl in her tutu. It was a break-through moment and gave me hope that we could have another success at Poppy's birthday party dinner the next day.

The kids and I got ready for the celebration earlier than we needed to on Sunday afternoon. It seemed wise to allow time for something to go wonky, since it often did with two kids. Eden loved having a chance to wear what she called her "pretty princess dress." I put Alex in his one and only button-down shirt with a bow tie that looped around his neck with elastic.

I wore the black boatneck top Tess had given me along with my most comfortable pair of black pants. They weren't the smallest size of black pants in my closet, but they allowed me the tummy room I needed to sit for many hours with Joel's extended family and eat all the delicious food my husband would undoubtedly have delivered to our table in abundance.

Even though I knew I would be carrying Alex a lot and he was still pulling on everything, I remembered Tess's tip and decided to wear a pair of dangling gold earrings I had worn a lot when Joel and I were dating. He used to tease me and say that they were fishing lures, and I was using them to catch him. I wondered if he would recognize them tonight.

One of the things that still bothered me from the unresolved argument Joel and I had a few nights ago was his accusation that I was "different" because I had lost weight, wore makeup, and stopped putting my hair up in a messy twist. He made it sound as if I had been doing those things for some other man. How could he miss the point that I was trying to spiff up my appearance for *him*? I wondered what he would think of the new top and the earrings.

It doesn't matter because tomorrow will be our day to get everything out in the open and resolved.

I needed an uncluttered heart.

And I need my husband back.

CHAPTER 22

Poppy and GiGi were already in the reserved room at the Blue Ginger when we arrived. Eden ran to hug them and told Poppy that we brought him a present, and she had made him not one card but two.

Poppy held up two fingers and grinned at her. "Two?"

"Yes." She mimicked the two fingers. "Two cards. For you, Poppy. Because I love you." Eden wrapped her arms around his leg, and I watched my father-in-law turn to mush.

I let Alex run around for a while because I knew he would be confined in his high chair for a long time. I left Eden with GiGi and followed my adventurous son around the back room. He had to examine the chairs, one leg of the table, and an edge of the tablecloth — and pick up the piece of something unidentified from the floor. I followed and monitored him until nearly all the other relatives arrived. Alex's older cousins wanted to squeeze his cheeks, pick him up, and feed him bread from the baskets delivered to the table.

My sister-in-law, Angela, sat Alex on her lap until he had downed the soft center from the piece of bread she gave him, and then he was determined to crawl across the table for more.

Everyone seemed to have an opinion about what Alex should do. The experienced moms warned against letting him fill up on bread. All the uncles told me to let him down so he could run around the room. I felt like I was locked into some sort of parallel universe where every other human on the planet was a clone of my husband, and I was the only one trying to maintain any sort of routine or control.

Just then, Joel appeared with four sharply dressed waiters who were filling our glasses and offering to place our cloth napkins on our laps.

"Welcome!" Joel stood behind his father and placed a hand on his shoulder. "I'm glad you're all here. Let's raise our glasses in a toast to the man we honor most in all the world. The man who raised us, who still puts up with us, and is the man who puts *that* smile on our mother's face. Yeah, that's the smile. That one, right there. To Poppy!"

We cheered and toasted, and the birthday feast began with family-style platters of fabulous looking and smelling food.

"Put the salmon there." Joel caught my eye as my favorite dish on the menu was placed in the middle of the table in front of me.

I smiled at Joel. He was shining. He looked happy that his family could see him in his domain. I thought of how well suited Joel was for being the manager-owner master of ceremonies. He needed to be noticed, not hidden in the kitchen.

Eden had to go to the bathroom, so I slid out with her. When we returned, I finally got my son back and put him into his highchair next to me. I calmed him with a sippy cup I had brought with me. The chair on the other side of me was left empty, in hopes that Joel would sit with us at some point. Eden was on the other side of that chair, and GiGi was next to Eden, telling her what all the yummy foods on the table were. I almost let out a cheer when Eden tried three of the items GiGi put on her plate.

The meal was superb. The conversation, lively as always. I could tell that Poppy was loving every minute. Joel was right. This was the thing we could give Poppy that would make him happy.

A beautiful, big birthday cake with many candles was delivered to our table on a dessert cart. Eden squealed with delight and helped Poppy blow the candles out. The ribbing about hurrying up before setting off the smoke detectors and the round of applause were silenced when two waiters sliced the cake and delivered generous wedges around the table.

Joel slid into the seat next to me, still wearing his chef's jacket. "Did I miss anything?" he teased.

"This was wonderful," I said. "All of it was so good, Joel."

He took a bite of cake, leaned back with his arm resting on the back of my chair, and seemed like the second happiest man on the planet — his father being the first. The conversation rolled on, with lots of praise for Joel and lots of comments as Poppy opened his cards and gifts.

"You look stunning," Joel said. "Is that a new outfit?"

I nodded.

He smiled. "I've missed those fishing lures." I thought he was about to kiss me. Our moment was broken by an outburst from Alex, who had reached his limit.

322

Angela offered to take him. I gladly let her. Now that her kids were way beyond the cuddling stage, she seemed to crave the snuggles of my son, regardless of how sticky he was at this point.

Eden had come over and crawled onto Joel's lap. One of her older cousins across the table was playing a game on his dad's cell phone. Eden wanted to do the same.

"So that's why you came to sit on my lap. I don't have my phone with me." Joel turned to me. "Do you still have those kids' games on your phone?"

I didn't like giving Eden a phone to occupy her, but the dinner had been long, and I knew Joel wanted a chance to sit and visit with his family. I pulled my phone out of my purse and handed it to him. "There's an alphabet game on there in the game file."

Joel tapped and swiped, telling Eden she didn't need to help him. "I'll get it ready for you, then you can have Mommy's phone. There. It's opening. Wait. There's a message."

"Daddy, I can do it."

Joel didn't reply to Eden. I turned and saw that his face was going gray.

The realization of what had just happened crashed down on me. I reached for my phone, but it felt as if my arm moved in slow motion. It was too late. The game he had opened by mistake was the one I had played with Garrett. I had forgotten all about it; I had never deleted it.

The game opened to the last message. I could see the words on the screen as Joel held it just out of Eden's reach.

Thanks for spending tonight with me, Jennie. Love you.

Without a word, Joel handed me my phone in a civilized manner. Calmly lifting Eden, he transferred her to my lap. He stood, gave his dad and mom a hug and a kiss, and made an apology for having to get back to work.

With a massive lump in my throat, I watched Joel as he strode away from me, from his children, from his parents, and from his family. He disappeared into the welcoming kitchen — the kitchen that had been my competition for the last two years.

I sat in heart-pounding, aching silence until Eden's wiggles were too much for me to contain. With a courageous fake smile and farewell to all the relatives, I gathered up both my children and hustled them out to the car and back to the familiar fortress of our home.

I texted Joel. I called him. I called the restaurant and asked the hostess to let him know I needed him to call me. I put the kids to bed and waited for him to come home.

But Joel didn't come home.

Throughout the night, I huddled under a blanket on the couch, waiting, listening for the sound of his key in the front door. I checked my phone every few minutes. I cried off and on for hours.

The agony that gripped me was paralyzing. I didn't know where he was. I didn't know if I should contact his parents. I let my mind consider the very worst.

Around three in the morning, a slow-burning anger set in. His tactic of disappearing wasn't fair. He didn't know all the facts. Only an assumption. If he was going to judge me and alienate me due to what he thought the message meant, then he was the one in the wrong. He was being jealous and petty and was out of line.

I made a cup of coffee and found that it fueled my thoughts on what I would say when I saw him. Even though he was supposed to have Monday off, I wondered if he might go into work or if he might even still be at the restaurant. I imagined going to the Blue Ginger and pounding on the locked doors.

Where is he? Where did he go?

For the next few hours, I fluctuated between being furious with him and being worried about him. I thought about how Joel's tactic was to step away from an escalating conflict. He put time and space between the outburst and the resolution. We had established a routine of letting our arguments become neutralized during the separation.

I now saw clearly how our pattern of coping had never given us space to resolve issues. We didn't dismantle our conflicts, examine the patterns, and mutually discover the source. We just went on.

Only this time we weren't going on. We weren't going anywhere.

My mind and my body were beyond exhausted when first light snuck in through the window over the kitchen sink. I knew Alex would be awake soon. If the reason for my exhaustion were different, I would see if GiGi and Poppy could watch the kids at their house so I could sleep. But that would invite too many questions. Besides, I didn't know if Joel was staying with them or what he already had told them.

My guess was that he hadn't turned to his parents. Not on his dad's birthday and not in light of the way his mom had been advocating for us to spend time together.

Joel had a thing about not airing our personal stuff to his parents. He wanted us to be us.

Ironic. We're not "us" right now, are we?

I made another strong cup of coffee and felt like a zombie as I went through the morning routine with Alex and Eden.

"Mommy doesn't feel well today," I told Eden. "Can you be a big girl and help me with your brother?"

"Sure, Mommy. Can I make you a feel better card? Alex can help me."

"Maybe later. Eat your breakfast first. You and Alex can watch a movie this morning."

"Yeah!"

Eden's cheer brought on the headache that had been pushing at my temples for hours. I went on a hunt in the vitamin cupboard and downed the pain medication with the rest of my coffee. I couldn't eat anything. I couldn't think. I had no tears left to squeeze out, and the flame of my anger in the early morning hours had smoldered to embers.

I slogged through the morning, still anticipating that Joel would walk through the door at any moment. I tried to remember all the explanations I had rehearsed throughout the long night.

The waited-for chime sounded on my

phone a little after ten, and I felt my heart leap. The text was from Tess, not Joel.

Dear DOEs, I don't need any of you to say anything right now. You can all have at it with me later. I just needed to tell you that I agreed to see Rick tonight. Don't judge me. Don't call me. Just pray, please. I think I know what I'm doing. We'll see.

I stared at the screen.

Alex was wailing in the background. Eden tried to pick him up. I had no place to put Tess's announcement in my exhausted mind. I kept going, focusing on my own personal mess.

If I had shared my messy story with the DOEs, I could text them now the way Tess did and ask them to pray for me too.

I decided to text Christy. I typed out a few words about how I needed prayer, too, but then I deleted it. I wasn't sure why.

By noon, when my texts to Joel continued to be ignored, I decided I could leave as easily as he could. I could pack up the kids, find a hotel, and disappear too. That way, when he finally tried to call me or when he decided to come home, he would be the one lost in a fog of confusion.

I'm sure I wasn't thinking clearly when I packed a suitcase for the kids and me and drove with no idea where we would go. All I knew was that I couldn't stay in my beautiful prison of a home and wait any longer.

I drove around for a while. Alex fell asleep in his car seat. I pulled into the drive-through of a coffee stand and ordered a blended iced mocha for me and a juice and cookie for Eden. She was elated.

"Where are we going now, Mommy? Can we go to the park?"

"Not today, Eden."

"Can we go to see Hana and Cole again? Pleeeeease?"

I hadn't texted Christy and asked her to pray, but somehow I knew that if I showed up on her doorstep, she would let me in. At this point that seemed like the answer to prayer that I needed.

I turned toward the coast and waited at the familiar intersection of 32nd and Newport with my blinker on. My thoughts were all over the place. The light for the cross traffic turned yellow, and two more cars hurried to get through. One of them was our car. Joel's car. Our Lexus.

I watched him drive through the intersection. He was focused, jaw set, looking straight ahead.

All my defenses crumbled. For the first time in the churning of all my thoughts and feelings throughout the night, I asked myself, *What if it were me?*

What if I had been the one who found an affectionate-sounding message on Joel's phone from one of his old girlfriends? What if I believed something was going on that he'd never told me about?

The car behind me honked. I looked in the rearview mirror with a scowl and then realized they were honking because the light had turned green. I needed to turn right.

Slowly driving toward Christy's house, I wondered if Joel had stayed with them last night. Was Todd and Christy's home his haven too? What if Joel was driving home now? What if he expected me to be there and wanted to talk?

Should I go home?

I decided to see if Christy could watch the kids for me. If Joel hadn't been there, I didn't need to tell her all my woes. I could just ask the favor and assure her that I would be back in a couple of hours.

If Joel had been there, if Christy and Todd knew all the messy details, then I definitely wanted her counsel. I had run out of everything, including objectivity. It would not be good for me to go home and meet Joel there in my present state.

Christy's car was in the driveway. I circled around through the narrow alleyway close to their house and found a parking spot, which is always a miracle in that neighborhood.

"I'm going to play princess dance with Hana," Eden said. "Mommy, did you bring my tutu?"

"No, Eden. Hold on a minute. I have to check with Auntie Christy to make sure she's home."

I sent a short text and received a quick reply. I'm home. Do you want to come over?

Yes. I'm already here. I got out and released Eden from her seat. I tried to unbuckle Alex without waking him, but my jostling was too much. He woke confused and mad and cried all the way to Christy's front door.

When I rang the doorbell, Christy called out for me to come in. We entered and found her seated at the kitchen counter with her laptop in front of her.

"Say hi to Katie," she called out over the sound of Alex's wails.

"Hi, Katie." I hoped I didn't sound as rattled as I felt. I pointed to Christy's refrigerator, and she nodded.

Helping myself to an applesauce snack tube, I opened it and handed it to Alex. His crying stopped. I pulled one out for myself, since I realized all I had consumed that day had been lots of coffee.

"Where's Hana?" Eden asked.

"She's at school, sweetheart. You can play in her room, if you want."

Four-year-old Cole was playing with trucks on the living room rug. He abandoned them and explained to Eden what she couldn't touch in Hana's room. In true little-brother form, he followed Eden upstairs.

The house suddenly seemed quiet after our rowdy arrival. I leaned over Christy's shoulder and waved at Katie, trying to appear composed. Alex was still in my arms. He reached for the laptop as if Katie were on a show for him to watch.

In a way, she was.

"Hi, Jennalyn. Hi, Alex. Look at you! You're such a big boy now. Wowee!" Katie waved at him. In the background her cottage appeared dark and very quiet for a home with three boys under the age of five. I realized it was the middle of the night in Kenya.

"I'm going to go and let you guys talk. Christy can tell you our big news," Katie said.

"Another baby?" I ventured.

"No!" Her green eyes grew wide, and she leaned in closer to the camera. "Jennalyn, please, don't even joke about that."

"Sorry!" As distraught as I was, I couldn't help but smile at Katie's wild-woman expression.

"No apology needed. Just . . . just pray for us and our little circus."

"Bye, Katie girl." Christy blew her a kiss, and Katie returned the gesture right before the screen went dark.

Alex leaned over and tried to reach the keyboard to make the Katie show come back on. Christy quickly closed the laptop and moved it into the guest room. When she opened the guest room door, I peeked in. The bed appeared slept in and was unmade.

Maybe Joel did stay here last night.

Christy returned with a concerned expression. She held out her arms to Alex, and he went to her without hesitation. "Is it okay if I give him a rice cake?"

I nodded.

Christy pulled her kids' old high chair from the corner and put Alex in it. She gave him a rice cake from the bag on the counter and then came over and gave me a lingering hug.

"You know, don't you?" I asked.

She pulled back and nodded, her expression showing concern. "You okay?"

"No."

"He stayed here last night," Christy said.

"I saw him turning at 32nd. Did he go home?"

"I think so. He was out on the beach for a while, but then I noticed his car was gone. I've been talking to Katie for a bit, so maybe he didn't want to interrupt to tell me he was leaving."

"It's such a mess, Christy. *I'm* such a mess."

"Do you need something more to eat?"

"No. I just need to talk to him. More importantly, I need him to listen to me."

"Then go home. He's probably there. Go. It's fine. The kids will be fine here."

"Are you sure?"

"Of course."

"Thank you, Christy." I hugged her again. "Pray."

"I am." She gave me a comforting smile.

Before I left, I turned and asked, "Was he really mad? Do you think he's still mad?"

"I think he was hurt. And confused."

"What did you tell him?"

"After he came here around ten thirty last night, he and Todd sat up for a couple of hours and talked," Christy said. "I didn't stay in the room, but I could hear bits of their conversation. I didn't think it would help if Joel knew that you had confided in me about Garrett. It might have hurt him more that you had told me but hadn't told him the details yet."

I thought about Christy's comment and decided it made sense.

"Todd didn't know any of the things you shared with me. I hadn't told him any of it. So, I think Todd and Joel mostly talked about how the two of you can work through this so that you come out closer to each other."

"Joel doesn't know, then. He doesn't know that nothing happened. He's still assuming I . . ." My throat felt like it was swelling the way it had at the restaurant. "I should go."

Christy nodded. "Joel loves you, Jennalyn. He really does. Remember that. Go share your heart with him. Your whole heart."

CHAPTER 23

The first tear crested as I hurried out Christy's front door and fumbled for my keys. I drove home by the shortest route, through a residential area. My chest ached, and my heart thumped uncomfortably as I pulled into our driveway behind Joel's car. I took a deep breath. After gathering my thoughts and emotions, I slowly stepped out and walked up the sidewalk. The front door was unlocked.

I found Joel in the kitchen, sitting at the counter. He had a glass of something in his hand and was swirling the ice cubes around inside. The faint clinking reverberated inside me as if amplified ten times as it traveled across the room.

"Joel, I'm sorry." My voice was steady. I took a few steps closer. I hadn't expected to lead with an apology, but I was glad that was the first thing that tumbled out of my heart.

Joel sat staring at the counter. "I'm sorry too."

Neither of us said anything for a moment. I knew this couldn't turn into one of our usual tiffs where we spoke the expected "I'm sorry" and then just went on.

"Joel, I need to explain."

He turned his head slowly, looking at me for the first time. "Did you sleep with him?"

"No!" I took five swift steps and stood next to my husband, looking him in the eye with a sense of rising fury. "Absolutely not. Nothing like that happened. Why would you —"

"Then explain why he would thank you for spending the night with him."

I remembered the message Joel had seen on the game app and ached inside even more when I realized what my husband must have been thinking all this time.

"Because," I paused, drawing in a calming breath. "Joel, I need to explain everything. Then it will make sense."

I pulled my phone out of my purse and opened the game app. I hadn't deleted it last night because I wanted Joel to see the whole conversation.

"After I saw Garrett at Eden's dance class, he messaged me and asked for my address so he could send me pictures he had of my mom."

Joel sat up straight. "Did you give him our address?"

"No."

"Has he been in our house?"

"No. Just let me explain."

I told Joel about the word game, the pictures he had of my mom, and how my heart went out to him when I found out his mom had died. I showed Joel the entire back and forth exchange that had taken place on those nights when I was so alone. He read each word slowly, scrolling up and going back several times to reread parts of the long dialogue. I sat beside him at the counter, feeling an odd mix of humiliation and indignation.

If Joel knew me, if he trusted me, he never would have asked if I slept with Garrett.

Joel reached the end of the feed and looked up at me. "Why did he say 'Love you'?"

"I don't know. I think he was trying to see how I would respond. You can see, I didn't respond. That was the end of the conversation."

"Did he ever give you any pictures of your mom?"

"Yes, he brought them to the recital. They're upstairs. I can show them to you, if you want."

"No, I believe you." He clenched and unclenched his jaw. "Was there anything else going on?"

"No." I wanted the tension and the conversation to end there. I wanted this to be over. I wanted to delete the game app in front of my husband and then turn the tables and release all my anger at the way he had treated me by leaving and not answering my calls all night.

"Nothing else happened."

I felt a nudge inside. This was my chance to get everything out. So I kept going. I told Joel how I had hunted for my yearbook and about the many nights when I crawled into a dark cave inside. I tried to explain how going there made my mom feel somehow closer because I held memories of Garrett in there too.

"I know that probably doesn't make sense. And I want you to know that I don't feel that way now. I want to keep everything out in the light and not hidden." I took a breath. "That's why I also need to tell you that I had a dream about him. We were at the park, and he had his arm around me and was offering me his soda."

"And then what?"

"That was all. I woke up."

Joel seemed more relaxed, but I wasn't

sure how he was taking all this. "Is there anything else?"

The only thing I could think of was that I had let Garrett carry Alex to the car. I told Joel, finishing my full disclosure down to the last drop by telling him how Garrett had thumped on the roof and said "To infinity and beyond."

During my long account of every detail, Joel had listened with the same expression. He was serious, thoughtful, as if he were taking it all in with a few flinches of anger mixed with a sadness in his eyes.

However, when I revealed the last part about "to infinity and beyond," Joel's eyes narrowed, and he looked down at his emptied glass. The side of his jaw flinched. He turned his lowered head and looked at me with his eyebrows raised and a repressed grin rising on his lips.

"To infinity and beyond?" he repeated.

I nodded.

My husband burst out laughing.

"What?"

He kept laughing; I didn't understand why. I had just emptied my heart to him, and he was chuckling.

"Joel, what is so funny?" I swatted him on the arm.

"To infinity and beyond!" he said in a comical voice.

I tried not to flinch, but when Joel looked into my eyes he must have seen how hurt I was because he dialed it back.

"I'm sorry." He took me by the shoulders and looked at me tenderly. "You have to admit, though, come on, that is the worst pickup line ever."

I wanted to agree with him and let myself smile, but a sense of self-protection had kicked in when he laughed. "It wasn't a pickup line. It was a high school thing. You can't tell me you didn't have any high school things like that."

Joel stroked his chin, still playing the comic, looking like he was trying hard to remember.

"You just don't understand because you were never serious about any of the girls you dated in high school. You were a big clown about romance, the way you're being right now. You don't get it."

Joel put up his hands in defense. "You're right. I don't get it. But what I do understand, as a man, is that he wanted more from you and you didn't see that."

I blinked but didn't have a clear enough thought in my head to reply. Part of me wanted to let it be done with and join in a round of laughter with Joel. Another part of me wanted to yell at him. I wanted to list all the ways he had failed to see me, hear me, know me. I wanted to make an earnest defense for why he should value me and care about my life, my world.

But I couldn't pull up any of the rage I had felt earlier. I was exhausted. All I wanted to do was shut down.

Joel's expression sobered when he saw that I was withdrawing and staring at him like I was trying to remember my own name.

He reached out and took my hand in his. "I'm sorry I laughed. I'm sure it was painful for you. You trusted the guy when you were young, and he betrayed your trust. You tried to figure out how to relate to him as an adult, and you didn't have anyone walking through that with you. I can see how hurtful and painful that could be."

I drew in a deep breath and reached over for Joel's glass, downing the last drops. It tasted like pineapple juice with a spritz of ginger ale. The bright burst gave me enough clarity to look at him.

"Thank you for telling me everything, Jennalyn," he said. "I didn't mean to make light of anything you told me."

"I wish I had told you sooner, Joel. I should have. I shut down and didn't include you in that part of my life. I feel like I left you. Not physically, but emotionally. Part of me divorced myself from you." I hadn't fully formed that thought until this moment. I was surprised at how raw and vulnerable I could be with him now that everything was out in the open.

"Joel, will you please forgive me?"

He paused before meeting my gaze. "Yes, I forgive you."

Neither of us spoke for a moment. We were used to apologizing. Asking for forgiveness felt different. Deeper and more freeing.

"Listen," Joel said. "I don't know what it's like to lose my mother, obviously. I don't have any of the shared feelings or the ability to empathize the way he did. Whenever you can help me to understand what you're going through, I appreciate it."

I nodded.

"What I do understand is the pull, the luring away from what is, and the temptation mentally and physically to pursue someone else. Do you understand what I'm saying?"

"Yes."

"It's intense for men. You know that."

"It can be intense for women too."

"I can't tell you how many times a day I remind myself that I chose you, Jennalyn. I chose our family, I chose our life together. Anytime you're struggling that way, I want you to tell me."

Even though I felt released after sharing so openly with Joel, and even though I sensed a freedom because of his forgiveness, part of me felt that he needed to understand more fully the struggles I had gone through.

"Sometimes it's hard for me to know what to say to you. I mean, I could sit here right now and admit that I'm struggling with grief over my mother, or that I'm having a hard time with my hormones and emotions. I could tell you that I'm lonely." I pulled my hand away from his and sat up straight. "The truth is, I'm not sure it would help. I don't know that it would make a difference to say any of those things to you because it hasn't made a difference between us for a long time."

Joel's expression remained solemn. "I know. But would you be willing to try? Because when you do let me in, it gives me a chance to at least try to understand."

I didn't answer right away.

A sadness seemed to come over him. "I'm sure you're thinking that you can't tell me things like this because I'm gone all the time."

"That's not what I was thinking." My wearied thoughts were a swirl, and I wasn't clear on anything other than that I didn't want us to go back to the way things had been.

"It's still something we need to address. I know I become defensive when you say that I'm never home. It's true, though. I haven't been here. I think part of me divorced you, too, when work became the most important thing in my life. My priorities have been twisted." Joel rubbed the back of his neck. "I can see how I made a lot of choices that put our family out of balance. I'm sorry, Jennalyn."

He reached for my hand again. "Will you forgive me?"

"Yes, I forgive you."

"I should have called you back last night. Please forgive me for not making myself available to you. Not just last night, but for the past year or more. I haven't been there for you. Not even when Alex was born."

"It means so much to me that you just said that, Joel. I forgive you. I know you've been trying. When Alex was born, none of us knew he was going to come when he did. Please don't think you should apologize for that."

"Okay, maybe not for missing Alex's birth. But I could have done other things differently over the last few years. A lot of things. I haven't been a team player. I haven't loved you the way I should. I want that to change."

"So do I."

The cleansing tears came effortlessly for both of us. I couldn't remember the last time we had both been so vulnerable and honest. We knew how to be uncovered and open with each other physically. Learning how to do that emotionally and mentally was new.

"Come here." Joel stood and opened his arms to me. I rose and rested my head on his shoulder. We wrapped our arms around each other, clinging tightly and whispering to each other all the deeper feelings our hearts were telling us to say.

I felt as if Joel and I had found our way back into each other's confidence and trust, into the deeper essence of who we both were at heart. A lot of truth was spoken between us that night, and I felt so free.

I also felt depleted. Beyond exhausted.

"Why don't you go to bed?" Joel said. "I'll bring up some toast for you. Do you want tea? Water?"

"Just water. A piece of toast would be nice."

"Slightly crunchy around the edges with honey melting into all the little holes?"

I looked into my husband's face. He remembered. "Yes, please. That's how I like my toast."

"I know." He grinned and added, "I'll be up in a minute, and then I'll pick up the kids. Are they at my parents?"

"No. I took them over to Christy's. I didn't think you would want your parents to know we were having an argument."

Joel kissed me. "Thank you. I love my family, but they don't need to know everything about our lives."

"I agree."

Our bed felt so good. I drank most of the water and had three bites of the toast before turning off the light and falling into a deep sleep. Sometime later I heard Joel coming to bed. I didn't ask about the kids, or what time it was. I kept my eyes closed and went back to sleep, only slightly aware of Joel's steady hand resting on my shoulder.

The world I awoke to on Tuesday morning was a different world than the one I had pushed through since Sunday night when I had left Poppy's birthday party. I felt unencumbered.

I set up my paints and nice paper on the kitchen counter and was working on the invitations for the Spring Fling beach picnic when Joel came into the kitchen with Alex in his arms. The two of them were playing a game in which Alex planted a slobbery kiss on Joel's face and then pulled back and laughed. Our happy boy did it over and over until Joel was belly-laughing too.

Catching his breath, Joel tried to pull away from the kissing bug. "Where does he come up with this stuff?"

I grinned. This was the life I had dreamed of.

Leaning over my shoulder, Joel glanced at the words I was lettering on the invitations.

SECOND ANNUAL

Daughters of Eve
Spring
Fling

WHERE: Sierra's Secret Beach
WHEN: Saturday, March 22, 5 p.m.

BRING:
A favorite treat to eat
and
A favorite bit of décor

"What are you going to take as your food item?" Joel asked.

"I don't know yet. Do you have any ideas?" Before Joel could answer, I remembered some of the sillier suggestions I had made when we first started to plan our gathering. I scrolled through a long group text. "I volunteered quail eggs with figs and cream."

Joel gave me an odd look.

"It was a joke. We were trying to come up with a theme. I think we were leaning toward all things *Downton Abbey* at that point."

"Figs and cream," Joel repeated. He put down Alex and pulled out one of his old cookbooks.

"It was only a joke," I said.

He shot me a playfully dramatic look. "Don't ever joke with me about food."

I grinned and finished adding the watercolor embellishment to the last invitation.

"Here we go." He smoothed down the page. "Figs and cream. Okay, hmmm. Mascarpone. Interesting. Oh, yeah. This looks good."

"Have you ever had figs and cream?"

"No, let's make it tonight. You and me."

I couldn't believe he was inviting me to cook with him. An invitation to share kitchen space with my husband was like being invited into Fort Knox to see where all the money was kept.

"We'll need some ingredients," Joel said. "Would you like me to take the kids with me to the grocery store to buy what we need?"

"Okay. Yes, sure. If you can wait a few minutes, these invitations will be dry. Would you mind mailing them for me? They have to go out this morning."

"I would be glad to."

When I helped Joel load the kids into the car, I couldn't believe how excited they were to go somewhere with Daddy. It reminded me of when Todd had taken Hana and Cole out for ice cream before dinner. At the time I thought I never would want Joel to do that with our kids. Now I loved that he was adding his own version of "pop-up events" to our family and giving our children great memories of their childhood, including their dad being around and involved and fun.

I used the free time to take a true shower. I shaved my legs, let the conditioner stay on my hair for two minutes, and even used a loofah on my rough heels. I looked at my naked toenails and said aloud, "It's time."

I wanted to start the mom and daughter pedicure tradition with Christy and Hana. I wanted fresher springtime beginnings.

Once I was out of the shower, I texted Christy and suggested we schedule our mother-daughter pedis. I opened the DOEs group text and told them the invitations for the Spring Fling were being mailed that morning.

Then I added the question none of the others had asked yet, which surprised me. I asked Tess how things had gone with Rick. Her reply came back while I was drying my hair.

I will tell all on Saturday.

I frowned and wanted to ask for more info. What would our favorite woman of options tell us on Saturday that she couldn't tell us now? I was nervous. It didn't make sense to me why she had decided to meet with him in the first place. Unless she intended to keep the relationship going. I thought about how I felt no need to have further communication with Garrett. Not that it was the same thing, but I felt that both Tess and I needed to protect our impressionable hearts.

As I dressed, I thought about how disconnected I was from Garrett. The game app had been deleted the same night I had shown it to Joel. If Garrett tried to message me through any other social media, he would be blocked. I put him into what Joel called the no-fly zone so that it would be clear to him that I had closed the door into my life.

The powerful part was that thinking of him didn't bring any feelings to the surface. Not good feelings, not bad — nothing. All the emotions had been unplugged. Diffused. He was no longer in my head and most certainly not in my heart. Memories like the prom had settled into a coming-of-age image in my mind that carried no complicated messages. I saw the past as *then* and my life in the present as *now.* My choice each day was to live in the now.

As for the dark cave where memories of Garrett and my mom had mingled in the deepest corner of my soul, that space had been filled with light. Haunting spirits can't float about in the light. Everything I remembered about Mom was now in the open air, alive and well in my thoughts. Nothing remained in the darkness.

I glanced at my reflection in the mirror and smiled softly. She was very much alive.

One day, I would see her again.

"I love you, Mom. I always have, and I always will." My voice was a whisper. A steady, confident whisper.

CHAPTER 24

I noticed a sense of calm during dinner and bath time that night. Our kids were different when their dad was home and connecting with them. They were happier, and so was I. I tried to describe the difference to Joel after the kids were in bed. He had his beloved fifty-year-old cookbook open and all the ingredients for figs and cream lined up on the counter.

Instead of diving into the prep work, Joel stood with both palms resting on the counter. "I've been doing a lot of thinking about work," he said. "Would you mind if I talked through a couple of things with you?"

"I would love it."

"I'm thinking about stepping into the manager position full time and putting Vincent on as head chef."

"That's a big decision," I said.

"I know."

Joel glanced at me. "What do you think?"

My heart did a little flutter. It had been so long since Joel had asked my opinion on anything related to his business. When we were only dreaming of a future restaurant for him, he asked my opinion on everything. Then the kids came, and he immersed himself in the world he was creating at the Blue Ginger. At that point our lives became more and more separated.

"I think you love to cook, and you will cook and bake and come up with delicious recipes for the rest of your life. It's in you, and it's not going to go away."

"What about the managing part?"

"You're good at that too. The question is, Do you love it? Do you love being a part owner and having the final say on things like the new stove and who you hire?"

"I do."

"Which do you love the most?"

Joel thought a moment. "If I was twenty-five, I would say I love being a chef more than anything. However, I'm going to be forty next year."

"I know." I grinned. "I'm going to be married to an old man."

Joel ignored my attempt at teasing him and stayed on topic. "I've learned a lot about the business side this past year. I would like to learn more. I like managing. I like being the boss." Joel grinned. "So, what do you think?"

"I'm one hundred percent in favor of you pursuing what you love to do. I'm also one thousand percent in favor of you having a life that encompasses us, your family. We want you, Joel. We want you to lead us."

"That's why I'm trying to make the change." Joel described how he was going to write his own job description. He already had talked with his assistant manager, and the two of them were coming up with a business plan and restructuring model.

"I would make a couple of other staff changes in the kitchen. I might even change the name of the restaurant and adjust the menu. I wouldn't do it all at once."

"When would all this start?"

He lifted his hands to me, palms open, as if inviting a response. "It will start whenever my life partner tells me she thinks it's the way to go."

I hadn't expected that. I answered him with the first thought that came to mind. "Maybe we should pray about it. Together. I mean, I think it's a good idea. But we should pray about stuff like this, right?"

"You're right. Absolutely right. Come here."

I went to the other side of the counter and

put my hand in his. Joel prayed with more confidence than I think I had ever heard from him. When he ended with "Amen," he gave my hand a squeeze. "Promise me you'll keep giving input if you have any insights into all this."

"Okay." I looked closely at my husband. "Joel, don't take this the wrong way, but what happened to you? Why are you being so attentive?"

He slapped his open palm to his chest as if I had wounded him. "Oh, that hurt!" The smile hidden in the corner of his eyes let me know that he was teasing. I still felt a little timid after the highs and lows of the last few days.

"All I meant was that you've changed."

"I knew what you meant." Joel pulled the hand mixer out of the cupboard and popped in the two blades. "So here's the truth. Please, don't take this the wrong way."

I waited, not sure how this was going to go.

"When I left the restaurant Sunday night, I wanted to leave. Go far away. I imagined the worst. I had been feeling so much pressure for so long, I thought the only way to be free would be to go. To be done with you, the kids, everything. I just wanted to get away."

I watched his profile as he spoke and felt sick to my stomach. Joel never said things like that. He rarely told me what he was feeling. What he said was raw and honest, but for a moment, his truth frightened me.

Joel put the ingredients into a mixing bowl. I knew he wasn't angry. He bakes when he's happy, not when he's mad. He even said once that if you cook out of anger you can taste it in the food. I knew that he loved to create out of his own contentment, the way I paint and sketch out of a place of my own personal bliss. When I was at peace, the art flowed from me.

"Are you okay with me saying this?" Joel asked. "I don't want to bum you out."

"You're not. I understand the feelings. Go ahead."

"When I left the restaurant, I drove around and found a drive-through coffee place. I was sitting in line, waiting to order, and I saw the love note you left on the seat. When I read it, I realized how off my thinking was, and how it has been off for a long time."

"What love note?" I asked softly.

"The one you drew with the word *love* and the verse."

I realized that I had taken his car to the movies with the DOEs and that my word-for-the-year card must have fallen out of my purse on the passenger's seat.

Joel recited the words I had penned from 1 Corinthians 13, looking like he had worked hard to memorize it. " 'Love never gives up, never loses faith, is always hopeful, and endures through every circumstance.' "

He looked at me. "I don't know when you left the card. It could have been weeks ago on Valentine's. But I didn't see it until Sunday night. It really got to me, Jennalyn, so thank you."

I smiled timidly and told him the card was my word for the year and how I had made one for all the DOEs. Those words were meant for my weary heart, and yet they found their way to Joel's.

He pressed the button on the mixer, blending the sugar, heavy cream, and mascarpone with expertise and a smile. He pulled a teaspoon from the drawer and tasted the mixture before setting the bowl aside to pull out what he called a simmering pot. He turned the flame on our gas stove to high, and I watched as he poured in the measured orange juice, balsamic vinegar, and orange zest.

"All I know is that I thought the message was for me," Joel said. "But I still wasn't

359

ready to come home. I didn't want to go to my parents' place. It didn't feel right to go to a hotel. The only safe person I could think of talking to was Todd. I'm just grateful that he answered my text and let me show up at his place. We talked for a couple of hours."

Joel lowered the heat and kept stirring, setting the timer for five minutes. He handed me a knife and the colander of rinsed fresh figs. "Down the center," he said. "And back in the colander."

I took that to be chef-talk for how to cut the figs and where to put them. He returned to the simmering pot and kept stirring.

"I showed Todd the card with the verse. I told him I was ready to give up, lose faith, abandon hope. He said I had an issue with love."

"What did he mean by that?" I knew Christy's husband could be direct and that he often had a big-picture, eternal sort of view on life. Even so, I had a hard time imagining Todd telling my husband that he had an issue with love.

"You know how I came to Christ right before I met you?" Joel said. "When I surrendered my life to God, I transferred my allegiance to the Lord. But maybe I didn't transfer my love."

360

"I'm still not sure what that means."

"Todd showed me the verse in Luke where Jesus told the disciples the most important thing was to love God."

I knew the verse he was referring to. I had read it when I was doing the search on the word *love*. I repeated it to Joel, " 'You must love the LORD your God with all your heart, all your soul, all your strength, and all your mind.' "

"That's the one." He looked at my sliced mound of figs. "Nicely done."

Joel took the colander of figs and slowly poured them into the fragrant glaze simmering in the pot. He had prepared a cookie sheet with parchment paper and set the oven to broil.

"My priorities got messed up. I would say that, when I was in my teens and twenties, I was in love with myself. I put myself first. Then I fell in love with you, and I put you first, or at least most of the time. When the restaurant opened, it became my first love. Does that make sense? I kept transferring my allegiance and worshipping what I thought was the most important thing in life at the time. With the restaurant, it was about being successful. Making my dad proud of me."

"Your parents are very proud of you."

He nodded slowly, thinking as he was cooking. I watched as Joel used tongs to remove each of the saturated fig halves and place them on the parchment paper, cut side up. He set the timer for six minutes and slid the tray into the oven.

"I don't think that's supposed to be my goal in life. I think I'm supposed to love God first, with my whole being. Then I'm to love my neighbor in the same way I love myself." Joel grinned. "And it just so happens, you are my closest neighbor."

"Hello, neighbor." I grinned back at him.

"I love you." He looked at me with clear-eyed sincerity. "You and the kids. And our family, friends, and coworkers. But I need to love God first. Do you know what I'm saying? I had it messed up."

I nodded and thought about all the times I had admired Christy and Todd's relationship. Their love for God and for each other seemed unwavering. Not that they didn't have difficulties, but I could see how they had the same foundation to go back to and rebuild together whenever the incoming grenades of life had blown holes in their relationship.

"After talking with Todd I knew I didn't want to have a life where I was off building my career while you're here alone building

362

a home and raising our children. We need to figure out how to do this together so that we're shoulder to shoulder, building our lives together."

"That's what I want too."

Joel's eyes and expression appeared the clearest, least burdened I had seen in years. I smiled at him and felt the blissful gift of springtime. Fresh new beginnings. Revived hope.

The timer chimed, and Joel pulled the caramelized figs from the oven.

"Those smell so good." I drew in another breath of their sweetness.

"Grab a couple of blankets," Joel said. "Let's take these out on the deck."

I pulled the throw blankets from the basket by the sofa and took them outside. Instead of turning on the bright security light, I went to the laundry room and found in the cupboard every tea candle, lantern, and battery-operated luminary I could find. I loaded them in a laundry basket and took them outside, scattering them on the deck around the two lounge chairs.

Joel joined me with the plate of warm figs now capped with fluffy mascarpone topping. He placed the plate on the low table between the two loungers and returned to the kitchen. Settling on a lounge chair under a blanket, I gazed up at the sky. A few stars were visible despite the glow that rose from our densely populated suburbs.

My mind was filling with artistic ideas of what we could do with this outdoor space.

When Joel came out balancing two cups of espresso on a small tray, I smiled.

"What?" he asked. "I know that look. You want to do something or make something, don't you?"

"You know it."

"I know you," he said. "I know your looks." Joel stretched out his legs. "And I like your looks very much." He grinned and reached for one of the warm figs, lifted it, and waited for me to salute him with mine. "Bon appétit."

We both closed our eyes. I took a bite and let the combination of flavors roll over my tongue and down my throat. "Wow," I murmured.

"Nice," he echoed. "I think I would add a pinch of nutmeg next time. Or a dash of clove. No, not clove — too strong. It needs something."

"I like it. It's different. I can't remember the last time I had a fig."

Joel tried another bite and followed it with a sip of his perfectly prepared frothy espresso. "A bit of crushed walnuts, I think.

That's what I'll try next time." He looked up. "Okay. I'm ready. Let's hear your creative idea."

I rambled. I know I did. I didn't need to go on and on, expressing every patio decorating idea that was flitting through my head. But Joel didn't mind. He listened, evaluating my ideas all the way through.

When I finished, he said, "How about if I get somebody out here this week to give us an estimate? You can describe the pergola and all the add-ons you're considering, and he can draw up the plans for whatever works best for this space."

"That would be wonderful."

My lips lingered on the edge of the demitasse espresso cup as I thought about what Joel had said in the kitchen.

"Can I ramble about something else?" I asked.

"Sure."

"When you were talking about loving God above all else, it helped me understand how I've been off track for years too. In high school, my focus was on Garrett. Then I transferred all my affection and loyalty to my mom. She was my closest friend. When you came into my life, you took over as my top priority. Over the last year, I think I shifted my first love to our children. I want to learn how to love God first too."

Joel reached out and took my hand.

"We'll figure it out together," he said. "We need to do a lot more talking. With each other, with the Lord. We can't go back to living two separate lives and only overlapping when we go to bed."

I gave his hand a squeeze. "I agree."

CHAPTER 25

The morning of our Spring Fling get-together, I found nothing in my closet that came close to the dress code Sierra had suggested. "Boho chic" was the name Emily gave it. Tess had added to the group text, "Spare not the accessories." I wasn't sure what the others were doing with Tess and Sierra's enthusiastic vision. My options were limited.

I dashed out with both kids and headed to the chain store by the dance studio. As I pushed the cart, I was grateful that Eden hadn't recognized the studio or brought up anything about Violet. She never had asked if her friend "By-let" could come play, the way she asked if she could go to Hana and Cole's house.

My quick grab was a floral-print maxi dress with bell sleeves and a long necklace that had a tassel and turquoise blue beads. Eden picked out the dress, which looked like something Sierra would wear, so I was feeling confident that my boho game was going to be strong that evening.

Joel came home at four. I was amazed that on a Saturday he could step away from the restaurant for the whole night. That had never happened before. The changes he was making were having an immediate effect.

He grinned when he saw me coming down the stairs in my flowing dress and several long necklaces, including the new one.

"Aren't you the belle of the ball," he said with a grin.

"She's not a bell," Eden said. "She's Mommy. Isn't she pretty?"

"She's beautiful." Joel still was grinning. "I like the flowers in your hair."

I had pulled a section of my hair to the side and made a single, narrow braid into which I had tucked half a dozen tiny blue flowers that grew on a bush we ignored on the side of the house.

"What about me, Daddy? Don't I look pretty too?"

Eden had joined the dress up fun and put on a dress over the top of her Christmas nightgown from GiGi. The nightgown was the longest "dress" in her closet. I guessed the extra dress was her idea of how to make her outfit look flowy. She wore a colored macaroni necklace that she had made last summer with Emily's daughter, Audra.

"You look very beautiful too," Joel said.

Eden beamed and gave us a twirl.

"Do you need help loading anything?" Joel asked.

"No, Sierra is setting up the beach table, and Christy is bringing the pillows. Everyone is bringing something. I have the food ready to go."

The doorbell rang. Joel reached over and opened the door. Christy was standing there, and the moment we saw each other, our mouths opened, and we burst out laughing.

We had on the same dress.

"Where did you get yours?" she asked.

I told her the store and confessed that I had grabbed it at eleven that morning.

"That's where I got mine. Last night."

Joel didn't seem to get why going to a party in matching outfits was funny, but Christy and I thought it was hilarious.

I kissed my sweethearts goodbye, and Christy and I took her car, which was loaded with pillows and blankets in the back seat. We were in Corona del Mar and nearly to the remote beach cove that Sierra had suggested as our picnic location when Christy said, "I almost forgot to tell you the good news. The deadline to register for the marriage retreat was yesterday and . . ."

"You're going? You got the money in time to register?"

"Yes! Todd is doing a backyard-deck renovation or something like that in Costa Mesa. The work doesn't start until we get back, but they paid him ahead of time. It's crazy. He said he knew the guy, and Todd is looking forward to working on it. I'm so grateful."

I smiled and said I was so happy for her. That was all I said.

Todd had recommended a contractor to Joel for building the pergola and the other additions we wanted to make to our deck. Todd had worked for the guy a few years ago, before Todd started teaching. In turn, Joel had requested that Todd be the one to do the building. I was surprised that the arrangements had been made so quickly.

Christy would find out soon enough that the project was our backyard. Until then, I loved seeing how excited she was about Maui. I was getting excited too.

We found a good parking place near the remote beach. Before we left the car, Christy handed me a small gift bag that she pulled out of her purse.

"Here. I wasn't sure when I would give

this to you. I found it the other day, and I had to buy it for you."

"Christy . . ."

"Remember what Tess said? You never protest when a sister gives you a gift. You say thank you, you give her a little kiss on the cheek, and then you wear it like you deserve to look as gorgeous on the outside as you are on the inside."

I grinned and opened the bag. Inside was a bottle of nail polish. "This is so sweet. For our mother-daughter pedis. Thank you, Christy." I leaned over and gave her the little kiss on the cheek as Tess had taught us.

Christy was still grinning, waiting and watching my reaction.

I looked at the polish again. It was red. I turned the bottle over and read the name, even though I didn't need to. I knew what the label would say.

"Oh My, Cherry Pie."

Christy smiled broadly. The glistening tears in her eyes matched mine.

"This might be the best gift anyone has ever given me."

"I'm glad you like it," Christy whispered. She hugged me, and as we pulled apart, our long necklaces tangled together.

We laughed hard. I had to remove the turquoise tassel necklace and loop it around her neck since it was caught on one she was wearing.

We were still laughing as we toted our baskets of food down to the beach. The moment Sierra and Emily looked up and saw Christy and me coming toward them in our matching long dresses, they stopped setting up the low beach table and stared. Their wide-eyed expressions changed to a moment of confusion as they glanced at each other and then back at us.

Christy caught on to their reaction sooner than I did and laughed. "Before you ask, the answer is no. We didn't plan this!"

Emily returned with us to Christy's car, and all three of us filled our arms with the assortment of pillows and blankets. We heard our names and turned to see Tess as she strolled toward us.

Her off-the-shoulder peasant-style embroidered top was cinched by a wide leather belt around her narrow waist. The full tapestry-like skirt skimmed the ground as she came toward us on red and purple slippers with stars appliqued on the toes. She looked as if she were modeling for an elegant gypsy woman magazine. No one in the world could pull off an outfit like that and look regal the way Tess did. A wide silk scarf held back her hair, with the long tail flowing over her bare shoulder.

Before any of us could summon a hello, Tess stopped, pointed at Christy and me, and said, "Hey, I have that dress! In yellow."

Our mixed laughter sounded like wind chimes to me on the gorgeous evening as we set up our special gathering in Sierra's recommended hideaway. She had brought a long, low table that was set up on the sand. It was covered with a swath of sky-blue fabric. Tess brought candles, including two white tapers in mismatched candleholders. She gave up trying to light the candles since the breeze off the water kept blowing them out.

"Guess I didn't think about that," Emily said. "Good thing everyone else brought something to help hold down the tablecloth."

Tess added a gorgeous low floral centerpiece with exotic-looking tropical flowers. Christy put her small-sized white plates at each place setting. I had brought our initial mugs but left them in my basket because Christy had brought peach-tinted juice glasses.

To Sierra's delight, Tess had brought her blue goblets with the polka dots and several small ceramic bowls that she said were for our olive pits. I had a pretty good idea that she had created one of her scrumptious charcuterie boards for us.

I helped Christy spread out the beach blankets on the sand on either side of the table and scatter all the colorful pillows so we could recline on them like ladies of leisure in our flowing outfits.

I commented on Emily's cute outfit as she was taking a picture of our set table. She was wearing a simple long gauze skirt, and her top was a scoop-neck white T-shirt. Over that she wore the highlight piece: a long crocheted vest with a dozen different saturated sunset tones descending from pink to orange to red. She wore a darling gold starfish on a long chain around her neck and had a matching starfish hairclip that pulled back her short, feathery hair on the right side. She gave a twirl to show off the unusual vest. Only someone as winsome and dainty as Emily could make a vest like that look like an artistic charmer.

"And, Sierra," I said. "I love your outfit too. It's so you."

Her poet's blouse flowed over a long, layered skirt that was a rich olive-green color. Sierra tipped the brim of her big floppy hat, drawing attention to the yellow-and-green striped scarf around the crown.

She had on her usual rows of bracelets and several beaded necklaces as well as dangling beaded earrings. If she took off the hat, she would look much like she always did.

"I brought iced mint tea with pomegranate juice," Christy said. "If that doesn't sound good to any of you, I also brought fresh squeezed orange juice. And wedges of avocado toast. One of Todd's students blessed us with a bag of oranges and a bunch of avocados."

"Nice!" Tess held up a fancy box tied with a purple ribbon. "Don't judge me. You all know I don't bake or sew, but I know where to buy the best chocolates in Southern California."

"Nobody here is judging you," I said. "Believe me."

"I also brought a mini charcuterie since everyone seemed to like it so much before." Tess carefully uncovered a square plate with raised sides. We admired the colorful mosaic of finger foods, including the aforementioned plump Kalamata olives.

"Well, I hope everyone has an open mind when you try what I brought. Joel looked up the recipe in one of his vintage cookbooks. Ta-da!" I placed the plate of figs and cream on the table.

"What is it?" Sierra asked.

"Figs and cream." I tried to gauge their reactions as the breeze kept blowing my hair across my face.

"Didn't you make a comment about those in a text a long time ago?" Emily asked.

I nodded.

"How fun, Jennalyn. I love trying new things," Emily said. "I think my contribution of rosemary ciabatta bread and olive oil is a little boring."

"I love ciabatta bread." Sierra placed a bowl of ripe strawberries on the table. "The guy at the fruit stand said these are from the first local harvest of the season. I hope they're ripe."

Before we settled on the pillows, I said, "Do you want to pray together first?" I held out my hands, and we formed a circle. My prayer was simple and came from my uncluttered heart.

I wanted to tell my friends why I felt that way. I wanted to recap the events of the last few months, and how Joel and I had reconnected earlier that week in such significant way. Yet, I knew everyone was waiting to hear what Tess had to say about Rick. I wanted to hear too.

"These are delicious!" Tess held up her half-eaten fig. "Did you guys try these yet?"

We tried everything, raved a little about

all the treats, and went back for seconds. Christy filled our vintage goblets from her two large thermoses. She raised a glass, and we all did the same.

"To the King and His kingdom," Christy said.

"To the King and His kingdom," we echoed.

"So, Tess," Sierra said. "We're kinda dying here."

Tess looked confused. "Why?"

"We want to hear what happened when you met with Rick," I said.

"Oh!" She grinned and reached for another wedge of avocado toast. "I met with him, and it was good. Really good, actually."

Tess stretched out her legs, looking comfortable in her clothes, in her skin, and especially with her decision to see Rick. "We met for coffee, talked for about twenty minutes, said goodbye, and it was good. I needed to see myself as an adult and treat him like one as well and speak truth."

"What did you say?" Sierra asked.

"I told him that he needed to figure out what had gone wrong with his marriage. He needed to own his part in the disintegration of their relationship and fix whatever he could. I told him he would keep repeating the same mistakes if he didn't work on it now and give his wife a chance to decide if their marriage could be repaired."

"That's pretty bold," Emily said.

"I know. I didn't owe him anything." Tess looked at me. "But I wanted to give him something — truth. You guys gave me truth. A lot of truth. Sometimes more truth than I wanted. In the circles I work in, very few people tell the truth. They don't talk about what's sacred and what lasts. They don't assign the same values to people and relationships that I've begun to since we started meeting."

"You gave Rick truth," Christy said thoughtfully. "Tess, what a gift. Really. I'm so glad you did that."

"I am too." Tess leaned back and reached for her goblet with the pomegranate mint tea. "I wish I could have had closure like this in all my past relationships. I apologized to him for leading him on. He apologized to me too. I don't know if he meant it at the same level I did. I had a lot of time to think about what I wanted to say, but he didn't. All I hope is that he and his wife figure out the next step, and that they do it together."

I felt a little hesitant, but this seemed to be the moment I had waited for. I wanted to open up to the DOEs the way Tess had. I wanted them to know what had been going on in my heart and life over the past few months.

I sat up straight. "There's something I've been wanting to share with all of you."

I caught Christy's glance. An affirming smile lifted the corners of her mouth. She may not have been a cheerleader in high school, like she told us at Alejandro's. But tonight, I felt that she was cheering me on.

I started with Eden's ballet class and how I felt when I saw Garrett. I gave a brief history of our years together and how his wife seemed to be "visiting her mom" a lot.

"No wonder you were so in tune to what Rick said at the movie theater," Tess observed.

I nodded and kept going, leaving out nothing except for some of the painful details about the way Joel and I worked through everything.

"That's so intense, Jennalyn." Emily looked concerned. "I wish you could have told us."

"I know. So do I. The thing I'm beginning to understand is how going into hiding can be a trap. The longer I stayed in isolation, the more fearful I was about telling the truth."

"It's Garden of Eden stuff, isn't it?" Sierra

asked. "Adam and Eve covering up, saying to God that they were afraid, and so they hid."

"Well, I'm not there anymore. I'm free, and I'm so grateful."

"Truth can do that. Set us free." Tess raised her glass to me. "Thank you for giving us your truth, Jennalyn."

"And for trusting us." Christy raised her goblet.

I recognized her word, *trust,* as well as Tess's word, *truth.*

I raised my glass to them and added my word. "I love all of you so much."

We clinked our glasses and sipped. All of us were smiling.

The sun slipped out from behind the hedge of fluffy clouds on the horizon. I gazed at the beautiful teal-colored water and felt the calm that always seems to accompany the golden hour at the ocean. In the distance a sailboat was skittering back to harbor. A few seagulls were circling above the shoreline, scouting for one last sand crab before flapping back to their cove.

"You know what I think?" Christy said. "Having friends in your life who are willing to take the time to know you by heart is a gift."

"Well, you and Jennalyn have apparently

reached a more advanced level of knowing than the rest of us," Sierra said. "Because obviously you two did a mind meld on your wardrobe choice. Are you two going to show up to all future DOE get-togethers in matching outfits? Or will we just need to wait and be surprised?"

"I think you should wait and be surprised," Christy said with a big grin.

"Speaking of surprises." Sierra placed her goblet on the table and looked at each of us with the sort of attention-commanding cuteness she wielded so well.

CHAPTER 26

"As you know," Sierra said. "Jordan and I have been looking for another place to live because . . ." She paused for dramatic effect. "Maybe, hopefully, if it pleases God and all goes well, we might manage to make another baby this summer."

We all gave a cheer.

"I don't recall ever hearing that was the reason for moving," Tess said.

"Well, tonight is full disclosure night, isn't it?" Sierra grinned. "My good news is that we have a place to live for the next three years at a price we can afford!"

"That's wonderful!" Emily said. "Where is it?"

"It's where we live right now!"

"At Jordan's parents' house?" Christy said.

"Sierra," Tess said, "that's not news; that's non-news."

Sierra lifted her index finger in the air as if she were Mary Poppins and about to pull something wonderful from her bag. "We are going to live there without his parents!"

I was confused. "Where are they going?"

"Oregon. They have a place there. A cottage by the sea, they call it. They decided that since my father-in-law can take early retirement, they would go live there. He wants to write a novel and was told he should allow three years to do it. So, that's what they're doing."

"I didn't know he was a writer," Emily said.

"He's not. He's always wanted to write, though. He's been a VP for a long time at a company in Irvine that makes contact lens solution."

"What's he going to write about?" Christy asked.

"I don't know. He's excited about it, though. So is Jordan's mom. I've been to the cottage. It's a really special place."

"I'm happy for you and Jordan," Christy said.

"Wait!" Emily said excitedly.

We all waited.

"No," Emily laughed. "I meant, your word, Sierra. Your word was *wait*. It's a good thing you didn't sign any of those leases you were considering. You waited, and this opportunity was just around the corner."

Sierra nodded slowly. "I hadn't thought about that."

"I have an update too," Emily said. "Trevor has had several significant real-estate sales, and he's working out a way for us to sublet our apartment. He found a house that's going to go on the market in June, and he would really like to buy it so we can move in this summer. I've come to love our little apartment, but if we could buy this small two-bedroom house, it would be wonderful."

"Where's it located?" Tess asked.

"On Balboa Peninsula."

"That's really close to us," Christy said.

"I know. I'm trying to not get too excited about it. It's small. But Trevor is all about the location."

"Let me know if you do end up buying it and want to sublet your apartment. I might have someone who would love your darling little nest," Christy said.

"That's good to know," Emily said.

"I know this is a long shot, but Katie, Eli, and their three boys will need a place to rent starting the end of August. I would love it if they could be nearby."

"Katie is moving here?" I asked.

"I thought I told you."

"No. I would have remembered."

"Really? Because I remember you being at my house when she and I were Skyping about their plans." Christy paused.

She and I both seemed to remember the strained details of why I was standing in her kitchen last Monday. I barely said hello to Katie before leaving my children with Christy and dashing home to talk to Joel.

"They're going to be here from August till the middle of May. Eli will be scouting at Southern California colleges to recruit students to work on the clean water projects in other places in Africa. The ministry they're with keeps growing, and no one is more qualified than Eli to communicate the need and how to get involved."

"I'm so excited they're coming!" Sierra said. She turned to Tess and Emily and said, "You're going to love Katie. We have to make her an honorary DOE and host a welcome party for her in August. Where should we have it? Does anyone know somebody who owns a boat we could borrow?"

We laughed.

"You sure do know how to dream big, Sierra," Emily said.

"As we've been sitting here, I've been watching the sailboats go by, and it looks like such a dreamy way to spend a summer evening," Sierra said.

"Our deck will be fancied up by then," I said. "We could have it at our house."

"Fancied up?" Tess asked. "Do you need any design ideas?"

"Yes, I do. We're adding a pergola and a built-in bench by the barbecue. I want to add some planters and more outdoor furniture."

"Nice," Tess said. "What colors?"

"I don't know yet. Do you want to come by sometime to make suggestions?"

"Sure."

Christy was sitting directly across the table from me and had been watching me closely. "A pergola? A built-in bench. Are you also adding railing?"

I nodded. She was on to me. I had forgotten all about Todd being the one who would do the work.

"Jennalyn," Christy dipped her chin. "You and Joel didn't need to —"

"Christy!" I interrupted her and simply pointed to my cheek.

Christy blew me a kiss and tapped the palm of her hand on her chest.

"Did you two just throw down some kind of gang sign?" Sierra asked.

I laughed and explained about the nail polish and remembering Tess's rules of etiquette for when a friend gives you a special gift. Then I concluded with how Joel wanted to bless Todd and Christy so they could go with us to the marriage conference on Maui.

It felt good to tell the DOEs that we were going to a marriage retreat. I even included the full title with the words *Rigorous Renewal*. Even though it felt a little uncomfortable to tell them that Joel was helping Todd this way, I decided to go ahead and say it.

"I feel elitist or something since we're going to the retreat on Maui," I said.

"Jennalyn, there's nothing for you to feel elitist about," Sierra said. "I see this as a chance for you guys to go to Hawaii as a lavish gift from God. You should send God kisses and tell Him thank you, not apologize to us. He's giving us other gifts. Different gifts."

I looked up into the sky as the sherbet colors of the spring sunset were curving over us like a banner. I put my fingertips to my lips and blew a kiss to heaven.

Thank You, Father. You are so generous and kind. I love You.

When I lowered my chin, Tess caught my gaze. "May I ask a favor?"

"Of course."

"Could you bring me back some Kona

coffee? There's a certain plantation on Maui that has the best, I mean, *the* best coffee. You can only get it there. I'll send you the name."

"Sure, I'll bring you back some Kona coffee. What should I bring for you two?"

Sierra wanted a little grass skirt for Ella Mae. Emily thought Audra would like to have a postcard sent to her.

"We can do better than that," Christy said. "We can send Audra a coconut."

"She would love that!"

"Are you sure we can do that?" I asked.

"Todd sent me one when I was in high school. I actually think I still have it somewhere in a storage bin in the garage."

Sierra laughed. "Maybe we should have an intervention for you, Christy, and have you bring your petrified coconut and any other scary memorabilia from high school so we can burn it here on the beach."

"My mom did exactly that with me. I burned all the stuff I had collected in high school from Garrett."

"It sounds like that scene in the movie *Emma,*" Tess said.

"That's where my mom and I got the idea," I said.

"Your mom sounds amazing. I wish I had had her as my mother," Tess said. "You said once that you started these gatherings because she set the example."

"She did."

"All of us will be forever grateful," Tess said. "You were the one who began this group, and you were the one who reached out to invite each of us. I don't know where we would be without each other in our lives." She raised her glass.

The rest of us did the same.

"To Jennalyn," Tess said. "Our favorite haven maker. And to Jennalyn's mom, who is the modern-day Eve to all of us daughters." Before Tess took a sip from her beautiful goblet, she pressed her fingers to her lips and blew a kiss toward heaven.

"I would like to give a benediction," Christy said.

"What's that?" Tess asked.

"A blessing. I want to speak some of my favorite verses over us as a blessing."

"Yes, please," Tess said. "Bless us."

Christy's blue-green eyes seemed to catch the waning sunlight as it reflected off the glassware on our table. She looked so content as she quoted from Psalm 139.

"O LORD, you have examined my heart
    and know everything about me.
You know when I sit down or stand up.

You know my thoughts even when I'm
  far away.
You see me when I travel
  and when I rest at home.
  You know everything I do.
You know what I am going to say
  even before I say it, LORD.
You go before me and follow me.
  You place your hand of blessing on my
  head.
Such knowledge is too wonderful for me,
  too great for me to understand!

I can never escape from your Spirit!
  I can never get away from your
  presence!
If I go up to heaven, you are there;
  if I go down to the grave, you are there.
If I ride the wings of the morning,
  if I dwell by the farthest oceans,
even there your hand will guide me,
  and your strength will support me.
I could ask the darkness to hide me
  and the light around me to become
  night —
  but even in darkness I cannot hide from
  you.
To you the night shines as bright as day.
  Darkness and light are the same to
  you."

I felt as if every word of Christy's blessing was for me. After struggling so much with my heart's desire to be known, she was now echoing what Joel had been telling me. I *was* known. Fully known by my Heavenly Father. He wanted me to know Him and love Him with my whole heart.

When I was in bed that night, reliving all the sweet little memories of our Spring Fling, I thought about Tess's spontaneous tribute to my mother. I loved thinking of my mom as the Eve to all of us Daughters of Eve. She would have loved that. I thought about Christy's benediction and felt as if she had handed me the truth my heart had been missing. I was known by God. In life and death and the darkest cave, He was already there.

I also thought about how everyone entered into the excitement of Christy and me going to Maui. If they were jealous or sad that they weren't all able to go, they didn't show it.

Their kindness to Christy and me continued in a string of text messages two weeks later, the morning we were heading to the airport. Tess, Emily, and Sierra all said they were praying for us and happy that we were going on what they were calling our second honeymoons.

391

Joel was in such a great mood. The changes at the Blue Ginger over the past few weeks had gone as hoped, and everything was running smoothly with Vincent and all the other staff changes. I loved seeing Joel so excited about our trip. He had a list on his phone of the notable restaurants where he wanted us to eat on Maui.

It had been harder than I thought it would be to say goodbye to our kids when we left them with GiGi and Poppy. Joel had us all hold hands and pray, the way he had been doing with us lately. Each morning we prayed as a family, and then Eden would announce her new made-up game of "A Hug and a Kiss." We would give each other a hug and a kiss after our brief prayer before Joel left for work.

The morning we left for Maui, we paused by our suitcases to join hands and pray. Eden called out, "A hug and a kiss," and with a final wave to Poppy and GiGi, Joel and I slipped out the door without any crying.

Except for me. I cried a little.

Once we were checking in at the airport, I felt little shimmers of happiness kick in. We spotted Todd and Christy at the oversized baggage counter, where he was checking in a surfboard in an orange zip-up cover.

I waved, and my heavy shoulder bag began to slide. I had packed so much. Way more than Tess had recommended. We had checked two suitcases, and I knew that Joel would have to lift my carry-on into the overhead because it was so heavy.

My problem was that I had waited too long before starting to pack. I didn't know what I would need. I had no idea how many books I would have time to read. Never having been to Hawaii, I found it hard to believe that the only shoes I would need was a single pair of flip-flops. I ended up packing four pairs of shoes. Joel watched me squash them into the second suitcase and was about to protest, but I said, "Don't judge me," and he kept his lips sealed.

Christy walked over to us with Todd right behind her. She had a small wheeled suitcase. "Ready?" she asked.

"What about your luggage?" Joel asked.

"It's just this," Christy said.

Todd turned, showing us his backpack and indicating that was all he was bringing.

Joel laughed. "If you guys discover that you need anything, anything at all, I'm sure we brought extra you can use." He took my hand and led the way to security.

I was a painfully inexperienced traveler. I really hoped my foibles wouldn't irritate everyone that week.

Relax. This trip is a gift, Jennalyn. A gift of love. Enjoy it. All of it.

I lightened up. This was going to be a great trip. We arrived at our gate and discovered that the flight already was boarding. Joel and I took our seats right behind Christy and Todd, thanks to the guys arranging that earlier.

Christy peered over the top of her seat and with a bit of mischief in her eyes and said, "Guess what? We're going to Maui!"

"I know!"

A passenger coming down the aisle caught my eye, and my mouth dropped. "Christy," I whispered. "Look!"

She turned to see Rick Doyle lifting a suitcase into the overhead luggage compartment. In front of him was a pretty, stylish young woman wearing a cute straw fedora.

Isn't she a sweet young thing? Man, he sure replaced Tess quickly! I'm so glad Tess didn't get tangled up with that guy. I can't believe he's on the same flight with us.

Christy rose from her seat and called out, "Nicole!"

That's his wife!? He's with his wife!?

Todd lifted his hand to wave. Rick grinned and came over. Todd stood, and the two of them gave each other a manly sort of shoulder-to-shoulder hug.

"So glad it worked out for you and Nicole to come," Todd said.

"Thanks to you," Rick said.

Todd ignored what seemed like a compliment and motioned to Joel and me, introducing us to Rick.

Rick looked at me. "Didn't we meet . . ." He suddenly seemed to remember. "Oh, right. The movie theater. You're Tess's friend."

Nicole had joined Rick and obviously heard him say Tess's name. Apparently, no shadowy unspokens would need to be tiptoed around between the two of them. I was astounded.

Christy gave Nicole a warm hello before introducing us.

"It's going to be a great week." Rick looked at his wife with the sweetest expression of admiration.

I felt as if I were watching a miracle.

What if Tess hadn't . . .

The announcement to take our seats came on over the Hawaiian music playing in the background. Rick and Nicole returned to their bulkhead seats in the center aisle. I reached into my shoulder bag, stuffed under the seat in front of me, and pulled out a pair of socks. It was one of Tess's top ten recommendations for comfort on a long flight.

Slipping one foot out of my sandal, I performed a bit of a contortionist act by bending my knee and raising my foot high enough to rest the heel on the edge of my seat. That was the only way I could scrunch up my sock and pull it on without kicking Christy's seat.

I heard Joel make a "hmm" sound. I turned, expecting him to look amused. I was ready to say "Don't judge me" once again. He looked sweetly sad and was staring at my foot.

"What?"

"You got your toenails painted," he said.

"Christy and I had pedis on Monday, remember? When we got our hair trimmed. Next time we go, we're going to take our girls and make a new tradition of it."

Joel's expression remained sober. "Your mom used to always have red toenails."

"You remember that?" I loved that he remembered.

"Yeah, but I don't know why. I liked her red toenails."

"So did I. It's one of the things I always remember when I think of her." I pulled on my sock and tried to be a little more grace-ful as I repeated the motion with the other foot. "Oh My, Cherry Pie," I murmured.

"What's that?" Joel asked.

"It's the name of the polish. It's the only one she ever wore."

"Oh My, Cherry Pie?" he repeated.

I nodded and pulled on the second sock, loving the way Joel noticed. I also loved that he had memories of my mom and that we could talk about her.

"She loved cherry pie," he said.

"Yes, she did."

"Your mom was a classy woman," Joel said. "Just like you."

I put down my foot and leaned my head on his shoulder.

Joel gave a chest-deep chuckle. "Do you remember how she said that after she was gone cherry pie would still be here, and it would carry on the sweetness into the next generation?"

I smiled. "Yes, I remember."

Joel kissed the top of my head. "She would be so proud of you, Jennalyn. So proud of the woman you've become, the wife and mother that you are."

He reached for my hand, and we laced our fingers together. "You know what I think?" he asked.

I lifted my head, looking at him with tears in my eyes.

"I think that all along, whenever she raved about cherry pie, she was dropping one of her clever secret messages."

"What secret message?"

"Don't you know?"

Joel looked at me with tears in his eyes and whispered, "It was you, Jennalyn. *You* were her cherry pie."

ABOUT THE AUTHOR

Robin Jones Gunn is the bestselling author of nearly one hundred books with more than five and a half million copies sold worldwide. Best known for her Christy Miller novels for teens and the Christy Award–winning Glenbrooke and Sisterchicks series, Robin's nonfiction titles include *Praying for Your Future Husband,* coauthored with Tricia Goyer, and *Spoken For,* coauthored with Alyssa Bethke.

Hallmark Channel created three movies from her Father Christmas novellas, which broke a record for the network by being the highest-rated and most-watched original Christmas movies.

Robin's love for storytelling and training writers has taken her around the world. She has served on the board of Media Associates International and has been a keynote speaker in Africa, Brazil, Europe, and Australia, as well as in Canada and throughout the United States.

Readers who grew up with Robin's books have written to tell her how the memorable characters in her stories have mentored and influenced them over the years. Robin and her husband have two grown, married children and live in Hawaii.

The employees of Thorndike Press hope you have enjoyed this Large Print book. All our Thorndike, Wheeler, and Kennebec Large Print titles are designed for easy reading, and all our books are made to last. Other Thorndike Press Large Print books are available at your library, through selected bookstores, or directly from us.

For information about titles, please call:
(800) 223-1244

or visit our website at:
gale.com/thorndike

To share your comments, please write:
Publisher
Thorndike Press
10 Water St., Suite 310
Waterville, ME 04901